Cast of Characters

Jane Amanda Edwards, a self-styled "full-fashioned" spinster, who terrorizes her family, irritates the local police and always gets her man.

Arthur Edwards. Jane's equally ample-bodied brother, he's a true lily of the field who can't stay out of trouble—or away from strong drink and weak women.

Annie Edwards. Jane's tenderhearted sister, who starts this adventure when she attends a meeting for British war relief.

George Hammond. Rockford's captain of detectives, he's willing to put up with Jane in exchange for a home-cooked meal.

Theresa. The Edwards' sharp-tongued cook, who's responsible for Jane and Arthur's girth.

Austin Barrett. Owner of the local defense plant.

Julian Norbury. A known idler and Barrett's nephew.

Steve Boyd. His design could shorten the war. He's married to Norbury's sister, Katherine.

Henry Platt. The plant's general manager.

Bill Randall. A technical expert from back east, he seems to have a few secrets of his own.

John Storm. A labor agitator.

Jappy Carillo. A very suspicious character.

Officer Blake. Hammond's right-hand man and Jane's arch-enemy.

Various other townspeople, relatives, plant workers

Books by Charlotte Murray Russell

Featuring Jane Amanda Edwards

Murder at the Old Stone House (1935)
Death of an Eloquent Man (1936)
The Tiny Diamond (1937)
Night on the Pathway (1938)
The Clue of the Naked Eye (1939)
I Heard the Death Bell (1940)
The Message of the Mute Dog (1942)
No Time for Crime (1945)
The Bad Neighbor Murder (1946)
Ill Met in Mexico (1948)
Hand Me a Crime (1949)
Cook Up a Crime (1951)

Featuring Homer Fitzgerald

Lament for William (1947)
The Careless Mrs. Christian (1949)
Between Us and Evil (1950)
June, Moon, and Murder (1952)

Non-Series Mysteries

The Case of the Topaz Flower (1939)
Dreadful Reckoning (1941)
Murder Steps In (1942)
Market for Murder (1953)

The Message of the
Mute Dog

A Jane Amanda Edwards mystery by
Charlotte Murray Russell

**Introduction by
Tom & Enid Schantz**

**The Rue Morgue Press
Boulder, Colorado**

The Rue Morgue Press
P.O. Box 4119
Boulder, CO 80306

PRINTED IN THE UNITED STATES OF AMERICA

About the author

WHEN CHARLOTTE MURRAY RUSSELL shipped off the manuscript of her first mystery, she sent it to the Doubleday, Doran Crime Club, saying, "I might as well start at the top and work down from there." But when a parcel about the same size as the one she sent off to Doubleday showed up in the mail a couple of weeks later, she hid it in the attic without opening it, reluctant to face that letter of rejection. Imagine her surprise two weeks later to receive a warm letter from Doubleday welcoming her to the ranks of Crime Club authors. Hurriedly, Charlotte rushed to the attic and discovered that the package she had secreted away was a box of stationery ordered by her husband Marcus.

Published in 1935, *Murder at the Old Stone House* was the first book acquired by longtime Crime Club editor Isabelle Taylor. In it we meet Jane Amanda Edwards, a self-satisfied spinster of 45 who tips the scales at 180 pounds—"full-fashioned," not fat, as she tells one and all, although she complains that "since Helen Hokinson began to publish I never look in a full-length mirror." "For some obscure reason," wrote a reviewer for *The New York Times*, "it seems that a story involving an old maid sleuth is always sure to be entertaining. This one is no exception to the rule, and we hope to hear more of Jane Edwards." The *Times* would not be disappointed, as the tart-tongued Jane would go on for another sixteen years gleefully meddling in the affairs of her neighbors in Rockport, Illinois (a thinly fictionalized version of Charlotte's own home town of Rock Island) at the slightest provocation. When murder strikes, as it does with alarming regularity given the fact that only 40,000 people call Rockport home, "old X-ray Jane," as she calls herself, is usually the first person on the scene.

Jane has a rare—and, she protests, unappreciated—talent for cracking murder cases, explaining in *The Bad Neighbor Murder* (1946): "I somehow, at frequent intervals, brush up against murder. Brush? Merely graze? No. It is not a delicate contact. Rather do I scent from afar, feel in my bones, ferret and fish for information, hunt and harry, and finally corner a guilty, wretched villain. Whereupon Detective Captain George Hammond . . . takes over, basks in the resultant publicity (always making use of a newspaper cut ten years old), hies himself out to our house for one of Theresa's chicken-and-dumpling dinners topped off with lemon pie, and explains the case to me. This pattern tends to repeat itself. I have come to accept the recurrence."

Happily, so did Charlotte Murray Russell's many readers. In all she published 20 mysteries between 1935 and 1953. Four of her books were non-series mysteries while four others featured Homer Fitzgerald, a small-town Indiana police chief. But her reputation in the field is based on the even dozen books in which Jane runs roughshod through one murder scene after another, unabashedly stealing evidence and excusing her indiscretions with exclamations like, "The police wouldn't know what to make of this anyhow." She points out in Cook *Up a Crime* that she does "not disparage policemen. They have organization, routine, experience, scientific aids, and, above all, the majesty of the law on their side. But they can't beat me on the observant eye."

This attitude doesn't exactly endear Jane to George Hammond, but he puts up with her and even, on occasion, actively seeks her help. Their relationship is a bit like that of Hildegarde Withers and Inspector Oscar Piper in the contemporaneous mysteries of Stuart Palmer. Jane is quite content in her spinsterhood and George, five years her senior, is a confirmed bachelor. There's not a hint of romance in the air, but from time to time the two appear together at the odd social gathering or spend a companionable evening together listening to the radio in Jane's home.

But Jane's domestic life clearly revolves around her siblings. Her family belongs to what passes for Rockford society, although in recent years they have fallen upon hard times. They have been reduced to living off their capital, perhaps because no one in the family seems ever to have held a job. Her sister Annie is a year Jane's junior and, according to Jane, too wishy-washy to make it on her own (although she seems to be a remarkably well-adjusted individual), while their younger brother Arthur is merely waiting for the right opportunity, employment-wise. In the meantime, Jane must be constantly vigilant lest the hapless Arthur fall prey to strong drink, as the poor boy's constitution is so delicate that it takes but a single glass of wine (or so Jane would have us believe) to wholly rob him of his faculties. Arthur also has a weakness for unsuitable women, which Jane does her best to curb. Theresa, their long-suffering and bluntly outspoken housekeeper and cook (imagine Thelma Ritter in the part), thinks Arthur is no more than a lily of the field, but her aspersions usually fall on deaf ears. In Jane's eyes, Arthur can simply do no wrong; she dotes on him totally and her attempts to manage his life are only for his own good.

Indeed, in case after case it's Arthur's Mr. Toad-like indiscretions that quite often require Jane's intervention in matters criminal. He always seems to be in the wrong place at the wrong time, and more than once the police have been poised to cuff this rotund good fellow and haul him off to jail until Jane pulls the real culprit out of a hat.

Charlotte Murray Russell's mystery writing career began in 1933 when she won a writing contest sponsored by a Rock Island newspaper in which contestants had to furnish the final chapter to a mystery plot devised by the paper's editors. She then began writing her first novel, which would take her some two years to finish. Her writing was no hobby. It was the height of the Depression, her husband had lost his real estate business, and Charlotte's books helped put food on the table. The Russells were forced to rent out their home and move in with Charlotte's parents until her royalties started coming in and Marcus found work with John Deere. They then moved back into their own house, which was not large, and Charlotte's daughter, Marianne Nelson (born the year Charlotte won the newspaper contest), remembers her mother pounding away at a manual typewriter on a dining room table strewn with papers, clearing it off only for meals. It was not until after the war that she acquired an actual desk to write at. At night, Marianne would lie in bed and listen to her parents discuss clues and alibis in the living room.

Charlotte was an avid mystery fan herself, especially fond of the English mystery writer Ngaio Marsh. Other favorites were Josephine Tey, Dorothy L. Sayers and Agatha Christie. Certainly, there's more than a touch of Miss Marple in Jane.

In 1953, Charlotte announced she was tired of writing and took a job as a book cataloguer at the Rock Island Public Library. She never again considered writing a mystery, though she worked off and on for several years on her memoirs, filling shopping bags and bureau drawers with handwritten notes that she never got around to organizing.

Born Charlotte Murray on May 22, 1899, in Rock Island, she lived most of her life there and was known as Chatty by her many friends. She graduated Phi Beta Kappa from the University of Chicago and did graduate work at McGill University in Montreal before returning to her home town to teach French and Latin at the Rock Island High School until she married Marcus J. Russell in 1925. She died on her birthday in 1992 at the age of 93.

One of the most successful early exponents of the American cozy school of mystery writing, Charlotte Murray Russell is a spiritual forebear of such popular contemporary farceurs as Charlotte MacLeod, Joan Hess, Deborah Adams, and the early Sharyn McCrumb. And in her blithe refusal ever to admit she is wrong, Jane foreshadows Elizabeth Peters' equally obstinate and meddlesome heroine, Amelia Peabody. Russell did not invent the old-maid sleuth—it was already an established convention when she began writing—but Jane Amanda Edwards was one of the most appealing of her generation of busybody spinsters and certainly deserves to be better known today.

TOM & ENID SCHANTZ
Boulder, Colorado

NOTE: Although food is an important element in all the Jane Amanda Edwards books, recipes were not included in the original editions, perhaps because the author herself was, according to her family, an indifferent cook. Not so the long-suffering but talented Theresa, and the recipes included here for the old-fashioned dishes mentioned in the book are all based on recipes from cookbooks of the period and our memories of how our mothers made the very same dishes.

Recipes from Theresa's Kitchen
ROAST LEG OF LAMB WITH GARLIC

1 leg of lamb (5 to 6 lb.)	1½ tablespoons coarse salt
¼ teaspoon black pepper	several cloves garlic

Rub meat all over with salt, pepper, and cut clove of garlic. (If a stronger garlic flavor is desired, cut deep gashes into meat and push slivers of garlic inside.) Place fat side up (do not remove fell) in an uncovered roasting pan and roast in a 300° to 325° oven until a meat thermometer registers 175° to 180° F., or 30 to 35 minutes per pound. Serve with fresh asparagus, new potatoes, and minted pineapple jelly.

NEW POTATOES

Drop small unpeeled new potatoes into rapidly boiling salted water to cover and cook uncovered until tender. Remove, let cool partially, and remove skins. Melt 2 or more tablespoons of butter in a skillet, add whole potatoes and shake gently over low heat until heated through and well coated with butter. Sprinkle with finely chopped parsley or chives and serve.

MINTED PINEAPPLE JELLY

½ cup fresh spearmint leaves	¼ cup water
3 cups sugar	2 cups tart apple juice
green food coloring	2 cups pineapple juice

Wash and chop mint leaves. Mash with 2 tablespoons sugar, add the water, and let stand overnight. Bring mixture to boiling in a small saucepan, strain, and set aside. Bring the apple and pineapple juice to boiling in an 8 to 10 quart kettle, gradually add remaining sugar, and boil rapidly until the mixture sheets off from a spoon. At this point add food coloring as desired and 2 tablespoons of the mint mixture. Remove from heat immediately, pour into sterilized 6-ounce jelly glasses, and seal with paraffin.* Makes 7 glasses.

If fresh mint isn't available, pour 1/3 cup boiling water over 3 tablespoons dried leaves, let stand 15 minutes, strain, and use as above.

*Modern preserving methods recommend refrigerating jelly and using within several weeks.

(more recipes after page 155)

CHAPTER ONE

I HESITATE TO BLAME MY SISTER Annie for the dark and tragic occurrences of last spring although it is extremely easy to blame Annie for almost anything. She is the essence of refinement, amiable and willing, but, I insist, muddle-headed. She seems to invite undeserved judgments. I am not one to say I told you so, and, naturally, Annie was not involved in the murder in any way. I want that to be understood here and now. But for a period her innocence was not unquestioned, and Detective Captain George Hammond gave her a few bad moments. Nevertheless, the fact remains that Annie was the first one in our family to become conscious of national defense. It was she who persuaded Arthur to attend the mass meeting for British war relief, and that really started the whole thing. Not the murder, of course, but Arthur's entanglement and my participation.

For me the recollection of my last spring hat—a chic model in pursuit red—brings an inevitable memory of those lost blueprints. The fragrance of a balmy evening snatches me back in horror to those dreadful moments in the deserted cotton mill, and I can hear again the locust tree whispering and the river swishing close beside our hiding place. Indeed, after these many months I can scarcely bring myself to pass Red Green's Bowling Alley. Would you think that my innocent entrance in search of Julian Norbury would necessitate the replacement of my pivot front tooth?

It seems scarcely essential for me to introduce myself, but there may be one or two who have not followed the adventures and admired the triumphs of Jane Amanda Edwards.

Rockport, my place of residence, is middle-sized, Middle Western, and, at the time of my story, midway between alarm at the changing world and determination to do something about it. Annie, Arthur, and I are middle-aged but not middle-sized. Annie is undeniably skinny. Arthur and I are large and well formed, as befits people of magnificent enthusiasms. Arthur's undertakings invariably lead him into trouble, while mine lead me into crime.

9

False pride does not afflict me, and I challenge any sleuth, male or female, thin or fat, amateur or professional, to point to a better record than mine. I do my own snooping and I tell my own tales. Let Sherlock Holmes have his Dr. Watson; let Philo Vance have his S. S. Van Dine; let Nero Wolfe cling to his Archie Goodwin. Jane Amanda Edwards makes her own way with a murder mystery, and no monkey business about her. She sees all, hears some, and tells everything.

Greenwood Avenue is a pleasant street, wide lawns, screened porches, old houses, old neighbors. Occasionally a new resident moves in to add a bit of zest, give us a terra incognita, as it were. But in a few months we know the newcomers intimately and can speak with authority on their tastes in movies, toothpastes, and politics.

Except Julian Norbury. We never did know him well. Certainly not favorably.

From the very beginning the war in Europe had greatly disturbed Annie. She had knitted feverishly for the Finns and canvassed for funds for the gallant Greeks. Now she was putting forth a mighty effort for England. She is the flighty type, easily agitated, apt to make a vocal fuss about every disturbing trifle. Not that I consider war a trifle. I deplore the catastrophe.

But Annie, obviously, is not the person to cope with a world upheaval.

"The country can fall in ruins about your ears," she complained. "What do you do? Nothing. What do you say? Nothing."

"What can I do?" I asked not unreasonably if a little absently. I was at the moment halfway through an excellent murder mystery in which a man was electrocuted in his bath and then frozen there. "What can I say?"

"Plenty," retorted Annie with unusual vigor. "Help others. Join the concerted efforts. Put your shoulder to the wheel. That Barrett girl has the oddest hat——exactly like a soup bunch."

I glanced up, mildly surprised, until I saw that Annie was standing at the front window looking through to the street. My gaze followed hers. Judith Barrett, one of our young neighbors who lives just opposite and a few houses down, was strolling along beside a most upstanding, handsome young man.

"Who's that with her?" I asked, joining Annie at the window.

"I don't know," said Annie regretfully. "What broad shoulders he has! What a military carriage!"

"He walks just about like anybody else, as far as I can see," I replied, returning to my book. "I've never noticed him in this neighborhood before."

The time was not far off when the blond young giant was fairly to haunt our avenue, but of those depressing days I was as yet happily unaware.

Annie may leave a subject, but only temporarily. Until it has been worn to a shred or completely evaporated she will return.

She dismissed the young couple with a wave of her hand.

"We were talking," she said, "about helping humanity in this crisis."

"You were talking," I corrected. "I was listening. And you were talking about Britain."

"Bundles for Britain," maintained Annie.

"What's in them?" I asked.

She gave me a cold, offended look.

"Does that matter? Would you look a gift horse in the mouth? I use the term broadly, in a sense meaning to help."

"Well," I said reminiscently, "when I think of some of the bundles I sent to our soldiers in 1918. Drop-stitch socks and those so-called trench mirrors— remember them? And that nightshirt you featherstitched in pink and—"

"That," said Annie with frigid dignity, "was long ago. The point is, will you come with me to the rally tonight?"

"No," I said firmly. "Take Arthur. I have to get this man out of the bathtub."

Arthur readily agreed to accompany Annie. He is social by nature and, moreover, had already glimpsed the speaker of the evening in a downtown hotel lobby. She was agreeably blonde and was rumored to possess delightfully shocking information concerning the goings on in air-raid shelters. It was also reported that she would model a siren suit. I cannot, however, give those details. I neither saw nor heard the lady. All I know is that Arthur attended the meeting, and she or something put him into a state of unprecedented exhilaration. Well, maybe not altogether unprecedented, but anyway regrettable.

At the moment of his return with Annie at his heels I was furiously engaged in pushing our dog through the front door.

This animal was a recent and thoroughly undesirable addition to our home. Theresa, who has been our housekeeper for many years, detested him; Annie pitied him, and Arthur adored him. I myself am fond of dumb animals, but I like to know where I stand with them. This canine did not, from the very first, take to me, and I entertained decidedly lukewarm sentiments toward him. His breed, I think, we might label triangular. He exhibited certain characteristics of the collie, the Airedale, and the German shepherd or police dog, the characteristics in each case being the worst ones. He had feet like an elephant, a tail like an anaconda, and Theresa claimed all four legs were hollow, as she could never succeed in satisfying his really astounding appetite. Although he seemed gentle he was enthusiastic, and she was constantly fearful that he might wind up a meal with a nip of her well-padded exterior.

Arthur had named the creature Win. This was partly a tribute to Winston Churchill and partly because Arthur suffered under the delusion that the animal was a "winner."

"What are you doing to Win?" he cried, now hastening his steps, his plump face registering concern. "Maybe he doesn't want to go out."

"Maybe he doesn't," I agreed, giving Win's huge rear another energetic shove. "But he's going out! He's lucky I didn't beat him. I shall certainly change his name!"

"He's named for Winston Churchill," said Arthur loyally. "And—"

"Well, he's going to be renamed for Mussolini," I retorted. "Mussy, for short."

"Why?" asked Arthur.

"Do we need to go into that?" I snapped.

"Oh, Jane," cried Annie, her lips quivering. "Don't depress Arthur with complaints about poor Win. We've had a most uplifting meeting. Really quite spiritual. Dear Arthur was so impressed. He has talked in such a spirited and patriotic vein all the way home!"

The dog, seeing I meant business, scuttled away to the back yard, and I turned back into the house. In the lighted entrance hall I regarded my brother and my sister.

Arthur dropped his hat and coat to a chair. They missed their objective and settled limply to the floor, but my brother made no move to pick them up. His complexion was unusually rosy, and he seemed very warm. He gave a lordly wave of his hand.

"'O Canada, terre de nos aieux,' " he began to chant in execrable French. "Ton front ta-ta, tum-tum-te-tum-te-tum."

Arthur has a certain weakness to which I dislike to allude but which must occasionally be recognized. I do not grant that he easily succumbs to temptation. Rather his friendly and obliging nature renders him too susceptible to suggestion.

"Annie," I demanded sharply, "was Arthur with you throughout the evening? The entire evening?"

Annie's head was bent as she tugged at her rubber overshoe.

"Just before the meeting ended he went out with Ollie Bengston," she admitted. "But he came right back and put a ten dollar bill in the collection box!"

I heaved a sigh. My suspicion was confirmed.

"Ollie Bengston!" I cried out in reproof to Annie. "You know he always leads Arthur astray!"

Annie hung up Arthur's hat and coat and turned to look at me earnestly.

"Jane," she said, "I believe we've misjudged Ollie. His heart is in the right place."

"I don't give a rap about his heart," I said crossly. "It's his head I object to. It's empty. But no more talk now. I'm going to bed. And I'll deal with you, Arthur, in the morning."

Arthur went upstairs humming "God Bless America," but I put that down to his condition rather than to any burst of patriotism.

Resolving that I would ignore the incident rather than make an issue of it, I enjoyed my usual repose. Hence I was totally unprepared for the startling announcement that Arthur made at the breakfast table.

"I have decided," he said, clearing his throat and giving the words proper rhetorical effect. "I have come to a conclusion. I have made up my mind."

"About what?" I inquired absently. "Theresa, I believe these corn muffins are a bit too sweet."

"I have decided," said Arthur, "to enlist in the Royal Canadian Air Force."

"Pass me the jelly," I said, and then as the full import of his words struck me I put the muffin aside. "What—what did you say, Arthur?"

"Oh, Arthur!" twittered Annie. "How brave of you! How fine! How generous!"

I stared at them. Theresa came in with fresh coffee and uttered an unbelieving snort.

"If you haven't lost your minds, such minds as you have," I said clearly, "will you please tell me what you are talking about?"

"Ollie Bengston has gone to Canada," Arthur informed me. "He left last night. He is going to fly for England. I'm to join him. Here I am, free, no dependents, capable—"

"That last, at least, is a matter of opinion," I interrupted. "Putting aside the fact that the Canadian army probably doesn't want you, what brought you to this remarkable decision?"

"The speaker last night," exclaimed Annie. "Oh, Jane, she was marvelous! You should have heard her. And—"

"I should, indeed," I agreed grimly. "Besides giving her ten dollars Arthur now desires to fly for her. Is that it?"

"Certainly not," said my brother, selecting several slices of crisp bacon. "You know as well as I do that I am a bit too—er—adult to learn to fly. But there are other duties."

"Arthur," I said patiently, "let me hear no more of this nonsense. You are a citizen of the United States. We are not at war. Even if we were, an army of young men is being conscripted. You didn't fight twenty years ago."

"I tried," said Arthur righteously. "Could I help it if my feet were flat? Now I may be too old for conscription, but I am not too old to volunteer. Just because I wasn't in a capsule in a fishbowl in Washington—"

"They'd have a hard time getting you into a fishbowl," I broke in with a meaning eye upon his curves, "let alone a capsule."

"Jane," broke in Annie tremulously, "Ollie has gone to fight for democracy, to keep the alien enemy from our shores, to—"

"Bosh," I snapped. "If I know Ollie Bengston—and I do—he's looking for an exciting change. Probably thinks it'll be cooler up North this summer and he'll get in a lot of fishing. Let me hear no more of this silly talk. If you want to help your country there are plenty of ways to do it right here. Why, the whole town is upset with the defense order the Barrett Company has! I understand the farms out that way are filled with tents and trailers. There's never any parking space downtown. And half the neighbors are taking in roomers. No need to leave Rockport to help in the national emergency and—"

"That blond young man was there last night," interrupted Annie. "He was with Judith Barrett. Her father was there too. There was something in the way he looked . . . . I don't think he likes that young man."

"Plenty of people don't like Austin Barrett," I replied. "And put me on the list. He's too self-satisfied."

"Canada is a long way off," observed Arthur just then, and his voice was tinged with doubt. "If I should be sent to Vancouver, for instance . . ."

"You'll get no more of my chocolate cake," Theresa reminded him as she filled his cup.

"That's right," said Arthur weakly, "and I have just this minute remembered how I dislike Canadian bacon."

I picked up my muffin. I could see that the present danger had evaporated. I did not anticipate the frowns of fortune to come.

That very evening Arthur arrived at another conclusion even more surprising than the first and so informed us.

"I see my duty clearly now," he said complacently. "I shall go to work."

"Work?" babbled Annie in a high, amazed voice. Naturally she was astonished. She actually tottered as she walked to a chair and sat down.

"Work!" I repeated and stared at my brother with new eyes.

It is not that Arthur is lazy. I have always stoutly defended him against this accusation. He would be glad to be gainfully employed for no other reason than the fact that our income is not what it used to be, but naturally he is particular about the type of employment. The right sort has never presented itself. At one time he fancied himself as a politician. Again he entered the oil business with disastrous results. But, on the other hand, his dramatic efforts practically *made* the Rockport Little Theater, and his attempt at mushroom culture in our basement was almost a success. I have always blamed the failure of the latter enterprise to Theresa's complete lack of cooperation. There may have been a slight smell of mold, but the odor did not, as she claimed, resemble asafoetida!

Still I cannot deny that Arthur and toil are almost total strangers. Hence our astonishment at his expressed purpose.

"Do you really mean it?" I inquired. "Where are you going to work?"

"I shall offer my services to Austin Barrett," said Arthur modestly. "The machine-tool industry is the core of defense production. Every pair of willing hands is needed!"

"Skilled," I said, "as well as willing."

Arthur gave me a glance of scorn.

"Brains," he said, "still surpass brawn. I fancy that I shall hold my own."

That wasn't quite what I meant, but I said nothing more. After all, it was Mr. Barrett's problem, not mine.

To our stupefaction Arthur actually got a job and was quite overpowering about it.

"Mr. Henry Platt happened to be in the employment office. You know he's general manager. He told them to put me on at once. It's a key position," Arthur told us. "Three thousand men look up to me."

"What are you doing? Mending the roof?" I demanded.

His glance reproved my levity.

"No indeed," he replied with dignity. "I'm an examiner. That is—well,

I'm a guard. At the gate, you know. Every employee in that plant carries an identifying photo. Everyone wears a metal identification tag. I check them in and I check them out and, believe you me, I'm on the watch for sab cats!"

"Sab cats?" echoed Annie questioningly.

"The usual term for *saboteurs,*" explained my brother. "There's a million of them loose in this country, sniping at American interests, taking American lives, destroying American property."

"Goodness!" said Annie, looking nervously about her. She elevated her feet to the rung of her chair as if at any moment a sab cat might leap upon her. "My goodness gracious, Arthur! Do take care of yourself!"

An unpleasant possibility smote me.

"You are not armed, of course?" I began.

"I certainly am," said Arthur proudly. "I have a dandy automatic. By the way, I must get in a little target practice. Of course I'm pretty good with a revolver, but I told Bill Randall that I was a crack shot."

It was then that I had my first real foreboding, my first faint premonition that trouble had put on its wings and was heading straight for the Edwards family.

"And who," I inquired, "is Bill Randall?"

"A swell fellow," said Arthur enthusiastically.

This meant nothing. Every man Arthur knows is a swell fellow, even Captain George Hammond of the Rockport police force, who has consistently misunderstood him.

"Bill is a technical expert of some sort," Arthur continued. "He knows all about the machines. He came here from the East. Big, fair, good-looking kid. Played pro football for a year. Seems to have his eye on the Barrett girl."

"Oh," said Annie and I simultaneously. "That's who he is!" And I repeated the name, "Bill Randall."

Arthur went to work every morning and came back about four o'clock. His initial enthusiasm wore noticeably thin and, in my own mind, I gave him another week. But he finished that week, and nothing happened save that he lost his lunch kit and had to take his sandwiches in a paper bag.

He made no complaint, however. The lunch kit was new and shining with a small vacuum bottle for beverages. However, Annie, in artistic zeal, had decorated the box with decalcomania transfers and the initials A. E. in gold. It was my personal opinion that Arthur had lost the box on purpose, and I did not blame him.

But I attached no importance to the incident. Not until later.

We went about our daily duties. Annie was getting together her spring wardrobe and was in the midst of her usual trying on, bringing home, and taking back. Theresa was talking about spring housecleaning. I was making plans for a movement against the bingo games that I consider a blot on the name of our fair city.

How useless these occupations seem as I look back. How trivial they were in view of the frightening complications in which we were soon to be concerned, in which our very lives were threatened.

One bright sunny morning in early April the telephone rang. I remember that I was looking through the window at the yellow bells of a forsythia as I answered the call.

"Jane," said Detective Captain George Hammond.

"Yes," I said, still looking at the forsythia and wondering if the bleeding hearts were coming along.

"Better drop in at my office," I heard. "Arthur is in trouble. Again."

I flared up at once. George Hammond has never been fair to Arthur. I could see him in my mind's mirror, grinning at the phone, his glasses slipping down his nose, his bald spot shining.

"I'll be down in a little while," I assured him calmly. "I fancy it's nothing serious."

"That's what you think! But I'm telling you it's bad, Jane. Very bad. They say he's guilty of subversive activities against the government. He tried to blow up the Barrett plant!"

CHAPTER TWO

AT FIRST I COULD NOT TAKE IN the meaning of those surprising words. Win, the dog, was sniffing in a disgusting manner at my heels and flopping his tail in a mighty arc.

"Get out!" I shouted. "You old fool!"

"What's that?" cried George Hammond wrathfully on the other end of the wire. "Now, see here, Jane, I call you in a spirit of simple friendliness and—"

"Oh, I didn't mean you," I said with an effort at apology. "Thank you, George. I'll be right down. But don't be utterly ridiculous. You know perfectly well that Arthur means no harm."

Nevertheless, in spite of my confident words, my heart did a flip-flop and I broke all records in getting downtown. Luckily I found a parking place just across from the city hall. In great haste I eased the family sedan inside the yellow line, jerked out the keys, slammed the door, and ran for the detective's office.

Well might George Hammond call me in a spirit of friendliness. Well might he remember me in gratitude. His recent promotion testified to his noteworthy success in solving startling crimes. But I can assure you that each remarkable solution was directly traceable to my tireless pursuit of detail, my zealous curiosity, and my astonishing comprehension of human nature.

Now as George Hammond himself opened the door he gave me a careful glance, as if he wanted to make quite sure of my identity before granting me admittance. As soon as I was fairly inside and took a look at my brother my stomach contracted. I knew the situation was serious. Arthur had that limp dishrag expression that comes over him whenever he has had a disillusioning experience.

At first the room seemed full of men, but in a moment I had identified them. There were only three besides Arthur and George.

Mr. Austin Barrett, head of the Barrett Machine Company, occupied the central position of importance. He sat behind Hammond's desk, his gnome's face pursed into a distasteful grimace, his manicured fingernails peaked before him.

There was a well-dressed man with a dark, clever face whose brow was twisted into a frown. There was the blond, athletic young man whom I had noticed with Judy Barrett.

"Mr. Barrett, Mr. Platt, Mr. Randall." Hammond introduced them. "Miss Jane Amanda Edwards. Jane, I was trying to call you back. This thing is cleared up as far as Arthur is concerned, I guess, and—"

"But it is just as well you came, Miss Edwards," interrupted Barrett fussily. He patted his fingers together. "Because we must make it clear to you, absolutely clear, that this business is to be kept secret. Not a word about it. Not—one—word. I've told Arthur that and I'm repeating it to you with all the emphasis possible."

Austin Barrett is exactly like the brook, and the only way to defeat his babbling is to interrupt.

"I shan't say a word, Mr. Barrett," I told him earnestly. "Only—just what is it I am to keep secret?"

Young Randall, seated on the windowsill, gave an irrepressible gurgle, and Henry Platt swept me with alive, observant dark eyes.

It was then I noticed Arthur's lunch kit, dreadfully soiled, standing upon a newspaper on Hammond's desk.

"Why, Arthur, there's your lunchbox!" I exclaimed, taking a step toward it. "Where did you find it?"

"I didn't," said Arthur with spirit, and I thought he sent a defiant glance to Austin Barrett.

"That's the secret, Miss Edwards," said Barrett. He gave an apprehensive glance to the tin box and shivered perceptibly. "That thing might have blown us all to kingdom come if it hadn't been for Bill Randall. Someone—someone concealed a bomb in it."

"A bomb!" I repeated and felt my jaw drop. "Not a—a bomb! Why, who in the world—?"

"Exactly!" said Mr. Barrett with a snap of his thin lips. Anger replaced fear in his pale eyes. "That's what we want to know. That's what we'll soon find out. I know the ins and outs of my plant and I'll have no spies or plotters or—"

"Sab cats!" I murmured involuntarily.

"Eh? What's that?" said Barrett. "Now remember, Miss Edwards, not a word. Not a syllable, Arthur! And you, Bill, forget that you found the bomb. I'm going to run this rat to his hole and—"

"You're wrong, Austin," protested Henry Platt. It was the first time he had spoken, and his voice was strong and convincing. "We must get the federal men in on this. If we're going to get out government orders we're entitled to protection. Tell the FBI to investigate."

"Nonsense," said Barrett impatiently. "There's too much government interference in my business now. Hammond here is as good a detective as you'll find."

I wanted to sniff, but I didn't. Bill Randall took a step forward.

"Pardon me, Mr. Barrett," he said politely, "but are you sure this is merely sabotage?"

"Young man," interrupted Barrett, adjusting his eyeglasses to peer coldly through them, "sabotage is never *mere.*"

"I didn't mean that," said Randall hastily. "I meant that all sides of the question should be considered. The bomb was ticking away pretty darn lively in that lunchbox on your table when I found it. Now had it exploded, what would it have accomplished? The destruction of your safe? Your files, perhaps? Or—if you had returned—your death!"

Barrett turned perceptibly paler and made a small choking sound in his throat.

"You intimate that it may have been a personal threat?" he said. "Somebody wanted to kill *me?* Why, I should say not! You're crazy, Bill."

"We'll investigate all angles," said George very importantly. "A slow job. You've got some three thousand employees . . . ."

"There's always the labor problem, of course," said Barrett thoughtfully. He took a cigar from his pocket and carefully cut the tip with a knife that hung from his watch chain. A small key hung beside it. "And this is the second instance of sabotage. Somebody helped one of our precision drills to wreck itself. That was about two weeks ago. I've got my eye on a fellow on the number-one line, Jappy Carillo. You might look him up, Hammond. He lives in the tent colony. And there's John Storm. He's an agitator. Half crazy, I think. I keep him because his mother is our housekeeper and a good one. Besides, it's our policy to watch any known Red. When they're on the payroll and under your eye it's easier to control them. And then, there's my nephew Julian Norbury—but he's just a fool."

Henry Platt arose, jerking back his shoulders in sudden irritation, whether at the garrulity of his senior or from some other cause, I could not tell. "Oh, let's not name any names," he said. "The point is, let each one of us here make up our minds to keep mum about this incident. Idle talk increases its importance and might really hamper the investigation."

He looked directly at me, and I resented it.

"My tongue," I said acidly, "is under control. And I can answer for Arthur. He won't say a word."

Something like amusement flickered in his dark eyes. He turned away. And with that we were dismissed. Platt and Barrett went off together, and Randall and Arthur went back to the factory.

I regarded the lunch kit.

"Do you want it?" asked Hammond, grinning.

"No," I said. "It's filthy. I wondered if there were fingerprints. What in the world is that sticky black stuff all over it?"

"No fingerprints." Hammond shook a regretful head. "Randall acted in great haste and bravery. He walked into Barrett's office—his secretary had gone out—"

"I know his secretary. Grace Ashford. She's been with Barrett for years."

"Randall heard the thing click," went on Hammond. "He recognized Arthur's fancy box and knew it had no place in Barrett's office. He rushed it out and dumped it into a tub of oil. The bomb has been taken out. I've sent it to Chicago for examination, but I hardly think a report of its construction will tell us who put it there. Well, they say there are fifth columnists all over the country. Bound to be some at Barrett's. But old Barrett will likely smoke them out for us. Arthur is lucky not to be suspected."

"Arthur's reputation is above reproach," I was beginning haughtily, but George was wagging his semibald pate.

"His ignorance, not his reputation," he said slyly and chuckled. "As soon as Platt inspected that bomb he said Arthur couldn't possibly have made it."

I elevated my chin.

"Indeed? And who is this know-it-all Platt?"

"The general manager. They say he's a demon for work."

"At least he doesn't babble all the time like Austin Barrett," I said. "But you know, George, I wouldn't be surprised if that was all put on. Barrett is no fool. He's as shrewd as they come. When are you going out to the factory?"

"Right now," he said, picking up his hat. "But don't say you're coming, too, because you're not. No scope for your talents in this little affair."

His rudeness was both unnecessary and ill-advised. I had, at that time, no desire to inspect the Barrett plant. And I can't say that I had a premonition or even a hunch. But George's opposition was provocative, and at once I was keen to keep tabs on his progress. Can I help the way my mind works? The merest scent of a mystery, and I am as eager for a solution as Win is for a meaty bone. And I know how to get around George.

"As I left the house I noticed Theresa was baking rhubarb pies," I said tentatively. "They're for dinner. With roast lamb and new potatoes."

"Is that an invitation?" asked George eagerly.

I went my way. I knew he would be ringing the doorbell come dinner time. George has a good appetite, and for years he has taken a personal interest in Theresa's culinary triumphs.

Although, up to this time, I had given but passing attention to the matter, I was well aware of the rush for national defense. Annie's twitterings and alarms were not necessary to apprise me that democracy was being attacked. There was Arthur going to work every day! The daily papers were full of headlines, and the air was full of words. With half the world in arms our security was precarious, and every honest citizen resented and opposed those who would seek to undermine it.

Not that I consider our government *perfect!* I've often thought of a campaign for Congress. I can imagine myself touring the country, telling it a few plain truths.

"Civilization is going to smash," Annie observed hollowly at intervals. "The world will never be the same again."

"Who wants it the same?" I would come back waspishly. "Seems to me it ought to improve *sometime!*"

Now the bomb focused all my interest. It was clear that our country needed better defenses, more guns, more planes, more tanks, and dozens of other things I had never even heard of. The Barrett Company was trying to provide machines to make them, and if some selfish, traitorous wretch was trying to stir up a rumpus and wreck the works, why, I was interested! I certainly was. Especially when the villain attempted to throw the blame on poor, innocent Arthur who was losing his late-morning sleep and eating a cold lunch for his country!

I gave considerable thought to the question as I drove home.

Austin Barrett kept aloof from the neighbors on Greenwood Avenue, but I knew him. Just a shrewd little eye for a profit—that was Barrett. Chatter he might and chatter he did, but he never lost sight of his objectives. Low taxes, high profits, a good dividend to his stockholders, fishing trips in summer, Florida in winter, and two expensive cars in his garage.

Mrs. Austin Barrett was dead. During her lifetime the family occupied an estate on the edge of town, but that had been sold during the depression, when the Barrett Company had almost hit the rocks. Now Austin and his daughter Judith, pretty and popular, lived on Greenwood Avenue in an attractive white clapboarded house surrounded by a garden. There were two servants, Susy Anderson, young and pert, and Mrs. Agnes Storm, the housekeeper. Mrs. Storm was a silent, gray woman with heavy-lidded eyes. Her few guttural words were difficult to understand, perhaps because she spoke so seldom.

"She's a servant," said Theresa, who considers herself my equal, if not my superior, "and she's a foreigner."

This dismissed the subject. To which race or nationality this term referred, I had never inquired. In Rockport the term "foreigner" was all-inclusive.

Austin Barrett had mentioned three names in connection with the attempted bombing: Jappy Carillo, John Storm, Julian Norbury. Mr. Platt had gently rebuked him. Evidently he considered suspicion without foundation dangerous.

Jappy Carillo was just a name to me.

John Storm was talked of in town as a labor agitator.

Julian Norbury was known as an idler. And he was Austin Barrett's nephew. He and his sister Katherine were the children of Mrs. Barrett's sister. Not that they seemed to have much in common with their cousin Judith. They were not even on visiting terms at the Barrett house, and the neighbors had deduced a family quarrel.

Julian Norbury was a descendant of pioneers, men who seized their opportunities and grew rich. His grandfather was a lumberman; his father was a judge, but Julian was satisfied to be an accomplished spender and an amusing conversationalist. He still believed in the divine right of kings and the general worthlessness of the lower classes.

I suppose I might just as well pause right here to relate the history of the Barrett Company and tell what I know about Steve Boyd and his wife Katherine, who was Julian Norbury's sister and Judith Barrett's first cousin.

You see, for some years the Barrett Company was Barrett and Boyd. The money that started the firm belonged to Barrett, but the particular machine tool, some kind of a drill, that made the money had been invented by Boyd. Steve Boyd was a big curly-haired fellow just past fifty. After eighteen months in France with the A.E.F. he came home and with a whirlwind courtship married beautiful Katherine Norbury. She had some money, an inheritance. Her brother Julian had the same. He spent his, and Katherine gave hers to Steve to put in the Barrett Company. Julian's money went quickly but, ultimately, Katherine's disappeared as surely. Barrett and Boyd prospered during the twenties, and then profits disappeared. Steve was impatient, went off to California, found things no better, came back. Barrett persevered. In 1936 he raised money to buy Boyd's share of the business. Steve and Katherine took the fifty thousand *and* Julian, and the three of them went to Florida, where the fifty thousand was soon as extinct as the passenger pigeon.

This is where Henry Platt comes into the picture. At the time of the reorganization he had been working for the company for two years. Barrett then made him general manager, and soon things began to pick up. Now, with the government contracts, the place was a hive of industry.

I knew Steve Boyd. He had keen, restless blue eyes and a thick, pendulous lower lip. He had lots of vitality. He never gave up. He came back from Florida and went to work in the Barrett shop. He was a skilled machinist. He could always return to that and he didn't mind getting his hands dirty or wearing overalls. But the Norburys were different. Julian was sour, and Katherine was furiously discontented, and right now all three of them were living in a small apartment a block from us on Greenwood Avenue. Katherine was snooty with the neighbors, and Julian was rarely seen.

As I had anticipated, Annie and Arthur and I entertained Detective Captain George Hammond that night. The roast lamb was done to a turn. Theresa rubs it with a clove of garlic and serves with it a minted pineapple jelly that is delicious. After I had apprised her of Hammond's probable appearance she made a trip to her asparagus bed and then whipped up her special hollandaise sauce.

But this delicacy was not to be ours. Instead, Theresa, black with anger and somewhat lame, planked down with a thud upon the table a dish of canned peas. Unfortunately, the dog Win had taken a notion to emerge from the basement and run between Theresa's legs as the sauce was being poured upon the asparagus.

I regretted my suggestion to George. He has a single-track mind, and it never left his food. That night I gathered very little information concerning affairs at the Barrett plant. In fact, only one item of interest came into the conversation, and at the time I didn't even know it was important.

George said vaguely: "Barrett is snooping around. That place is a whirlpool. Nobody knows what the other fellow is doing. It's a laugh. That Carillo, for instance. We couldn't link him up with the bombing, but he got fired just the same. Come to find out, he'd been drawing three paychecks, his own and those of two men who quit three weeks ago. Nobody knew the difference until today. Can you feature it?"

In spite of the secrecy order there was talk in the plant about the bomb.

John Storm knew about it. He told his mother as he sat in the Barrett kitchen and scowled at the sounds of revelry from the living room where Judith entertained friends. He was a small man, about thirty, pale, and inoffensive looking. His hair was smoothly brushed and indeterminate brown. His fingers, long, with broken nails, were deeply stained with nicotine.

"There'll be others," he said calmly. "There'll be parts missing and breakdowns, and then, when the right time comes, we'll strike."

The woman went on about her work, making the sink immaculate. No flicker of expression crossed her gaunt face.

"Have care," was all she said.

Steve Boyd knew about the bomb. He went home, excited, and told his wife about it.

"Somebody tried to blow up your dear uncle Austin," he said, his pendulous lower lip thrust forward. "They say somebody got the bomb in time. Maybe it was a dud. Maybe next time it won't be."

Katherine Boyd regarded him critically. After almost twenty years she was never sure of him, could never judge of his intent. She lay now on the davenport in her small living room, her thin, handsome face petulant, her finely arched brows twisted into a frown.

"You wouldn't be taking that way to bring him to terms, would you?" she asked levelly.

"Terms? Now, see here, Katherine, don't begin on that stuff again," he said roughly. "I sold out to him. I used the money. Now I'm working for wages again. For a while. Until my new trick is perfected I wouldn't ask Austin Barrett for a plugged nickel. He'll make on it, but I won't stand by and see him profiteer. He'll play fair with me and with his labor or else. . ."

"Or else!" she mocked. "You're anti-everything. You and Pegler."

"Austin Barrett will make no millions from munitions while I'm around," he said heavily.

"You're a troublemaker. And Austin Barrett is a stuffed shirt. Henry Platt is the big shot." A small secret smile touched her painted lips. "I like big shots," she added slowly.

He strode over to her, his face flushed with dark fury, but when he came to her side he stopped and looked at her lying there. His expression softened, and he dropped down beside her.

"Don't let's quarrel, Katherine," he said. "I'm getting sixty a week. That's not chicken feed. You're comfortable, and I'll be on top again just as soon as the government men finish the tests. You'll see. It's Julian who gets you all stirred up."

She shrugged, the faintest possible movement of her shoulders.

"Comfortable! What a middle-class word! Anyway I'm not comfortable. I want a new car. I need clothes. I want to go to Asheville with Peg. And I do not intend to stay in this hole of an apartment."

"Ah, honey," he pleaded. "Don't be that way. Move over and let's plan something."

But she stretched one slender white hand to pull on the lamp and with the other picked up a magazine from the coffee table beside her.

"Go away," she said evenly.

He flushed as if she had struck him, rose, and walked heavily from the room. His eyes were glazed with ugly speculation.

There was nothing, however, to disturb the even tenor of my life until Monday night about two weeks later. The April skies were simply flooding us with rain, and I was worried about Brother Arthur.

He was working on the second shift at Barrett's. This necessitated going to work at four in the afternoon, a detestable hour, I thought, but Arthur does, of course, enjoy a morning sleep. He remained on duty until twelve-thirty with half an hour off for lunch, from eight to eight-thirty. Arthur has a distressing tendency to bronchitis that we have to consider, and as the rain continued I feared that the damp night air might be harmful to him.

Annie was knitting and yawning. I was trying to read, being greatly distracted by the strange and unnecessary and simply frightful things a radio orchestra was doing to "Jeanie with the Light Brown Hair." Poor Jeanie was almost done for when the announcer interrupted.

"We have a special news flash," he said, excitement hoarse in his voice. "Fire has broken out at the Barrett plant. Hose companies are at the scene, and it is hoped to have the flames under control shortly. Keep tuned to this station for further details."

Before the words were well out of his mouth I had my hat and coat and was poking about in the hall closet for my umbrella.

"I'm going to the fire," I called out.

But my sister was right at my heels, pulling on her overshoes with hurried determination.

"Me too," said Annie.

CHAPTER THREE

AS I CLOSED THE HOUSE DOOR behind me I could hear in the distance the stirring sounds of the sirens and gongs and, like any old fire horse, I lifted my head and pricked up my ears.

It was a wretched night. The chill seemed to penetrate to the very bone. It was dark as Erebus, and the driving rain made visibility practically nil. The gusty wind banged the garage doors and almost blew them off the hinges, but I managed at last to get them fastened. With Annie beside me in the front seat I drove out of the yard.

The Barrett Company occupied a great rambling factory on the outskirts of town. In fine weather the trip takes about ten minutes, but on that April night we crawled over the wet and slippery pavement at a snail's pace.

In a moment we heard again the wail and the roar of additional fire engines. I pulled over to the very edge of the road and let the impressive, demanding trucks sweep past.

They were followed by other cars, one after another, and I had a difficult time getting into the stream again.

"Oh, dear me, I hope Arthur is safe! Oh, goodness me, I hope it isn't a bad fire!" Annie chirped continually. "Wouldn't you think this rain would put it out?"

I took a firmer grip on the wheel and stepped on the gas. It wasn't that I actually wished the Barrett plant or, indeed, any structure to go down in flaming destruction, but as long as there was a blaze I wanted to be on hand to see it.

Another five minutes and the Barrett shops with their long rows of lighted windows came into view. I maneuvered the car into a vacant space in the line of cars already parked. Firemen, floodlights, great panting engines, curling lengths of hose, took up all the available space before the plant. People were milling about, some in raincoats, some with umbrellas. Shouts echoed.

I knew the lay of the land. There was a high, stout wire fence around a great enclosure. Just inside the double front gates was a small brick structure with a door, a window, a desk, chair, light, and telephone. This was Arthur's post. Here he checked the numbers of incoming and outgoing work men, examined the credentials of all visitors. Beyond Arthur's office was a stretch of lawn, muddy now but turning green. The main office building of the factory was parallel to this grassy strip, and the various shops branched off at right angles in the rear. Beyond all this were the storage buildings and the company railroad tracks.

"Well, here we are!" I said to Annie. "But the firemen won't let anybody in. Look, the people are getting back into the cars."

"Why, would you look at that fence!" clucked Annie indignantly. This was her first sight of the plant. "It's just like a cage. One would expect to see the animals. But where is Arthur? And where is the fire?"

I poked my umbrella outside, elevated it, and edged into the rain beneath its shelter. At once I discovered that Arthur was not in his coop. An electric bulb gave illumination, but the tiny room was empty.

Advancing boldly to the gate, I decided to cross forces with a fireman. A pleasant firmness is my usual policy.

Thunder rolled a reverberating peal and added impetus to the downpour. There was nothing warm or comforting or full of the promise of summer about this rain. I saw only rheumatism and influenza in the immediate future, but something seemed to tell me to make sure that Arthur was not concerned with the fire. Had I seen him happily busy in his little hut I believe I should have driven thankfully and hurriedly back into town. But such conjecture is in vain.

At that hesitant moment a man came rapidly from the left, almost collided with me, and slid through the gate.

"Good evening," I began cheerfully. "Can you tell me if—"

The man did not wait for me to finish my sentence. He gave a violent start, and I had the impression of extreme haste. I realized, too, that he had not seen me. His head was down; his collar was up against the rain. While floodlights made the building before us bright they threw into greater shadow the region of the fence.

Annie, who was sitting in the car with the window open and ears and eyes straining, must have heard me speak. She said afterward that she had caught the movement of the man and thought it was Arthur coming to the car. She leaned forward and turned on the bright lights.

The man, caught in the glare, tall and mysterious in a black slicker, gave a muttered exclamation, turned sharply, and ran into the darkness.

But not before I had a brief glimpse of his features.

I knew him. Those deep-set, hollowed eyes were quite unmistakable.

It was Julian Norbury.

"Well," I said indignantly, going back to Annie, "a fine way to act! That was Julian Norbury. "

"Do you suppose he works here?" she asked, craning her neck in a vain effort to see what had become of him.

"Not him. He simply sponges on Steve Boyd. At least, that's what people say. I know that he spends most of his time in that bookie joint above Red Green's Bowling Alley."

I may be—in fact, I am—old-fashioned in habit and principle, but I'm not such a back number that I don't know what's going on in my own home town. I make it my business to find out things, and sooner or later the information comes in mighty handy.

"Very rude of him, I'm sure," said Annie judicially. "Jane, this rain isn't going to do my throat a bit of good." She coughed in a tubercular manner. "And I don't see any fire."

"Stay in the car where it's dry," I bade her. "I'll be back."

I had the cringing and crawling up my spine that told me something was going on. Why did Julian Norbury run as if pursued? Where was Arthur? Suddenly I wondered if Austin Barrett had ever discovered the source of the attempted bombing.

I went back to the gate, but a fireman barred my way.

"You can't go in, lady," he said.

"I want to find my brother," I told him. "Where is the fire?"

"You can't go in," he repeated stolidly. "The fire was in one of the offices and no one hurt. All over now. We're getting our lines out, lady, and you'll likely get hurt if you're in the way."

His pleasant firmness surpassed mine. I left him and went along the fence until I was well out of his range of vision. There is something about opposition that always develops my tenacity of purpose.

I discarded my umbrella and investigated that fence.

The mesh of the wire was too small for a toe hold, but I could get my fingers through the holes and pull myself up almost to the top. I did so, and there I hung—wondering.

I had never heard that the fence was electrically charged, but there was a chance. I put up a careful finger. No shock. But I discovered at once that sharp barbed wire ran all along the upper edge. With luck I felt able to cope with that.

I removed my coat and felt the cold rain on my silk-clad shoulders. Throwing the heavy garment over the barbs, I made one mighty effort, pulled myself over the top. It wasn't easy. It's many a day since Jane Edwards was known as the tomboy of Greenwood Avenue. And I wrenched my ankle as I hit the ground on the other side.

Hastily I shrugged into my water-soaked outer wrap and pondered a report to Mr. Barrett. His fence was not invulnerable. It would be comparatively easy for a spy to effect an entrance to the factory. Climb the fence and then, if no one saw him . . .

But I was not in that situation.

An authoritative hand seized me by the collar and spun me around into the beam of an investigating flashlight. Then the hand dropped and a voice stammered

"Oh, I say, Miss Edwards! Did—did you climb that fence?"

"I certainly did, young man," I said with some pride. "The fireman wouldn't let me through the gate. Oh, it's Mr. Randall, isn't it? How serious was the fire, and where is my brother Arthur?"

"Arthur should be at the gate," he replied instantly. "He's supposed to know exactly who came in tonight and—"

"That's what I thought," I said sadly. "He seems to have stepped out for a moment . . . ."

Bill Randall wore no hat. His hair was wet and darkened by the rain.

"This will be bad for him, the poor sap!" he said explosively. "First the bomb in his lunch pail and now a fire with the gate unguarded . . . ."

"I'll run inside and find him," I offered. "I'm going to wait and drive him home."

"I have to locate Richards. I have to get on the phone," he murmured more to himself than to me. "O.K., Miss Edwards. Just look inside the main building there as soon as the firemen will let you."

He set off at a run for the gate. I could practically read his mind. He was thinking, "The old girl can't possibly do any harm, and maybe she'll get Edwards back on his job."

I went to the front entrance of the office building and walked inside. The firemen were busily removing their paraphernalia and made no attempt to stop me. The wide hallway that bisected the place was muddied and wet and bore the deserted look that all offices, busy by day, wear in the silent night.

At the far end of this central hallway was another door leading outside and to the shops in the rear. It was closed. Halfway to it were two wide arched openings to corridors right and left, both flanked by offices.

I advanced a step softly, my rubbers making no sound on the marble floor. The light was none too bright. Suddenly the first door to my right was pushed aside and a figure wavered toward me. I started in involuntary fright.

But it was only Arthur.

He brushed past me and sought the outer air. He looked white and green and as if he were going to be sick.

I followed him. He was.

"Honestly, Arthur, you're worse than Mussy," I said in quiet vehemence when he had at last recovered and had come inside again.

"His name," said Arthur, feeble but firm, "is Win. The fire is over, Jane. It certainly was exciting while it lasted. But the smoke finally got me . . . ."

"Bill Randall seems to think you'll be in trouble for leaving the gate," I said to him. "I think he's out there now using your telephone."

Arthur dismissed this airily. He seemed very sure of himself.

"Come on, I'll show you where the fire was," he offered. "Don't worry about me getting called down. They'll be mighty thankful I did leave the gate. Don't worry about that."

He led the way down the corridor to the left, and I walked after him straight into excitement.

The head of the Rockport Fire Department stood there talking to two of his men.

"Couldn't you use your nose?" the chief was saying irritably. His name was Brownlee. He was a short, thickset man with a faint, black film of beard pushing through his jaw. "I'm sure, I tell you. Stay right here, Jim, and don't let anybody in. First thing is to find out who turned in the alarm."

"I did," said Arthur in proud confidence behind him.

The chief turned and looked at us, not in welcome but in cold doubt.

"You did?" he said. "Stick around here until I can ask you about it." His eyes were frankly suspicious as they rested on me.

"I'm just waiting for him," I said meekly. "I'm his sister."

Sometimes meekness is helpful—not often.

Men talked and shoes clattered and the Rockport chief of police, two uniformed policemen, and Captain George Hammond in his winter overcoat and old felt hat came down the hall.

George hesitated when he saw me and to my greeting returned only a very strange look. I couldn't quite interpret it. A compound perhaps of suspicion plus resignation. He looked somehow as if he thought I had started the fire.

"What's up, Brownlee?" asked the chief of police.

"God knows," said Brownlee piously, "and we got to find out. This feller here discovered the fire."

He pointed to Arthur.

Hammond looked at Arthur as if he had seen him before but wished he hadn't. Then he stepped to the door of the burned office. I looked over his shoulder until I was elbowed aside none too gently by the two uniformed policemen. But I could see that the once-beautiful paneled room was a smoked and dripping ruin.

"Didn't discover it quite soon enough, did you?" Hammond observed to Arthur.

Bill Randall came hurriedly down the hall, shaking the rain from his coat and slicking back his wet hair. He gave Arthur a cross look.

"The gates are locked, and your man is on the watch," he said to Hammond. "And it's a damn queer thing where Richards is. I—"

"Where can we talk?" interrupted Brownlee. "We got to get these statements. I'm all in. I got to get through. These doors along here all locked? Who's got keys?"

"Richards," said Bill.

"Well, who the dev—?" Brownlee began but caught my stony glare and coughed. "Who is Richards, and where is he?"

"I don't know where he is," said Bill, scowling. "He's the night watchman, makes rounds all night, but I run all over the place. Anyway, there's the general reception room on the other side of the central hall. Come along."

We trailed after him, but the man left behind cried out.

"I gotta have a chair, Chief. If I gotta stay here I gotta have a chair!"

"For God sakes," began Brownlee angrily.

"I'll bring you one," offered Bill Randall hastily.

We returned to the room from which I had seen Arthur emerge only a short time before. The lights shone now. It was warm and bright and orderly with desks and chairs, and we all sat down. Except Hammond, who prowled about. And Bill, who went out with a chair.

A faint thought of Annie patiently waiting in the car, listening to the tattoo of the rain on the roof, crossed my mind but did not penetrate.

Arthur cleared his throat and began his story.

"I was sitting in my office at the gate," said Arthur importantly. "I was just looking out at the rain when I noticed a strange light in the last window on the left-hand side. It didn't seem like electric light. I can't explain exactly, but it was redder somehow and more flickering. Or maybe I am just psychic enough to—"

"Yeah," said Hammond dryly. "We know. Go on."

"I rushed into the building and down that corridor. When I reached the door it was closed. I opened it and saw a mass of flames."

"All over the room?" asked Brownlee. "The walls? The rug?"

"Mostly in the corner by the desk," said Arthur. "But, yes, I think the floor was burning too. The smoke was terrible. I ran back to this office and called the fire department."

The outer door opened then, and we heard it. And Bill Randall's voice speaking. Then Henry Platt appeared in the doorway, and with him was Judith Barrett.

"Good evening, gentlemen," said Platt abruptly. He was in evening dress, his white scarf immaculate above his black overcoat, his dark eyes concerned. "I didn't hear. We've been at the country club. I wish I had been at home to get the call. What happened? How did the fire start?"

Brownlee opened his mouth, but Hammond said quickly, "We don't know yet."

"It's out now," said Brownlee. "Only one office. Fortunately we got here in time to save the rest."

"But how did it start?" insisted Platt. "What office?"

Judith said nothing at all but looked excited and very pretty. At least I thought so, and I could see that Bill Randall agreed.

"Did you see Richards?" Randall asked Platt. He could not get the watchman out of his mind and was determined to make someone take an interest.

"For that matter," put in Arthur suddenly in a loud tone, "where is Mr. Barrett?"

The fire chief turned to Judith.

"Do you know where we might locate your father?" he asked. "We've already called several places . . . ."

She shook her head. She was all in white—long, soft chiffon skirt, white fur jacket, white spangled handkerchief tied down over her curls behind the artfully rolled pompadour. Only her eyes were very blue.

"But Mr. Barrett was here," Arthur said then. "Why, surely he wouldn't leave when—"

"Here?" Randall asked sharply, and all of them turned to Arthur, who was not abashed but nodded his head in certainty.

"Of course. He came about nine-fifteen, I imagine, parked his car right in front of the gate in his reserved space. He didn't speak to me but nodded as he went past."

"He must have gone away again," said Platt definitely.

"No." Arthur was stubborn and sure. "He didn't leave before the fire. Because I was right there at the gate until I saw the funny light in his office. And surely he didn't go *after* the fire had been discovered."

"But did you see him when you opened his door?" Hammond pinned him down.

"He wasn't there then," Arthur conceded slowly.

Judith Barrett shuddered suddenly, a long convulsive quiver, and Henry Platt stepped close to her and put a protective hand on her arm.

"Now don't get excited," he said soothingly. "Your father always knows quite well what he's doing. This fire seems very strange, and I'll bet he's checking up on it some way. Bill, run out and see if Mr. Barrett's car is still there, will you?"

Randall looked rebellious, but however much he would prefer to be the one who stood beside Judith with his hand on her arm the request from the general manager could not be disregarded. He went.

"And just to make sure," Platt began with a suggestive nod of the head to the detective, "you'd better—"

But Brownlee and Hammond were already on a dogtrot down the corridor, and Arthur and I were at their heels.

"There's a lavatory off the office," panted Arthur. "Maybe he was overcome by the smoke. It almost got me, I tell you. And there's a big closet where the safe is. It's a small room with shelves."

"I went in there," said Brownlee grimly.

The man at the door looked up inquiringly as we bore down upon him.

"Jim, are you positive there isn't anybody in that room?" asked the chief.

Jim's eyes looked surprised and then amused.

"Not unless it's the invisible man," he said smartly.

It was that—almost.

The office, as I have said, was a sodden ruin. It was wood-paneled, with the usual rugs and chairs and cabinets. A large walnut desk was ranged across one corner.

Brownlee made for the desk, scooted around one end, axed stopped short. The rest of us stopped just behind him, but we could see what he saw.

On the charred floor behind the desk lay what had been Austin Barrett.

CHAPTER FOUR

"HE'S DEAD!" SAID BROWNLEE quite unnecessarily.

Captain Hammond made a decisive step forward and at the same time motioned the rest of us back. I was the only one who disobeyed him and I took but two steps and a brief look. That was enough. The fire was infamous outrage, yet the work of destruction was not complete. Even to the casual glance of a neighbor it was apparent that the remains were those of Austin Barrett.

"A heart attack?" I wondered aloud. It seemed essential to at once seek the cause of this disaster. "Perhaps he fell and dropped a match or a cigarette. No, he smoked cigars."

"The fire was hottest in that corner," put in Chief Brownlee. "We doused it good and proper there. But I can understand why none of us saw him. We stood this side of the desk, and when we knew the fire was out there was no reason to go poking behind it. Besides, I had a particular reason to leave things undisturbed."

Hammond stepped to the door. I was quite unable to remove my eyes from the burned desk. I suppose Austin Barrett had been busy there. The once shining and smooth walnut was blistered and still wet. Feathery gray ashes were all that remained of papers. The telephone was blackened. But at one end stood, unharmed and audacious, a small china dog.

"Jim," Hammond was saying to the man at the door, "get on the phone. I want men from headquarters. The regular once-over, tell them. Photographs, fingerprints, and everything. Get the coroner. Jane, you'd better go back down the hall and break it to Miss Barrett."

I have no fund of smooth phrases and I did not relish this task. But I was spared, for Judy, white and shaken, was suddenly behind me in the doorway.

"Don't come in," Hammond ordered. "You mustn't see—now."

"What is it?" she cried, and then she understood and big, slow tears welled into her blue eyes. "That's my little dog," she said then irrelevantly, darted to pick up the figure, and stood there shivering.

"Come now, Judith, be brave," I soothed her. "I'll take that home for you." I slid the animal into my coat pocket. "You must have courage."

She allowed me to lead her down the hall where Henry Platt was hurrying to meet her.

"I was called to the phone," he said, shocked and solicitous. "Why did you run down here, Judith? Don't cry. I'll take care of everything. Just try not to think about it now. I'll tell Hammond . . . . I'm taking you home."

"Mr. Barrett's car is still outside," said Bill Randall, choosing just that moment to hasten into the building. "And he must be out in the shop or— Now, what's the matter?"

"Mr. Barrett was somehow caught in the fire," I told him. "He—he has— passed away."

Randall stood absolutely still for a moment. I felt that he had taken in the meaning of my words, but he made no reply. Swift thoughts seemed to be pressing behind his narrowed eyes. And then he crossed over to Judith and took her small white hand.

"Come on, Judy, let me drive you home," he said gently. "I'm so sorry. I'm terribly sorry."

"No," said Henry Platt abruptly and then reconsidered. His strong fingers stroked his chin, and he frowned as if he found himself in a maze from which he could not see the way. "Very well, Randall," he said as if he gave permission. "Perhaps that would be best. Certainly I am needed here. See that Mrs. Storm is there and, also, call some one of Judith's friends."

Bill Randall's eyes flashed, and I thought there would be friction, but the moment passed. Bill and Judith were going out of the door when Platt's eyes suddenly rested on me.

"Why, you should be the one to take that poor girl home!" he exclaimed as if he hated himself for not having thought of it before. "A woman's understanding . . ."

"No indeed." I shook my head and nipped that notion right at its blossoming. "Comforting the afflicted isn't my forte. This is."

"What is?" he asked coldly.

"Investigating deaths that occur under peculiar circumstances."

He flushed and looked more worried than ever.

"Mr. Barrett's death has occurred under sad but not mysterious circumstances," he denied stiffly. "I don't believe, Miss Edwards, that you will find anything here that pertains to your—er—hobby."

I didn't bother to contradict him. I knew his remark was only wishful thinking. At the time a mob of Hammond's followers was crowding through the door. Blake, a policeman with whom I have had frequent unpleasant altercations, headed the parade, and Mr. Jenks, the coroner, ended it. The sheriff was there and the photographers and two reporters and Dr. Hamilton, the medical examiner. Austin Barrett's death was not to go unheralded in our town. Any death makes a ripple, but a rich man's makes a splash.

A hum of speculation arose, but no pronouncement was made. At least I, loitering in the corridor outside the office, had a thin time trying to pick out illuminating phrases. Arthur had gone back to his position at the gate. As the men went about their necessary tasks they gave me many a curious look, but no one said anything. Most people in Rockport know me and my ways. Before the job was finished Bill Randall came back.

"Judith's at home," he said gloomily. "Fortunately Mrs. Storm turned in at the same time. Where do you suppose that old dame was at this hour of the night? We sent a wire to Judith's aunt. Say, your sister called out to me as I parked just now, Miss Edwards. She wants you to drive her home."

I passed that off. Is it my fault that Annie has never learned to drive?

"Mr. Randall," I asked, "have you located Richards, the night watchman?"

"Not yet," he said, "but he'll punch in here any time now. It's almost time for the shifts to change."

A few minutes later one mass of workmen made way for a new crowd. Arthur, relieved of his duties, came in.

"The rain has stopped," he said. "Annie insists that one of us take her home, Jane. I—"

"Wait in that office," commanded George Hammond. He jogged hurriedly past us down the corridor. "We're having a little conference. Both of you stay right here."

I had no intention of leaving. The great silver bulbs were flashing as the photographers continued to take pictures of the burned office. Mortuary assistants came with a stretcher. Detective Hammond, the sheriff, the doctor, the coroner, the chief of police, the fire chief, dodged back and forth. The telephone jingled busily.

I stood in the central hall. A policeman was guarding the front door now, and I could hear him refusing admittance to many workmen who, on their way home, were trying to get a glimpse of the fire.

And then, just as Mr. Platt came down the hall, there came the metallic click of a key turned in the lock. We whirled as the closed door at the back opened and a big broad-shouldered man entered.

"Here, you!" shouted Platt, his dark face suddenly alive and furious. "Come here! What are you doing with a key to that door?"

The burly fellow approached, and I saw that it was Steve Boyd. His grin was insolent.

Platt recognized him at the same time, and his countenance grew more suspicious and his eyes more watchful.

"Oh, I've had it these many years," Boyd retorted easily. "I owned the joint; didn't you know? Where's Austin? Your stooge there in front wouldn't let me in, and I wanted to find out what's going on. The rumor through the shop is that the office has been bombed."

"No," said Platt shortly. His eyes on Boyd were speculative. "It wasn't a bomb. Just a fire."

"Somebody tried to burn the place, eh?"

"Nothing like that," evaded Platt. "It seems to have been purely accidental."

I was then aware that Detective Hammond had been watching from the door of the reception room. He spoke now.

"Mr. Boyd, would you mind joining us for a minute? Come along, Miss Edwards and Mr. Platt."

The room seemed full of men, sitting and standing. Mr. Platt placed a chair for me.

"If this is an inquiry," he said in a low voice to Hammond, "might it not be better to postpone it until morning? It's almost that now. Tomorrow will bring many problems. Mr. Barrett's office can be guarded."

"We want something to go on," said Hammond equably. "Let's take a whirl now. Arthur Edwards, I'll begin with you. At what time did Mr. Barrett enter the plant tonight?"

Arthur thought a moment and then put it at nine-thirty.

"What time did you discover the fire?"

"Somewhere near ten-thirty. I can't be exact . . . ."

"The alarm," said Chief Brownlee, "came in at ten thirty-five."

"All right, Brownlee, take it from there," said Hammond. "I drove in right back of the first engine. Edwards met us at the door of this building. The office was in flames, but it didn't take us very long to get them under control."

"Have you a theory concerning the origin of the fire?"

"You said it. Someone started this fire—intentionally."

"Arson," I put in helpfully, but no one paid any attention.

"From an odor apparent upon my arrival—it has since evaporated—and from the intensity of the flames in certain portions of the room, I would say that gasoline or naphtha had been poured about. Laboratory tests will confirm this. Moreover, windows on opposite sides of the room had been opened a little to create a draft."

Steve Boyd made a sound, an angry grunt. He was listening intently.

"Mr. Barrett was in his office," Hammond went on then. "We found him dead on the floor behind his desk."

That time Steve Boyd made no sound at all. It was hard to interpret the expression on his face. Surprise. Perhaps incredulity. Definitely not regret.

"Gentlemen," said Hammond deliberately, as though addressing a jury. He ignored my presence. Certainly he could not have forgotten it. "Gentlemen, does the intent seem plain? Whoever started the fire did so in the hope that the flames would consume the body of Austin Barrett."

I sniffed loudly. Platt made a gesture of repugnance and fingered his white tie. Bill Randall spoke up with frank curiosity.

"Did the fire," he asked briskly, "cause or contribute to Mr. Barrett's death?"

Dr. Hamilton answered.

"Mr. Barrett," he said with conviction, "was killed before the fire started. The fire was an afterthought. Death was caused by, a severe blow on the back of the head. The skull was seriously fractured. He may have lived a few minutes. Not long."

Curiosity is one of our most elemental human instincts. There wasn't a person in that room who, as soon as the fact of murder was out, did not ask themselves who did it. Who? Seeking eyes went from face to unrevealing face.

"Murder," said Henry Platt heavily. He looked older. Sudden lines showed from nostril to mouth. "Murder! My God, Hammond, we can't have that!"

"You've got it," said Hammond gloomily. His eyes always seem to be cold hard slate when he looks upon crime and intends to inflict punishment. "Could he conk himself and then set fire to the room?"

Austin Barrett, according to the doctor, had been struck with one of those well-known blunt instruments. I've read of those cases for years and had thought it likely that sometime I'd meet up with one.

"We've got to make a start somewhere," Hammond was saying. "Barrett was killed between nine-thirty and ten-thirty. There were some nine hundred men working here at the time. Presumably every one of them was checked in . . . ."

"In view of the fact that Mr. Edwards left the gate," said Platt vexedly, and his eyes dwelt most unfavorably upon my brother, "any assassin could have effected an entrance."

"Not at all," I put in quickly and firmly. "Whoever struck Mr. Barrett did so before the fire started. Arthur was on duty until that time. Besides, the killer could have climbed the fence. I did myself. Tonight."

Every face in the room changed expression, and I hastened to justify myself.

"That had nothing to do with the murder. I didn't get here until the fire had been extinguished. But—that fence can be climbed. The killer could have entered and, during the excitement caused by the fire, he could easily have escaped. Maybe that's why he started the fire. To attract Arthur from his post. And—"

"Is there only the one entrance?" Dr. Hamilton asked.

"There's the truck gate in the rear. It's always locked and barred at night," Platt answered.

It was then that I remembered Julian Norbury.

"I've got something," I cried to Captain Hammond. "The other day, in your office, Mr. Barrett mentioned the name of Julian Norbury and mentioned it in an angry manner. Do you remember?"

He did.

"Well, Julian Norbury was out here tonight. He slipped through the main gate while the firemen were busy."

"He didn't!"

Steve Boyd uttered the exclamation with almost a roar of rage. His little eyes blinked, and he stood up, tall, head lowered.

"I *beg* your pardon!" I said in my most frigid manner. "*I—saw—him!*"

We could notice Boyd relax as if he willed himself to do so.

"I'm sorry, Miss Edwards," he said after a moment and managed a smile. "I didn't mean that I doubted your word. It—it upsets me to have Julian sticking in where he doesn't belong."

"Norbury is related, isn't he?" said George meditatively. "Your brother-in-law and Barrett's nephew. What was he doing here tonight? He doesn't work here."

A wry smile drew down the corner of Boyd's wide mouth.

"No," he agreed. "He doesn't work here. As for what he wanted—I can furnish no explanation. I didn't see him. I'm afraid you'll have to ask him."

"I shall," Hammond promised.

"See here, Hammond," began Platt anxiously. "We'll have to get quick action on this. Here I am making every effort to speed up this defense program, increase our production, everybody all over the country yelling for us to hurry on our tool orders. We've got labor trouble, material difficulties, and spy scares, and now—murder! Why don't you begin with these unauthorized entrances into our plant? Miss Edwards, for instance, and Norbury. And I know that Boyd here, supposedly at work in the forge shop, wouldn't have much trouble getting in and out with a key to the back door!"

"Trying to hang it on me, Platt?"

Boyd's hands were clenched until the knuckles were pale against the reddish skin, but his voice was even.

"No," said the harassed Platt defiantly, "but I think you ought to come out with an explanation."

"I had nothing to do with the fire or with the murder," said Steve Boyd, "and there's no evidence against me." He walked negligently to the door. "Any time you want amplification of that, Hammond, you know where to find me. I'm going home."

Hammond nodded. Not that it made any difference. Boyd had already gone.

Arthur sneezed. It was a really explosive sound and made us all jump. At once I was troubled, remembering his tendency to bronchitis.

"Arthur," I said, fishing about in my purse, "here are the car keys. Do take Annie home. I'll get back someway."

I glanced at George, but he has a disconcerting habit of forgetting our long friendship whenever he is busy with a case.

Arthur obeyed, passing a policeman at the door who had a whispered word for Hammond.

"This night watchman now," said Hammond, turning back to us. "This Richards you were looking for, Randall. Our man can't find him either. Doesn't seem to be around."

"Run off!" said Brownlee sagely. "Maybe he's the man. Did he have anything against Mr. Barrett?"

"Oh, he did a lot of talking," said Randall, smiling. "Just the other day he was telling me that he wouldn't give a dime a dozen for men like Mr. Barrett. He said the Barretts of the world are holding back civilization, hoarding instead of helping . . . ."

"Richards is an oldish man," broke in Platt impatiently, "and given to ranting. Townsendite, you know, and all that. Wouldn't it be better to locate him and ask the questions? And here's something I'd like to ask. What about the weapon?"

Hammond shook his head and passed a hand over the top. His forehead gets higher year by year, and arranging a few wisps horizontally deceives no one.

"No sign of a weapon," he said ruefully. "It's gone."

"The weapon has disappeared," I observed with fine oratorical emphasis. "Richards has disappeared."

"And Annie," echoed Arthur's frightened voice from the doorway. "I've looked everywhere, Jane. Our car is there, but it is empty. Annie has disappeared!"

CHAPTER FIVE

MY INITIAL REACTION TO Arthur's blunt announcement of Annie's disappearance was exasperation. You simply cannot count on Annie. Absolutely all in the world she had to do was to sit warm and dry in the car, nap if she so desired, while I dashed from pillar to post, climbing fences and wrenching ankles and getting rained on and viewing death at unpleasantly close quarters. It is easy for even the casual observer to realize that in my family I must be triple-minded.

"Oh, she must be somewhere about, Arthur," I exclaimed in frank annoyance.

"But she isn't. I looked everywhere and called and called. The car is empty."

I grumbled impatiently. Crossing to the phone, I dialed our number. I could hear the repeated ringings, and finally Theresa's vexed and sleepy voice came to me.

"Is Annie at home?" I demanded.

"I presume she is," said Theresa tartly. "Where else would she be? I thought you were here too. I thought you were in bed."

"Obviously," I said coldly, "I am not. Oblige me by looking in Annie's room—and get a move on."

Theresa, beginning to be alarmed and exclamatory, reported Annie's bed unslept in. Cutting off her questions, I replaced the telephone and felt a gnawing unease.

The men paid no attention to my problem, and I had to be quite plainspoken before George would even listen to me.

"Oh, Annie's all right," he reassured me, bluff and unconcerned. "She's gone home with a friend."

"A friend! Annie doesn't know a soul out here. I presume the members of the Tuesday Club are working the third shift!"

"Blake," said George in resignation, "take Miss Edwards out and scout around the parking lot. Then you'll be satisfied, Jane, that Annie isn't here. You and Arthur cut along home and catch some sleep."

I didn't want Blake, and Blake most assuredly didn't want me, but he had a good strong flashlight, so I made the best of him.

The cars that had been parked with ours had been driven away. Our chariot stood alone and was indubitably empty. Blake, the sooner to get rid of me, was very thorough in his exploration. To my horror he even looked in the trunk. He went up and down the lines and flashed a beam of light into every car. He investigated the little gatehouse where a new man was on duty. I went up along the fence and retrieved my umbrella.

We did not find Annie.

But even then I did not suspect the worst. A vision came to me of my sister, sniffling and damp, nursing her grievance, trotting the five miles into town. Just the silly sort of unconsidered thing Annie would do.

"I'll get Arthur," I told Blake, "and we'll pick Annie up on the way back home. She'll be in bed with tonsillitis tomorrow."

Blake grunted, and I followed his dark blue width back to the main building. But there, instead of entering the now familiar front door, I strolled off at a tangent.

"I'm going to circle around here and see what the setup is. It will take only a minute."

Blake hesitated, and I heard him mutter beneath his breath. I suppose he was wondering whether he'd get in more trouble or less by following me. In the end he came.

The rain had stopped, but the wind was raw and repellent. The great factory buildings in the rear loomed up, long rectangles of steel and concrete and glass, mysterious hives of activity. I knew in a general way that machines to create more machines were made here. I knew that there was a forge shop, a tool shop, storehouses, assembly lines, and so on. More buildings were under construction.

I stood on a broad paved area palely illuminated by lights high on the building. The plant proper was on my right, the office building on my left. I could see the glass upper half of the locked back door, a yellow square.

Austin Barrett's murderer had necessarily come and gone. Had he emerged from one of these roaring buildings and returned to lose himself therein?

Blake, plodding methodically, was now ahead of me, intending evidently to take me at my word: circle the offices and return to enter at the front. I proceeded more slowly, my mind busy and my eyes darting this way and that.

Between the last two shops was a narrow passage partially blocked with bulky canvas-covered machines. And as Blake passed this obstruction, the yellow circle of his torch bobbing at his side, I stopped in my tracks and felt the sharp exultation of discovery shake me.

"Look, Mr. Blake," I cried and heard my voice squeak upward into strange frightened accents.

"What is it?" he asked stolidly, not even bothering to turn his head.

"What is it?" I repeated testily, recovering myself. "It looks like a foot. At least, it's a shoe, and I assume there is a foot inside it."

Blake's bulk quivered, and his light followed my pointing finger. Then he quickly lifted away the concealing canvas.

A man lay there, an oldish man with thin gray hair, a plaid wool jacket, heavy boots.

"He's alive," said Blake. "He's breathing."

And with the words I was running as fast as I could back to light and life and help.

In the reception room Hammond was at the telephone. Platt was writing at the desk. Bill Randall and the sheriff sat smoking and looking at each other.

"We've found Richards," I announced. "He is injured. Get an ambulance at once."

George automatically whirled the dial. With one motion Platt and Randall slid from their chairs and ran for the door.

But the discovery of Richards told us nothing. Not then.

The watchman had been struck upon the head very much as Austin Barrett had been. The intern who came with the ambulance told us that. Either the blow had been delivered with less force or Richards had a thicker skull. At any rate, he had a fair chance to survive and was whisked off for treatment.

"It's traitors to the government," the sheriff made pronouncement. "It's foreign spies. Don't you think so, Mr. Platt?"

Henry Platt passed nervous hands over his smooth dark hair.

"I don't know what I think," he confessed. "In fact, I'm not thinking. I'm so concerned about the emergencies that will be staring me in the face tomorrow that my mind won't work. It's worn out. I'm going home. I've got to get a little sleep."

Sleep, I thought longingly and wavered as I stood. And Annie, timid Annie, trudging the long road with farm lands dark on either side. Past the mushrooming trailer town with its wraithlike tents. Why, Annie must be almost home by now!

"Where's Arthur?" I asked.

"He's gone out to your car," said Hammond.

"See here, George," I said firmly. "I'm coming here tomorrow. I want to see this place by daylight. Give me written permission, please, because tomorrow your policemen will be all over, trying to be important. I'm not at my best just now. Arthur is catching cold, and I must try to catch up with Annie."

Hammond regarded me with deep disfavor. I simply cannot understand why, in the beginning of a case, George is invariably loath to have my cooperation. He knows perfectly well that he owes his reputation and his success to my uncanny ability to nose out and interpret infinitesimal clues.

"Hurry up, George," I said sharply. "Scribble on a card and sign your name. I've got a feeling for this case. I don't believe I would have been projected into it if I wasn't meant to solve it. Fate—that's what it is. And whatever people may say about Jane Edwards—"

"And they say *plenty,*" interjected Hammond gloomily.

"They are forced to admire my achievements in the cause of justice."

The sheriff came to my rescue. I had never regarded him as an ally so that I looked at him in mute apology.

"Give 'er the ticket, George, and let 'er look around," he urged. "Two of them's been knocked cold already. Maybe there'll be a third."

My glance changed, and I hope he felt it.

There wasn't much of the night left, and I said as much to Bill Randall, who walked beside me to the gate.

"Will you be here tomorrow? Or do you work at night now?"

I spoke the words idly enough, but with their utterance a sudden suspicion smote me. I stopped short and thought, as I have often enough before, that attack is the best defense. Merely because Bill Randall had rushed at me as I came over the fence I had plunged at once into excuses. Trying to justify myself, I had not thought to question him. I could remedy that oversight.

"Young man," I said sternly, "how did you happen to be there at the fence tonight? Where is your office? What is your position?"

We walked on, and he didn't answer for a minute. I had the impression that he disliked my questions.

"Oh, I'm an inspector," he finally replied. "I've got a little cubbyhole back in the shop. I came out tonight as soon as I heard the fire alarm."

"But what were you doing when I came over the fence?"

He laughed easily.

"Now don't suspect me of anything nefarious. I'm harmless, really, Miss Edwards, perfectly harmless. I was on my way to see if Arthur had notified Mr. Barrett and Mr. Platt of the fire and—I chanced to observe your informal entrance."

He halted and stared. The policeman opened the gate, but Bill Randall did not move. His lean young face with its firm jaw and full-modeled lips was a ludicrous mixture of dismay and perplexity. Then an idea seemed to strike him, and he turned to me.

"Your sister has taken Mr. Barrett's car," he said surprisingly. "That's how she got home. It was parked next to yours. I saw it."

The cold and trembling fingers of alarm clutched me. Something was wrong with this picture.

"Annie wouldn't take the car, Mr. Randall," I said earnestly. "Annie can't drive. That's the reason she kept sending for me. And even if she could drive she would never, without permission, take another's property. And where would she get the key? No, there is another explanation far more logical. The key was taken from Mr. Barrett's dead body. The murderer escaped in Mr. Barrett's car!"

For a long comprehending moment we stared at each other, and then a different expression crossed Randall's face and he shook his head.

"No, that isn't reasonable," he said decidedly. "That can't be true. Not unless the criminal was here until long after the murder. Because your sister and Mr. Barrett's car were both right there at twelve-thirty!"

"Well," I said, wearily climbing into my own car, "tell Hammond to trace the car at once. Annie hasn't it. That is one thing certain."

Arthur was in the rear seat, dead to the world, not even giving out his little whistling snore. I started the car without waking him. Driving slowly, sending my spotlight along the roadside and honking occasionally, I startled several rabbits, but no Annie, weeping or otherwise, was to be seen, and eventually I found myself in my own driveway.

My mind was not in high gear. Absently I noted lights on at the Barrett house. Faintly I resented the doleful bays from our own back porch with which Win welcomed our arrival. I nudged and poked Arthur out of his place.

"I'm asleep," the poor boy protested.

"Then walk in your sleep," I snapped as, lame and cold and tired, I entered the house to meet real, honest-to-goodness trouble.

Not until that very moment did I believe in Annie's absence. Not until Theresa, curl-papered and anxious-eyed, confronted me. Back in the recesses of my mind was the comfortable conviction that my sister would turn up safe and sound. I had even formulated replies to her inevitable complaints.

Now I was frightened. I was almost frantic. But I took instant action. Hysterics reach no good end, and I never lose my head. I sent Arthur to bed. He was safe there, and I could put my whole attention upon essential details. I told Theresa to make a pot of strong black coffee. With me, effort requires sustenance.

"Better put together a few substantial sandwiches," I said.

Then I called the police station, the hospitals, the radio station, and five of Annie's close friends.

To no avail. Annie was not a corpse, a patient, or a guest.

"Amnesia," I muttered sadly to Theresa, who was holding a roastbeef-and-dill-pickle sandwich under my nose. "There is no other explanation."

Finally I called Captain Hammond. He had just returned to the room he calls home and was, no doubt, entertaining dreams of his downy couch.

"George," I said in a despairing voice. "A life is in your hands. Annie's. You must find her. Forget the murder of Austin Barrett. Call out the whole police force. Call out the militia and the CCC, and how about the Boy Scouts? Everything depends upon you. And call me back, George, in half an hour."

He didn't call me, and neither did Theresa. It was seven o'clock when I awakened. The sun was up. The birds were chirping gaily, and all the new leaves looked fresh and bright in the rain-washed world.

Though I had been rain-washed I was distinctly not fresh or bright. No doubt the sleep had given me strength, but I was as limp as a rummage-sale necktie.

No word had come from Annie. Arthur coughed distressingly, and Theresa moaned at intervals. Breakfast was as dust in my mouth.

I put on a hat without a glance in the mirror. My tweed coat was heavier on one side, and, remembering, I removed Judy Barrett's china dog from my pocket and put it on the closet shelf.

An engaging spaniel with long curly ears. I was observing his cocked brown head when the telephone rang.

"Jane," said George Hammond with honest sympathy, "I'm sorry. We've had a dozen reports, but, on investigation, they all fall through. Now I'm tracing a woman that bought hamburgers with onion about one o'clock in Modina. "

"If Annie bought hamburgers with onion," I said drearily, "she is in another incarnation. She prefers mustard relish."

"Well," said George, "it's early yet. And I got a lot more leads. And you might be interested to know that the nightwatchman has recovered consciousness."

"Richards? Does he know who knocked him down? And who killed Barrett?" I asked dully.

"Not exactly. But he sure narrows it down. He was just coming up to that back door when this man ran out."

"What man?"

"Why, the murderer! The firebug! It was one of the workmen. Richards will swear to that. He wore mechanic's overalls and goggles. And he carried a hammer."

CHAPTER SIX

IN MY DISTRESS AND CONFUSION there seemed but one place for me to go. Our doorbell was ringing; our house was already crowded with well-meaning friends and neighbors with whom Theresa could cope as well as I. In fact, as I edged with the hangdog air of the conspirator through our side door I could hear her coping with Mrs. Gilmore, whose fresh morning frock was conspicuously dotted with Win's muddy footprints.

I fled to the Barrett plant. There Annie had disappeared. There murder had been done. There alone could I hope to pick up the trail. I had found Richards—and alive. How would I find my sister?

Many cars were on the highway. The small truck farmers on the outskirts of town were busy in the gardens. The trailer town was buzzing. Women were hanging up freshly washed garments. Children were trudging along the highway to school.

In the clear sane light of day the manufacturing plant presented an ordered, normal appearance. A uniformed policeman was at the gatehouse. He looked at my card and allowed me to enter. The main hall was being scrubbed and restored to its usual state of cleanliness. The offices were full of girls and men at work. I glanced at the lettering on the doors identifying various departments: Purchasing, Employment, Shipping, and so on.

Halfway down the corridor to the left stood two policemen. The offices of the president were barred.

I was about to angle for an entrance when Captain Hammond and the sheriff came down the corridor behind me. I turned, my question in my eyes.

"Nothing certain yet," said George, taking off his glasses and polishing them. "We're bound to get news shortly though. You're doing just the right thing, Jane. Get busy on this case. It's likely Annie saw something here, got scared, and ran off . . . ."

"Sure," the sheriff backed him up. "You just keep on investigating this case, Miss Edwards. Your sister will come back today, sure."

My surprise at this astonishing cooperation faded as I realized it was prompted only by sympathy. Still, in a way, they were right. In trying to solve Annie's disappearance I might ferret out the murderer of Austin Barrett.

I followed the men into a room adjoining the burned office. Mrs. Grace Ashford, Barrett's secretary, was typing busily. Her hair was black, arranged in tight curls, and her manner was intense and feverish. She had a dramatic way of talking, making the simplest announcement important. Her husband had been killed in a motor accident six years ago, and since then she had devoted herself to her work at Barrett's. She was about thirty-five.

She rose to her feet as we entered.

"Captain Hammond," she said, "I have *one* request. The contents of Mr. Barrett's office must be checked immediately so that I can go in there. Business must go on, and there are a great many *vital* things —"

"Yes," said Hammond. "We'll get right after it. The keys to the desk and the combination of the safe—"

"I have *everything,*" Mrs. Ashford said competently. "Except the key to *that.*" She pointed to a small green filing cabinet beside the door leading to the adjoining office. "Mr. Barrett has—had—the key on his watch chain. But the contents of that case are not company business but *private.*"

"I'll get that key too," Hammond promised, and Mrs. Ashford shivered suddenly.

"See here," the detective continued, "they always say a man's secretary knows more about his business than he does himself. What do you make of the murder last night? Who did it?"

Far back in Mrs. Ashford's eyes a small spark glowed and faded. Her thin lips closed firmly.

"I don't know," she said primly. "I haven't the slightest idea."

"Had he received threatening letters? Had he had any quarrels?"

Mrs. Ashford made a flyaway gesture with her hands.

"Oh, quarrels," she said tolerantly. "You know Mr. B. Every now and then he simply goes—went—to pieces. I'd sit in here and listen to the *words* in there! Heavens! How the fur would fly. One had to know how to handle Mr. Barrett."

"One had to let him think he was having his own way," I said dryly, and she looked at me with sudden respect.

"But get down to brass tacks," urged George.

She looked prim again. "I don't know," she said doubtfully. "It is *quite* against my principles to repeat things. But under the circumstances . . . This all links up with the preparedness program, doesn't it? *Someone* is trying to stop us. The drill that was wrecked and the bombing . . . Mr. B. was *very* busy about that. He told me just yesterday that he knew who was behind it."

"He did?" Hammond jumped at her. "Who?"

"Jasper Carillo."

"Oh," I recalled, "the man who drew three paychecks and was then discharged."

"But he's still around," Mrs. Ashford said. "I saw him come out of the employment office yesterday. He's trying to get back. And have you considered John Storm? Mr. Barrett and John Storm had a frightful row yesterday just before noon. The language then was simply sulphuric. He shouted, 'I'll string you up as an example, you low-down traitor!' "

"What?" Hammond cried. "Storm talked like that to Mr. Barrett?"

"Oh no!" Mrs. Ashford was shocked. "Mr. Barrett said that to Storm. He thinks—thought—that Storm was urging a strike. With all these new men there's a good deal of unrest."

"What else went on yesterday?" Hammond insisted. "What callers, and so on?"

Her hand flickered to a book on her desk. "His business engagements are right here. Oh, and Mrs. Steve Boyd was in here yesterday. And I'm positive Mr. Barrett was furious when *she* left because—well, I can always tell if he is angry. I don't know what Mrs. Boyd wanted."

From Mrs. Ashford's intonation I could see that her opinion of Katherine Boyd coincided with mine.

"I suppose, Mrs. Ashford," I said, "that you've been asked over and over again about the bomb in the lunchbox. Do you think Carillo is guilty?"

"If he had proof Mr. Barrett kept it to himself," she said, and her intelligent eyes slid from me to Hammond. "But—I'm still wondering . . . . How did Mr. Randall happen to be in here Johnny on the spot? I was gone only ten minutes. Mr. Randall's work is back in the shops, and yet he's here, there, and everywhere. He came from the East, and everyone says that the East is simply a hotbed of fifth columnists and—"

The door to the hall swung abruptly open, and Mr. Platt looked in. He had a sheaf of papers in his hand.

"The fire must have knocked your buzzer out, Mrs. Ashford," he said. "I need your help—if these gentlemen can proceed without you."

"Go ahead." Hammond nodded to her, and she walked briskly after Platt to the doorway where she turned, frowned, made violent silent mouthings, shook a fist, nodded toward Barrett's door, and disappeared.

"For the love of heaven," asked the sheriff, "what was that?"

"I think," I said, "that she was trying to indicate without direct talebearing—after all, this job is her bread and butter and Platt is the man in charge—that a quarrel between Barrett and his general manager should be put on your list."

George gave a thoughtful nod.

"I had kind of a run-in with Platt myself this morning. I left plenty of men here last night on guard at this office, and over in the shops I had men watching every move. As soon as I heard from Richards that he actually saw the guy I decided to search the lockers. Platt said it wasn't necessary. He could give us a list in five minutes of every suspicious man, and there was no use nosing into the lockers of all those with good reports. I told him nothing doing. I wanted all master keys and I got them. I know what's eating him. He doesn't want the fact that the officials can go through the men's possessions any time to be brought out too much. It's one of their grievances. Anyway, I better get at the search. Can't keep guarding the lockers forever."

"What are you after?" the sheriff asked. "The weapon?"

"Yes. And maybe the overalls will show something. Blood or even the smell of gasoline . . . ."

Henry Platt stopped us in the hall.

"Something occurred to me this morning, Hammond. Seems a starting place. Why did Austin come to his office last night? He never comes here at night."

"Never?" repeated Hammond.

"Well, seldom. And I can't imagine why he would come out last night. No special job was on. It was raining. Mrs. Ashford, too, thinks it was very odd."

"I'll try to find out," Hammond agreed. "You've got a point there. Why did he come?"

Many days were to pass before we knew the answer to that question.

I went my own way. A pleasant young man was detailed to take me through the plant.

"What do you think of the fire?" I asked him. "What of Mr. Barrett's death?"

He was voluble.

"A firebug, naturally. One of these subversive aliens, I bet. He was trying to burn the factory, and Barrett caught him in the act."

My search was not rewarded. I saw enormous machines and long lines of laboring men. But I saw nothing to tell me where Annie had gone.

While I was so busying myself certain conversations were taking place. At that time they would perhaps have had no meaning for me, but had I understood their implications I could later have clarified some puzzling points and hastened the ultimate solution.

Judith Barrett was facing Bill Randall. The sunshine flooded through the long windows of her living room and struck warm color from the crimson draperies. Judith's softly rounded chin was elevated; her blue eyes were cold.

"My aunt Elsa will be here at noon. There is nothing you can do. Thank you. You've already done—enough."

"Now, Judy, don't be that way!" he begged. "Be reasonable. You invite me to a dinner dance. I couldn't go because I had to work. Surely—"

"You didn't have to work last night," she interrupted. "I asked Father yesterday at noon, and he said he didn't know why you should. He—"

"Your father, president of the company! Did he know every order the superintendent issued?"

She trailed to a chair and sat down.

"My father knew a lot," she said colorlessly. "But he didn't seem to know much about you, Bill."

"So he scratched me from the list. And spindle-shanked Platt is at the top. Ever since he came in as general manager the Barrett plant has made money. So you're thrown to him as a bonus. Of all the dirty, ugly, calculating— Why, don't you know that everybody in town is talking about Henry Platt's affair with Katherine Boyd?"

She rose from the chair and marched to the door, scorn and disdain in every line of her slender body.

The tall blond man shrugged his shoulders.

"All right, I'll go. I'm sorry. I know this is no time to bother you with arguments. And I'm darn sorry I didn't go with you to the club last night. I didn't accomplish anything else."

"Are you sure?" she cried and whirled. Indignant color flooded her cheeks. "Somebody accomplished something out at the plant last night. Somebody killed my father!"

"Judith!" he protested angrily, but she had gone. He could hear her light running footsteps on the stair. Muttering furiously to himself, he strode to the hall and picked up his hat.

A movement in the rear caught his attention, and he swung about.

"Mrs. Storm," he said sharply, and the gray woman halfway through the door at the end of the dim hall halted and then moved silently toward him.

"Were you listening?" he demanded, careless of courtesy.

"No," she denied. Her queerly accented voice was low, unflurried. "But I heard loud talk, and after what happened last night . . . The policeman was here this morning early. He told us to be very careful until they find out who attacked Mr. Barrett."

Randall pulled on his light topcoat and stood considering her.

"Where's John?" he asked abruptly.

Something about her gave the impression of complete withdrawal, although only her eyelids with their scant colorless lashes moved.

"At work. For a couple of days. I lave not seen him."

"He didn't tell you that Barrett fired him yesterday?"

"No," she said. "No, he didn't tell me."

"Do you know Jappy Carillo?"

"No."

Randall didn't believe her. Untruth seemed to deaden the air. But her closed countenance promised neither conversation nor information, so he turned and left the house.

He drove out to the factory then, where I encountered him in the main hallway. I had just finished my tour of the plant and had dismissed my obliging guide to look for Captain Hammond.

"Discovered any clues, Miss Edwards?" Randall asked me. "I hear you're famous as a detective in these parts."

There was more than a shade of superiority in his remark, and I resented it. I dislike being considered a mild eccentric.

By this time George had acquired a small room in which to work, and we found him exultant. A folded suit of mechanic's overalls lay on the table before him. A yellow pencil bobbed as he busily made marks in his little book.

"Made in Waterbury. Average size. If I get these on the afternoon plane . . ."

He looked up as we entered, and his eyes had a speculative glint as they rested on Randall. But that expression changed immediately to his usual pleasant vagueness as Platt came in behind us.

"What have you there, Hammond? Whose overalls?"

"John Storm's. And there's this thing too."

Hammond pointed to an ordinary red-painted oilcan, a one-gallon measure.

"Held naphtha. He had it hidden in his locker."

Bill Randall gave a sharp little whistle and stepped forward to inspect the overalls.

"Put those down," Hammond roared, and Bill dropped the suit like a hot potato. "I'm sending those to Chicago. That suit under a microscope may tell us a lot of things."

"You're positive they belong to Storm?" insisted Randall. "Anything in the pockets?"

"Not a thing," said the detective. He picked up the garment in careful fingers and shook it vigorously. "I looked in every pocket. Of course it belongs to Storm. It was in his locker 168."

I turned around to Henry Platt. He was staring at the overalls and the naphtha can, his face frankly puzzled, his dark brows twisted.

"I don't see," he objected. "He might have given the key to someone else. And we—the management has a master key. And Richards had one."

"Why are you protecting Storm?" asked Hammond.

"I'm not," denied Platt. "The point is, I don't think Storm worked here last night. He was given his time yesterday."

"Fired, eh? There's your motive. He came back last night and took his revenge."

Hammond wrapped the overalls in paper. "We've already sent a man to pick up Storm. He's probably down at headquarters right now. Looks like the case is settled."

"Any day it is, it isn't," I said. But I spoke to myself. I had nothing concrete upon which to base my objection.

"George," I said in the hallway, "give me that locker key. I want to take a look."

"Nothing to see," protested George.

"Do you always have to make objections?" I burst out pettishly. "I should think that just once I could do something, even if it is silly . . . ."

"Oh, here now," said George hastily, staring at me as though he expected to see a flood of tears, a sight he has never yet seen. "Take the key. The locker is in—"

"I know where the locker is," I snapped. "And see that you have it finger-printed right away."

I sailed away, leaving him closing his mouth, and in a few moments I reached my destination, the locker room I had passed in my tour of the plant. I located the particular row that contained locker 168. Upon first glance the locker was uninteresting. Likewise upon the second. A look around the bare interior. An inspection of the narrow shelf. But on the third glance I had re-sults. I am nothing if not thorough.

The locker room was dim and shadowy. Strong upon me was that crawly, unpleasant feeling of unfriendly eyes upon me. So before proceeding further I located the light switch and illuminated the place. After that I felt better. No one came to disturb me although I could hear fading footsteps in the hall.

After a minute I knelt down and peered carefully at the floor of the locker. There was a strip of molding, very loose molding that ran around the inside.

Something had slipped behind it on the right-hand side.

Opening my purse, I found a nail file. Often have I heaved a sigh for the good old days when I wore my long hair in a sensible bun at the back and anchored it firmly with strong wire hairpins that frequently came in handy in an emergency. But those days are gone forever, so I made shift with my nail file and poked out my find.

"Have you found something?" boomed a voice behind me.

I straightened up so quickly that I got a crick in my neck. Steve Boyd stood not three feet behind me.

"Yes," I snapped tartly, "I've discovered that a lady can't stoop to tie her shoelace without being scared to death. Otherwise, my search here was fruitless."

I marched away and left him standing there with a half-smile on his big pear-shaped face.

I admit the lie, a small white one I considered necessary in the emer-gency. Besides, it was none of his business.

But, safely concealed in the palm of my hand, I held a small flat key.

As soon as I reached my car I put the key into my purse and, to make concealment more certain, within my powder compact. I seldom open it. There are always problems more pressing than the shine upon my nose.

I was not deliberately withholding evidence. I knew quite well that there wasn't a bit of use giving that key to George Hammond while he was hot on the trail of John Storm. Besides, with every passing moment my worry about Annie grew until I could have no other thought or feeling. I decided to hurry home and see if there might be news.

There was.

I entered the front door to hear Theresa shouting into the telephone.

"It's long distance," she yelled at me, maintaining the same volume she uses for the extremely deaf. "They want to know if they can reverse the charges."

"Certainly," I said.

"Certainly," she screeched into the mouthpiece.

If Theresa had to telephone to California I don't believe her vocal cords would stand it. I snatched the instrument from her.

"Hello, hello," a small, weak voice was saying, a voice that, however exasperating, was very dear to me. "Jane, is that you? Jane, I want to come home. This is Annie, and I'm in Chicago."

CHAPTER SEVEN

"WHY, ANNIE EDWARDS!" I cried, stern in my relief. "What are you doing in Chicago?"

"Nothing," said Annie miserably. "Jane, I want to come home and I haven't any money."

"Where are you?" I said again.

"In Chicago," said Annie, getting pettish, "as I just told you. And it's raining here and my neuralgia is making my whole head jump and my hat got stepped on and really, Jane, I really don't see how—"

"Annie!" Quietly and firmly I interrupted the flow. "I realize that you are in Chicago, but exactly where? After all, it's a big city and—"

"I'm in a drugstore," said Annie surprisingly, "on the corner of Ashland and something else. I can't quite see the name of the cross street from here, but—"

"Your three minutes are up," interrupted the operator. "Do you wish to continue?"

"Oh yes, yes," I broke in anxiously. "Don't cut me off, for goodness' sakes! Annie—"

"Jane," my sister was reiterating patiently from the other end, "I haven't any money and I want to come home. I've endured a good deal, and it does seem as if you could listen."

"Get into a taxi, Annie, and go to a hotel. The Palmer House, say, and—"

"I look like going to the Palmer House!" cried Annie indignantly. "I've been out all night! Didn't I tell you my hat got stepped on and it's raining? I want some money, and where shall I get it? I want to come *home.*"

There was a certain wild note in my sister's voice that alarmed me.

"Take a taxi to the railway station," I said. "I'll wire you money and a ticket at once. If there is any hitch call me again. You ought to make that two o'clock train."

Long-distance telephone is a wonderful thing. I could hear my sister sniffling two hundred miles away.

"Will the taxi-man take me to the station when I haven't any money?" objected Annie.

"Wait there in the drugstore until I have some time to make arrangements. Then call the cab and go. How will the driver know you haven't any money? Did you take your purse?"

"Yes," sobbed Annie. "I have three pennies in it."

I felt the old familiar exasperation steal over me. Annie's current handbag was almost eighteen inches long. In it she carried everything but money.

"Annie," I said distinctly. I could feel gray hairs sprouting. "Listen and do just as I tell you. When you get to the station take the cabman in and pay him. And one more thing. This is most important. How did you get—"

"Your three minutes are up," cooed the operator. "Do you wish three minutes more?"

"No," said Annie bitterly.

"Yes," I cried. "Annie, tell me. How *did* you get to Chicago?"

But Annie had hung up, and the connection was broken.

I turned away and found Theresa and Arthur waiting, visibly anxious for my report.

"Annie," I told them, "is safe! She'll be home tonight."

"Thank heaven," said Arthur piously.

"I believe," said Theresa thoughtfully, "that I'll stir up one of those banana cakes she likes."

I made arrangements for Annie's money and ticket home. I called George Hammond and gave him my good news. But to all wheres and whys I made no reply. I used Annie's simple device of hanging up the receiver. After my night of anguish and excitement and my morning of investigation I was a wreck. I was not capable of further effort, mental or physical. I consumed a large bowlful of Theresa's soup, filled with every handy vegetable and meat and barley, and then I went to bed.

No sooner had my head gratefully touched the pillow than I remembered the key from locker 168.

Crawling out of bed, I took the powder compact from my purse. The small key was safe within it. Had I known to what dangers it would eventually lure me, I probably would not have so tenderly placed it beneath my pillow.

I slept for several hours; then, somewhat restored, I arose to an unpromising world. The dog Win was shaking the house to the echoes of his furious barking. Theresa reported a photographer, a reporter, and a policeman on the front porch.

"It's Hades, that's what it is," she said with unaccustomed fury. "The doors are locked and so are the windows. And if those fellows rattle the knob again I'll sic that Win on them. It's time he did something useful. And I think you ought to know that Arthur's cough is worse, and he says he's got a fever."

She had not exaggerated matters. Nor was the situation in any way improved by Annie's arrival in a taxicab. Exhausted from her journey, irate over my failure to meet her at the station, her undoing was completed by the trio on our porch.

Annie's hat, oddly mashed, was askew. Her hair wisped forlornly about her small, pinched face. Clutching her large handbag as though it contained her entire patrimony, Annie gave a harried look at the three men before her and seemed to contemplate further flight.

I opened the door and I had opened my mouth as well to call out a cheery and reassuring welcome when the photographer suddenly focused his camera and squinted his eye.

Annie uttered a shrill protesting scream and flung herself through the doorway. The reporter jumped after her, but I weighed forty pounds more than he did, and the door clicked shut.

"My poor darling Annie," I cried sympathetically, stretching out compassionate arms, but my sister eluded me.

"It's all your fault," she screamed and then, uttering further demoniacal cries, she burst into frenzied tears and ran like a rabbit up the stairs. Into her bedroom she plunged. The door banged. The key turned.

Arthur in the room next to hers gave vent to a series of loud, hollow, reverberating coughs.

It was too much. Only flight could save my sanity. Well, anyway my temper. I counted to ten.

"Send for the doctor, Theresa," I ordered with assumed calm. "Tell him to bring a nurse. I'm getting out of here by the back door. Murder I can cope with, but before Annie's hysterics and Arthur's bronchitis I bow in defeat."

Nor did my reception at the police station soothe my ruffled spirits. George Hammond was not glad to see me. There was a complete absence of that generous sympathetic camaraderie which he had manifested that morning. It wasn't that he was busy. His feet were on the desk, and he was reading the funnies in the evening paper. His friend, the sheriff, was smoking a thick cigar, filling the office with noxious fumes. My perfunctory knock brought their heads around. They arose with visible reluctance.

"Good evening," I said brightly. "I came to find out the latest. When is the inquest? What did John Storm have to say? Did you find Carillo? Did you question Julian Norbury? Annie is in a state of nervous collapse and under the doctor's care. So we'd better let her rest until morning."

"Yes. Sure. Well, I'm glad Annie's back. I knew she could take care of herself. You get a good night's rest, Jane," urged Hammond, his eyes straying back to Cap Stubbs. "Inquest tomorrow afternoon. I've taken care of every-thing."

"Yes, everything is shaping up fine," chimed in the sheriff with all the effect of showing me the door. "Not a thing to bother your head about, Miss Edwards. Now that your sister is back you got nothing to worry you, and you're well out of it!"

"Yeah," agreed George indifferently, and this time he actually picked up the paper. "This case isn't your type, Jane. Just a common labor dispute. No beautiful woman. No eccentric old millionaire. Probably we'll wind it up to-morrow."

I just stared. I can read them like books, the dull, boring kind. Their friendly encouragement of the morning was only to occupy me for the mo-ment until Annie was found. It was not the sharing of a task with a fellow worker. Oh no! It was merely the expression of sympathy for a suffering woman. Now that Annie was back they took it for granted that her absence had been some fickle feminine vagary. Now that George saw, or thought he saw, a solution to the murder problem neither my assistance nor my presence was desired.

My fingers slipped into my pocket and touched the compact that held the key I had found in the locker.

"Well, well, that's simply dandy," I said casually. "I'll run along home then. I can see that I'm as welcome here as a storm trooper in the ghetto. But just between friends and not for publication, George, tell me what happened. Then I won't even have to attend the inquest tomorrow."

As I spoke I made sure that the door was shut, and I have no doubt George noticed a certain determination, an acid, in my voice. I can be put off, but not without some small effort. He shot an apologetic glance at the sheriff. He knew he had to tell me something.

"It's in the bag, Jane," he said easily and tilted back in his chair. "But Carillo isn't in on it. We couldn't locate him at all, but we went all over the trailer he lives in. There's no radio. No telephone. *He's* no spy! It's John Storm, all right. I think Richards will be able to identify him."

"So it's John Storm," I repeated.

"Yep. You know, don't you, that Barrett's is still an open shop? But just the same, there are organized units of the CIO and the AF of L too. Storm's been in and out of both of them, and just now he's in neither. We can't find out who he is tied up with. But he's been working up grievances among the men. Barrett had information that a strike was imminent. He fired Storm, who threatened retaliation. Storm entered the plant last night, killed Barrett, burned the office, escaped in Barrett's car. We haven't found him yet, but give us until tomorrow and we'll have him."

I looked at the two of them, complacent and triumphant, and knew that the explanation of last night's happening was not so simple.

"I see." I nodded. "All you have to do is find John Storm and he'll confess. But tell me, George, did you get that key from Barrett's watch chain? The one that Mrs. Ashford spoke of?"

"No," said George and looked at me suspiciously. "He didn't have any key on his watch chain. He must have put it somewhere else. Anyway, what's that got to do with it?"

"I just wondered," I returned airily. "I thought there might be something spicy and interesting among his private papers."

George grunted, skeptical and almost contemptuous, and as I opened the door I could see him promptly forget all about me.

Outside I stood in the spring darkness and pondered. Maybe John Storm had killed Austin Barrett. Perhaps he had delivered those violent, frantic blows. It seemed probable. And yet, he had not been on his job that night. Why then would he bother to get into working clothes and replace them later in his locker? If he had acted in this fashion why hadn't he left the weapon as well?

Mentally turning over these questions, I walked across the street and down to where my car was parked. The air was soft, and could one look higher than the neon lights of Main Street, the stars were out. A line formed at the ticket office of the Rockport Theater to see the motion picture *Awake, My Love.* I was in front of the drugstore, trying to put aside the notion of a hot-fudge sundae, when a man emerged and turned in my direction.

It was Julian Norbury.

"Oh, Mr. Norbury," I spoke up impulsively and put out a hand, but he made no reply. Walking rapidly, he passed me as though I were a disembodied spirit. Yet I was certain that he had both seen and heard me. How could he help it? No eye could skip a woman of my size. Nor does my voice resemble that of a cooing dove.

Halfway between chagrin and anger I hesitated. My car was parked not six feet away, but I am not one to procrastinate. I was as sure as a human could be that George Hammond, convinced of John Storm's guilt, had not even questioned Julian Norbury. Certainly someone should. Why not I? If he had a legitimate reason for his presence at the Barrett plant on the previous night why shouldn't he state it?

I turned and plunged down Main Street after the gray-coated figure. He walked rapidly, but so did I. He came to the corner and scooted across while the light was green. I had to wait and I saw him turn and slide a cautious glance behind him. That convinced me. He did not want to talk to me. Moreover, there was something harried, something unquestionably furtive, about his thin, white face and encircled eyes. I broke into a run, but even as I puffed across the street I lost sight of him. But he had not yet escaped me. Just there was the entrance to the Rockport Hotel. Pushing hurriedly through the revolving doors, I entered the warm, lighted lobby and in time to see my quarry whisk into the elevator.

"Up!" I called entreatingly. "Up, please!"

But the operator did not heed, and when I reached the spot only the blank brown door confronted me.

"Up, lady?" said the lad in the next cage, but I shook my head, ignoring his critical glance. I sank into a lounge chair to recover my breath and my aplomb.

Almost at once a descending elevator reached the main floor and a dark well-dressed man emerged, gravely nodded as he recognized me, and then, after a moment of hesitation, came toward me.

"Very glad to hear that your sister has returned," Henry Platt said to me. "I don't want to be intrusive, but I earnestly hope that the tragedy at our plant was not the cause of her—her—flight. The radio bulletin did not explain her absence."

"I don't know why she went away," I told him honestly. "Annie is exhausted and cannot be questioned until she has had rest. But I am quite certain that she knows nothing significant about Mr. Barrett's death—if that's what you mean. We didn't get there until the fire was almost out, and he had been struck down before that time. Besides, Annie would never conceal evidence. Never! But tell me, Mr. Platt, what was the connection between Julian Norbury and Mr. Barrett?"

"Oh, I guess Norbury is more or less a harmless sort of a leech," he told me readily. "He is Steve Boyd's brother-in-law, but you know that. He makes frequent slurring remarks about Mr. Barrett's honesty and claims to think Boyd was eased out of the firm. As a matter of fact, it was Boyd who proposed the dissolution of the company. And at that time the fifty thousand that he was paid represented more than a fair price. It was a generous one. That the Barrett Company since then has made large profits is merely a result of the times."

"I happened to see Norbury go upstairs just now," I said, "and I wondered . . ."

"You did?" exclaimed Platt and actually jumped. "Then I'm getting out in a hurry if you'll excuse me. He's probably gone up to find me and make a touch. Five minutes' conversation with that fellow and he wants to borrow a ten."

Clapping his hat to his head, he strode to the stairs that led to the hotel garage at a lower level. But he was not to escape so easily.

Julian Norbury stepped from the elevator, saw him, and pursued. I followed too.

"Platt!" said Norbury in almost a whine. "Platt. Wait."

The other man was through the swinging door at the bottom of the flight. He must have previously phoned down for his car, for there it stood, waiting. But before he could get in and drive away Norbury was beside him. I could see neither face, but I could well imagine that Henry Platt's controlled manner masked his vexed impatience. He shrugged a shoulder, motioned Norbury into the car, and they drove into the night, the outer doors sliding together behind the car.

I walked back upstairs through the lobby and out to my car, thinking busily. It was only seven-thirty. The night was very young, but so far it had been wasted. I wanted to search, to question, to make some effort in this case, but I hardly knew where to start, my suspicions were so nebulous, so un-formed.

If only Annie had confided in me. If George Hammond had been more open-minded and less smug. If Judith Barrett . . . But to what avail this idle conjecture? I had both feet into this case and I was determined to wade right along out of my depth if necessary. That night must tell me something, but before I listened I felt obliged to return home, make sure that Annie and Arthur were cared for, and secure my large flashlight.

Greenwood Avenue was faintly illuminated at each corner. Our house was lighted. The Barrett house was lighted. I could see, too, that the Gilmore attic light was on, and Mrs. Gilmore would doubtless be complaining again about her electric bills.

I discovered a young nurse, starchy and assured, in our kitchen. Theresa, she informed me, had gone to her room. The doctor had given Annie and Arthur each a sedative, and now they slept.

My dinner had been too light. I buttered myself a couple of raisin buns and poured some milk and invited the nurse (her name she said was Miss Deering) to partake, but she refused in favor of an apple and, murmuring something about starchy foods to which I paid no attention, although I knew what she meant, went into the living room to get the evening papers.

I took my flashlight from the shelf in the hall closet and then hastened upstairs.

Arthur was entirely comfortable. I could tell from the tone of his snore. A tiny night light burned in Annie's room. She, too, was quietly asleep, looking younger and thinner and extremely vulnerable. I felt suddenly sorry for my frequent harshness. After all, Annie can't help being wishy-washy, and it is my good luck I was born with an independent spirit.

I spied her purse, the large one that contained three cents in money! It lay on the floor beneath her bed. Automatically I stooped and pulled it out, in-tending to place it in the dresser drawer. But as I picked up the patent-leather monstrosity the unusual weight of the thing startled me and, without thinking, I pulled it open.

Then, indeed, I started back in astounded horror. My eyelids were stretched, my eyeballs popping. Why my nerveless fingers didn't drop the dreadful burden I cannot tell.

I was staring at a hammer. In Annie's bag was a hammer!

It had a handle about a foot long and a heavy iron head rounded on one end and narrowed on the other.

Forcing myself to move, I put the open bag close to the light. Yes. It was a hammer. The rounded end was smeared, and two or three hairs clung there.

My bursting lungs finally exhaled a long breath. I had not a doubt in the world that my sister's purse concealed the wanted weapon, the blunt instrument that had so brutally caused the death of Austin Barrett.

CHAPTER EIGHT

ONLY THE FOOTSTEPS OF THE nurse in the hall roused me from those chilly depths of dismay. Almost running, I hurried into my own room and slammed the door behind me. I knew that Miss Deering looked at me with a disapproving gaze, but what did I care about her?

What was I to think of Annie?

I deposited my grisly burden upon my table. I locked my door and pulled down the shades. Gradually the clean and ordered sanity of my quiet bedroom with its old mahogany and ruffled curtains calmed and collected my scattered thoughts.

Obviously *Annie* had not used the hammer. Even in the extremities of self-defense Annie would not commit a crime. Besides, when Annie is frightened she is weak as wet tissue. No. There was another explanation.

Probably someone had given the hammer to Annie. But, who? Annie, to my knowledge, was acquainted with but few of the people who have entered this story. Of course she had a neighbor's acquaintance with Judy Barrett. And Steve Boyd . . . . Yes, she knew Steve Boyd. And she knew Mrs. Ashford. But the hammer! Certainly I could not connect it with Judy Barrett or Grace Ashford, and as for Boyd . . .

Then a thought struck me. Arthur! Suppose the killer, fleeing from the scene of his crime, had dropped or tossed the hammer through the wicket into Arthur's gatehouse? If Annie had seen it there she might have jumped to a foolish conclusion and taken it to protect Arthur. The more I thought about it the more logical this explanation seemed. I could visualize Annie in the very act. I could even imagine her in frenzied flight to Chicago in a mistaken effort to protect Arthur. But there was nothing I could do about it now, and meanwhile time was passing.

I took the purse downstairs and put it into the drawer of the hall table. I locked the drawer and I took the key.

Dazed and baffled but determined as ever, I backed the car from our driveway. By the time I was well out in the street a new idea struck me. So I pulled up against the opposite curb to consider it.

There was that affair of the bomb in Arthur's lunchbox. I had looked upon that as a deliberate effort of a saboteur to throw off suspicion or rather throw it upon an innocent person. Was the hammer a similar red herring? Had the killer deposited the weapon in Annie's purse? If so, when? And where?

I sighed. Since Annie had been for some twenty hours out of my sight and was now unconscious beneath a soporific, the answer to that must be postponed.

I was parked across the street from our house and a bit south, about twenty feet from the Barrett house. Suddenly, without a whisper of warning, a bright light flashed into my eyes and was at once turned off. A dark, unrecognizable figure stood beside me. The window was closed. I felt immediately thankful for the glass between me and whoever it might be who leaned so close. The unexpected apparition was most disquieting.

Before I could draw a full breath the person put out a bold hand, opened the door beside me, and said hoarsely: "You'd better get for home."

The human voice, even though I did not know it, brought me back to normal.

"And who are you to give me orders?" I inquired coldly.

At the same time I located the flashlight on the seat beside me and gave the fellow a taste of his own medicine. But my bravery lessened and my high hopes of an exciting identification collapsed, and I saw lined in the pale circle of light the broad, disapproving countenance of Officer Blake.

"Oh!" I said in deep and inconsistent disappointment. "It's you."

Why I should not have felt relief at the sight of that dull, reliable face I don't know. Certainly, alone and unprotected as I was, I would not have welcomed an encounter with a dangerous criminal. But squeezing out of tight situations has developed my optimism.

"What are you hanging around here for?" I snapped at him.

"Just what I had in mind to ask you," said Officer Blake, heavily sarcastic. "Would you be going home and not be parking here in the dark? Or maybe you'll stay, and I might as well go get my own sleep.'"

"I always thought you slept on your feet," I rejoined politely and drove away down the street.

I knew quite well that Blake was watching the Barrett house. George Hammond wanted to arrest John Storm if he made an effort to communicate with his mother.

I hadn't the foggiest notion of the wanted man's whereabouts, but I dallied briefly with the notion of interviewing his mother. I thought in passing fashion of further talk with Mrs. Ashford. But all the while I knew that there was only one promising avenue of investigation, one avenue that George Hammond showed no disposition to tread.

I must return to the Barrett plant. It seemed a good idea to view the scene of the crime at night when circumstances would approximate those surrounding the murder. Now was my chance while George, slothful and inert, elevated his feet and put his mind on the comics.

In every murder the first inescapable reaction is a question. Who did it? To find the answer we must often first reply to other questions. If we can but say how and when and why, we can, perchance, answer the original query. In this affair we knew how and when. Suppose my little key, the key reposing in my vanity case, would unlock Barrett's private filing case? There was a possibility—and a strong one—that its contents would tell me why.

But I had plenty of time. There was another curious insistence in the back of my mind. The clock on the front of the Power Company office said eight-twenty. Eight-thirty ended visiting hours at the Rockport Hospital, and with that fleeting recollection I decided to see if I could get in under the wire and call on the injured night watchman, Mr. Richards.

It took me three minutes to drive to the hospital, three to run into the next-door florist shop, pick up a small pot of tulips, and throw down a dollar bill. That brought me into the hospital with three minutes to go.

The girl at the desk was crisp and businesslike. Reminded me of Miss Deering. "Sorry," she said, so that you could see she wasn't. "Visitors' hours are over."

"Oh no, they're not," I said firmly and looked down my nose in my most determined fashion. "I'll have time to leave this pot of flowers. Tell me, young lady, where is Mr. Richards?"

She hesitated, and the big hand of the clock hunched along to cover another minute. But Mr. Richards' room, it seemed, was just down the hall on the first floor, so the girl decided not to force the issue. At least, she took one more look at me and then indicated the wanted room.

Mr. Richards was better. Moreover, he was resentful because he had been neglected by the police. His wife, who was operating an old-fashioned rocking chair, was equally indignant.

"The police were at him this morning before he was hardly back in this world," she said. "The reporters were here and took his picture before he even had a chance to get his hair combed."

"And then that's the end of 'em," said her husband bitterly. "They haven't got the guy who knocked me out, and the picture was no good. All bandage."

"You talk to me," I advised flatteringly. "I'll follow up your ideas. I'm Jane Amanda Edwards and—"

"Yes, I know," said Mrs. Richards, nodding energetically. "I just got through telling Ira that I bet if you took a hand in this affair you'd soon find out who hit him."

I looked at the good woman again. She was really most intelligent.

"Have you remembered any further details that might help us, Mr. Richards?" I asked. "Tell me just how it happened."

Mr. Richards was willing and his wife was more than willing, but the joint recital was barely begun when the receptionist tapped on the door.

"All visitors must leave," she said glibly, and Mrs. Richards bounced up in a flurry. I waved her back to the rocker.

"Now, my dear young lady," I said with decision to the girl. "You run along and tend to your own knitting. This is a police matter, and I hate to bother the superintendent with it, but if you don't scoot down that hall you'll be very sorry for a very long time."

She scooted, and Mrs. Richards regarded me in even deeper admiration.

"I keep making the rounds at night," said Richards, setting back against his pillows and speaking with relish. "I punch in at every shop. I don't pay any attention to the front gate because there's the regular man there. Well, I was coming along in back of the office building at ten-twenty when the back door opens. Now that door is always locked at night. If I had seen Barrett or Platt or anybody in authority maybe I wouldn't have thought much of it because they'd have keys, but this was one of the shopmen."

I made an interrogative sound, but he shook his head.

"No. I don't know who it was and no way to tell because I didn't have time to look closely enough. He had on dark overalls and a cap and the goggles they wear to protect their eyes. I just opened my mouth to hail him when he came at me and bashed me on the head. That's all I know. But he must have dragged me back behind that machine and covered me with canvas, because he hit me when I was standing right at the back door."

"Could it have been a hammer he struck you with?"

"It sure could." His eyes were bright under the white bandage about his head. "It was. I saw it. Say, you been investigating already, huh? You the lady that came to see Mr. Barrett last night?"

"Lady?" I asked quickly. "You mean that a lady came to Barrett's office last night? Why, maybe she was the one—"

"That's what I've been telling him right along," chimed in his wife. "Barrett was killed, and they always say look for the woman."

"This lady didn't kill him," maintained Richards irritably, as if he had made the same objection several times. "Haven't I told you it was one of the shopmen? I saw this lady on her way out. And I saw Mr. Barrett after that. She went out of his office at five to ten, and at ten I passed his door and started my rounds. He was alive then and talking on the phone."

"What was he saying?" I asked curiously. "Do you remember or did you hear any of his words?"

"Gosh," he confessed regretfully. "I don't know. I did hear him talking, too, but I disremember just now—my head's pretty fuzzy yet. Maybe it'll come back to me."

"Maybe it will," I said hopefully. "And if it does, be sure you let me know. I'll be in to see you again, Mr. Richards, and between us we may be able to smoke out the murderer."

Mrs. Richards and I walked out past the young woman at the entrance but suffered no visible wounds from her piercing regard.

"My, I feel just like I had a police escort," prattled Mrs. Richards happily.

She meant well. She could not know my momentary opinion of the force. Ordinarily I'll give policemen their due. They work in a definite routine manner that puts to shame any amateur-detective efforts. They have organization, equipment, and experience that get results. But that night, after George Hammond's rude disposal of my help, I was sour about them all.

I drove Mrs. Richards to her home and ten minutes later I was in front of the busy manufactory of the Barrett Company. Quietly I turned into a space away down at the end of the parking line. I had no notion of how I was going to effect an entrance. Another man was in Arthur's place at the gate, and two policemen were patrolling the grounds. Still, I felt that persistence would find a way, even if it lay once more over the fence.

I dodged and prowled about until finally I had made a half circuit all the way around to the back of the grounds. The wire fence here gave way to a high brick wall. In its center was a heavy gate. This, I knew, was open during the day for trucks to drive through. At night it was kept locked.

No workmen were to use it. Even officials coming at night to the plant were supposed to enter at the main entrance and identify themselves at the gate.

But tonight there were some variations. At my first experimental push the solid gate wavered and opened, and I went in.

There was no one in sight as far as I could see, but I didn't trust to luck. Scurrying close to the wall of a partially constructed building, I stayed for some moments hidden behind a cement mixer. Then I saw the two policemen. They made their rounds in stolid indifference. Neither paid any attention to the gate that I had pulled carefully shut behind me.

After they passed I mustered up courage to leave my shelter, hurried through the shadows, avoiding the lighted areas until I was near the office. The whole expanse of the immense workshop both fascinated and intimidated me. The surroundings were, no doubt, natural enough to the men who were busy in those long shells of glass and concrete, but to me the place was weird and overpowering. I could hear the resounding metallic clank of the heavy machinery. I could see the glow of strange blue lights. The movements of many men flung grotesque shadows on the vast windows.

I came at last to the front and entered the dimly lighted hall of the main office. Now, if I ran into the watchman who had taken Richards' place or if Barrett's offices were guarded, all was lost. I might even be forced to call upon George Hammond for rescue, an eventuality that always dismays me, for it makes me feel a mere snooping old maid, which I certainly am not!

I walked softly along the side corridor. All the doors were closed. Barrett's door was not only closed, but a solid plank had been nailed across. But my interest was in the adjoining office, the one in which Grace Ashford held sway, the one containing Austin Barrett's private filing cabinet.

The doorknob was round and cool beneath my tremulous touch. I went in. Not daring to turn on the lights lest they be seen by the guards outside, I nevertheless risked flashing my torch about to make sure I was quite alone.

All the while down in the depths of my consciousness was a prophetic uneasiness. My entrance had been too easy. Was I expected? Had someone seen me take that little key from locker 168? Or had someone another reason for a stealthy entrance into the plant by the unused back gate, the gate that should have been locked?

I shook off my premonition. Maybe someone had entered unlawfully, but he wasn't here now, and it behooved me to get busy.

The green cabinet was small, only three drawers. The key slipped easily into the lock. I opened the top drawer.

First I took out a package of papers. I unfolded one, a blueprint with drawings that I could not in the least understand but that I took to be designs of some sort of machinery. Then I picked up a sheaf of letters. The top one bore Steve Boyd's address. It was not of recent date because the address was Miami, Florida.

There might be something pertinent here, but I had no time for detail now, so I slipped both the letters and the slim packet of blueprints into my capacious coat pocket.

Then I examined the second drawer. The papers here were jumbled together as though they were of small importance. I ruffled through them hurriedly. There was a stack of insurance policies. I replaced them. There were various business letters and some old bankbooks and a lot of receipted bills. I could not take all this stuff with me nor could I read it all now, but somehow I had a feeling that the clue for which I sought was not among these remnants.

I pulled open the last drawer.

All this time I had found it most difficult to hold my torch in one hand and turn over papers with the other. Now my caution yielded to my interest. I knelt upon the floor and placed the light at an angle so that I might more easily read what lay in the last drawer.

I picked up a large manila envelope, looked at it, and murmured in satisfaction. As I did so a stealthy sound behind me made me pause. The envelope slipped back into the drawer. But before I could pick up my torch, before I could even turn my head to look back into the dim room behind me, someone sprang.

My attempt at a strong and piercing outcry resulted in a mere gurgle. My assailant had closed a powerful hand over my mouth. I struck out with my feet, and my arms flailed wildly, but since I was already kneeling upon the floor it was child's play to bowl me over. The back of my head struck the floor and, at the same time, I felt a violent blow crash against my temple.

Despair, painful and overwhelming, flooded my mind. I moaned in anguish. But deeper than pain, sharper than fear, was the memory picture of the envelope I had just fingered.

It may have had an address, but that I had not seen. What had caught my eye was a scribble in heavy black pencil:

"Look into this at once."

And below had been drawn a rough representation of a black hooked cross.

CHAPTER NINE

I CAME BACK TO CONSCIOUSNESS, thinking that the room seemed overfull of bright lights and voices. My head ached and my mouth was dry and my feet and hands pricked unbearably.

"Miss Edwards, Miss Edwards, are you all right?"

"Don't yell at me! Of course I'm not all right," I wanted to say but couldn't. Then as I became more fully myself I realized that the voice was not loud, that the words were spoken close to my ear.

It was young Bill Randall, and he was endeavoring to be of assistance.

I opened my eyes and blinked up at him. There was no one else in the room.

"Just relax," he said earnestly. "You've had an accident. Take it easy. The doctor will be here shortly."

I boosted myself to a sitting position and, after the room had whirled around a few times, I spoke.

"I've been relaxed for some time," I said grimly. "Help me to a chair, young man, and get me a drink of water. I'll be all right in a few minutes."

He blithered for some moments, trying to make me stay stretched out until the doctor arrived, but I paid no attention to him. When I struggled to my feet under my own power he sprang to bring me a chair. Then he went after the water.

Painfully I turned my head. I took a look at the filing cabinet and saw just what I expected to see.

The manila envelope marked with the portentous black cross was gone.

"Mr. Randall," I cried then, my spirit stronger than my voice, "call George Hammond at once. I must tell him—"

"Yes," he said eagerly and came back to me. "What is it, Miss Edwards?"

I don't know whether it was the avid unrepressed curiosity in his eyes or the sudden feel of the packet of letters in my inside coat pocket, but I hesitated. My head ached abominably, and black spots whirled before my eyes, but I am not one to lose my self-control. The sight of that cross scrawled on the manila envelope had done something to me. I was tense and apprehensive. I felt as though three or four of the Gestapo or the Ogpu were on my trail, and it was within my power to outwit them. I remembered that among the papers in my pocket were blueprints that, for all I knew, might be of utmost importance. Why, an Edwards fought at Bunker Hill. An Edwards was with Andrew Jackson at New Orleans. Could Jane Amanda allow an unwary mind and a loose tongue to betray a secret of value to her country?

"Nothing, young man," I said blandly. "Nothing at all. I merely wanted to give George Hammond a quick report of my—accident. But, on second thoughts, don't call him. I'm going home."

"Oh no, you're not!" he said, and I glanced at him quickly. For a moment I thought I had detected a threat behind his easy words. But he was smiling.

"You must sit still, Miss Edwards. The doctor will be here in a minute. You might keel over if you try to leave. What happened to you, anyway?"

I didn't reply, but I looked at him and again I suspected him, but Dr. Hamilton did walk in just then and began an impertinent poking and questioning. After that he gave me something powdery mixed in water. I drank it, and my head cleared so that I was quite able to cope with Captain Hammond and Officer Blake and the sheriff as they tramped in.

"But what were you doing here?" George asked me a dozen times. "What brought you out here tonight?"

I kept giving him evasive answers and black looks. You would have thought that even one of his limited intelligence could have grasped the fact that I had a reason to postpone the conversation.

At one time I used to wonder if my platonic affection for George might not sometime develop into something deeper, but whenever I work with him on a case I thrust this idea far from me.

"Ask until doomsday and hear nothing," I said testily. "I was working out a reasonable theory. I returned to the scene of the crime. I have even risked my life. And what do you care? All you do is bother me with foolish questions. You should be tracing the miscreant who attacked me. All I know about him is that he walked softly and carried a big stick. Probably was a Bull Moose."

George gave up. "Blake will drive you home," he said shortly.

Officer Blake made a sudden startled sound. I knew he was remembering another ride with me in the course of which he fell from the car, an accident due entirely to his own lack of self-control.

I was too spent to argue. All I wanted was to get out of there with the papers in my pocket and I would have ridden with Ribbentrop if I could have done so speedily and no questions asked.

Our house was quiet. Arthur snored in his heartening manner. Annie's light was out. I resolutely put from my mind the thought of the dreadful instrument concealed within her purse.

I locked myself in my room. Tiptoeing, I pulled the shades to the very edge of the windowsill. Pulling my table well to one side so that not even my shadow would be visible outside, I spread out the papers I had brought with me.

The letters were from Steve Boyd to his wife's uncle, Austin Barrett. They spoke in glowing terms of a new invention. Each letter reported progress.

"I've got it," wrote Steve Boyd. "The United States Navy wants it. You can see that any country would jump at it. They suggest that I make a complete working model at your plant, secretly, of course. Then it will have to be tested. I'd expect to make arrangements as to your share of the profits. But with an order to manufacture in quantity you'd be all set."

I nodded my weary, aching head. That was why Boyd had come back to Rockport. Had he completed his model while he worked obscurely in the forge shop? Did the wretch who struck me down want these papers? How many people besides Barrett and Boyd and certain Navy officials knew of the invention? And what was it, anyway? Not one of the letters mentioned it by name. I could think of any number of things that would be invaluable to a navy, ours or another's.

Then I unfolded the blueprints. My eyes glistened as I opened the crackling pages in utmost anticipation, but as I perused them my heart sank in disappointment. Turn them about as I would, they meant nothing to me. I held tracings of some kind of a machine. I knew that. But what it was I could not discover. The angles were carefully lettered; the lines were painstakingly drawn, and the various and sundry parts were so much Greek to me. I am not machine-minded and have had no mechanical training. The blueprints were not labeled or headed or anything else. The only mark of identification that I could see was on the largest and most complete. Steve Boyd's name was in the right-hand corner and the notation B M S 333.

I put the papers back with the letters and, feeling a real touch of inspiration, I concealed the whole packet inside my new spring hat. The hat, red and more fanciful than I usually allow myself to buy, stood within its transparent cellophane box upon my closet shelf. No one but myself would touch it.

My heart was heavier than my head as I crawled into bed. Sleep was my only ally now. For certainly I had no idea what to do next. It seemed indisputable that a foreign agent was at work in the Barrett plant. He had killed Austin Barrett. He had tried to kill me. He had taken the envelope marked with the hooked cross and no doubt he wanted the one I had abstracted. Why hadn't he searched me? Perhaps there hadn't been time.

I thought of Bill Randall bending over me and I wondered if I had returned too quickly to consciousness. Had he thought it better not to kill me? Or had his arrival been fortunate, frightening away the assassin and saving my life?

How could I tell George about this? It would be dangerous to question anyone. For whom could we trust? The alien agent might be Platt or Randall. Was John Storm or Jappy Carillo in hiding near by? Or maybe the queer, elusive Julian Norbury was responsible. Painfully I turned in my bed.

In the morning I had a minor battle with Theresa, who appeared at eight o'clock with firm intention in her eye.

"What you got that drawer in the hall table locked for?" she demanded.

"Because I don't want it opened," I said crossly. "Bring my coffee up here, will you? I feel like the walking dead."

"I got to have that drawer opened," she insisted, paying no attention to my sorry condition. "My insurance books are in there, and the agent is in the kitchen right now. I have to pay him."

"Well, pay him," I said, " but don't bother me about it. And make that coffee strong . . . ."

"When I pay him he marks it in my books," she maintained stubbornly. "I like my records clear and shipshape. I want my insurance books out of that drawer and I'll thank you for the key."

"That's all nonsense," I grumbled, "having that insurance man run here every week. Insurance, bah! You just want somebody to talk to in the kitchen."

"I work for my money, and what I do with it is my own business," she remarked pointedly, marched out, and flung the door shut behind her.

I arose wearily and dressed, knowing quite well that if I wanted coffee, strong or weak, I'd have to go down to the dining room to get it.

On my way I stopped in Annie's room. Miss Deering was putting the room to rights, and Annie was propped up on pillows with the bed lamp on.

"Well, Annie, you look like your old self this morning," I said brightly. "As soon as you have breakfast we'll have a chat. Anything I can do for you?"

"Yes," said Annie malevolently. "Go away."

Miss Deering seemed to second this, and I gave her a glance that made her bridle and start fussing with the blinds.

"Now, dear Sister," I chided, "I have much to tell you. Most interesting. There's a lot going on around here."

"It can go on without me," rejoined Annie bitterly. "It's no fault of yours that I'm alive today. You—you old bottleneck!"

"Annie!" I said, scarcely believing my shocked and angry ears. "Control yourself. And don't use words whose meaning you do not understand. For some reason that I cannot fathom you seem to seek a term of opprobrium. Bottleneck is not such a term."

"It is, according to the newspapers," said Annie stubbornly.

I know when to retreat, so I went to the dining room, reflecting that my innings would soon come. I ate a few pieces of French toast along with my coffee, feeling that a hollow stomach would not help my injured head. Then I had a couple of little crisp brown sausages and some rhubarb sauce. Theresa was fixing Arthur's tray, but the nurse came in just then and, with a gasp of disapproval, took over. She removed the eggs, the sausages, and the rhubarb sauce, leaving only dry toast, put on a glass of orange juice and one daffodil in a crystal bud vase. Theresa watched her carry the tray upstairs.

"That one'll be out of here by nightfall," she remarked with satisfaction.

But she spoke to herself. She would not reply to my sallies, being still moody about the locked drawer. I gathered that the insurance man had departed and I deemed it best to say no more.

George Hammond rang the bell just as I emerged from the dining room. Decidedly diminished was his cocksure manner. His confident certainty that he had the murderer under his thumb had lessened.

"No sign of Storm," he told me sadly. "No sign of Carillo. I've just been to see Mrs. Storm again, but she sticks to it that she knows nothing. Says she was in John's room–he lives down over Becker's Drugstore–all Monday evening and waited until late, but he didn't come in. Says that if he was fired he's gone to look for another job. Carillo's trailer is locked and empty, just as it has been for two days. And those two guys are the only suspicious characters connected with the case."

"Oh, I wouldn't say that," I retorted. "You mean they are the only ones you suspected. I told you right in the beginning that Julian Norbury was where he had no business to be Monday night, and I'd like mighty well to know where he was last night. I've tried to talk to him, but he always runs away. Mark my words, that man doesn't want to be questioned."

Rueful recollection looked from Hammond's eyes.

"That's right," he admitted. "I'll have him on the carpet this very morning. Just now I want to ask Annie if she saw anything—"

"Come along," I said and led the way upstairs, formulating my plan of attack as I did so.

Arthur was talking in a loud firm tone in his room, and Miss Deering was expostulating.

"A light diet!" I heard her repeating in agitation. "A very light diet. . ."

Annie looked frightened when she saw the detective. She is timid by nature, and George, being worried, looked threatening. I closed the door.

"Annie," I began, speaking with great decision, "the time has come to talk. I call upon you to tell everything you know about this murder. There's no use at all claiming to be exhausted and ill and so on. You're hiding here in bed, and I know it. You've refused to explain why you went to Chicago, but you can't put it off any longer. Speak up, Annie Edwards, before that piece of starched broadcloth comes in here again. Tell me! Where did you get the hammer you have hidden in your purse?"

Of course George looked more surprised than Annie. His eyes bugged out and his jaw swung loose. Annie merely looked resigned.

"I might have known," she said. "But I didn't have a chance to take it out of this room. . . ."

"Why?" I asked angrily. "Why in the name of sense, Annie, should you be hiding the weapon that killed Austin Barrett?"

Annie gave a small, smothered shriek and turned the bluish white of skimmed milk.

"Jane! It didn't! You're trying to scare me!"

"I'd bet my last cent on it," I told her coldly, "and you know very well I'm not a gambling woman. Barrett was struck in the back of the head, Annie. His skull was fractured. There were several blows. That hammer is heavy. And it has smears of blood on it and a few hairs."

"No," she wailed again and put up a protesting hand. "I don't believe you."

"Didn't you know that?" I pressed her.

She shook her head. "I never looked at it in the light."

"Just a minute," interrupted George heavily. He took out his handkerchief and wiped his forehead, although the room was not uncomfortably warm. "Would you mind telling me what you are talking about?"

"Annie has been to Chicago," I said. "And she came back here with a heavy hammer concealed in her purse. A hammer with blood and—"

"Don't say that again," interrupted Annie sharply. "I'll tell you how I got it."

There's one thing about Annie. She knows when she is at the end of my patience.

"I sat out there waiting for you in that—that blasted rain for hours and hours," she said. "My face pained with neuralgia, and I was so tired and the policemen were so rude and wouldn't answer a single question. So finally, after I had sent for you so many times and you refused to come, I decided that I'd give you a scare. There was a big black limousine, a very beautiful car, parked right next to us."

"It was Austin Barrett's car," I said.

"I know," she agreed. "But I didn't recognize it at the time. It was dark, you know, and I was upset with my neuralgia and the rain and all . . . ."

Hammond cleared his throat and shook his head slightly, as if trying to clear himself from a surrounding fog.

"I decided I'd get in that lovely car and relax in the back seat," Annie went on then. "So I did. And the first thing I knew, or rather I didn't know or I wouldn't have done it, I fell sound asleep."

I opened my mouth but closed it again. Annie is Annie and there's nothing to be done about it, and what use to upbraid her? Although she can do the silliest things . . . .

"I went to sleep," continued Annie, getting more interested in her story. "Really, that back seat was a marvelous couch. Wide and soft. And when I woke up the car was moving, and moving very fast indeed. It took me quite a while to realize where I was and what had happened. Luckily I didn't say anything. At first I thought it was our own car and you were driving, Jane, and then the man began to talk . . . ."

"What man?" I said sharply.

"Why, the man who was driving the car was talking to the man with him," Annie explained. Her voice was matter-of-fact, and her eyes were innocent.

"Who were the men?" asked Hammond hoarsely.

Annie shook her head.

"I didn't know," she said. "It was dark, as I have said, and I was very sleepy and confused and, of course, I was terribly frightened when I realized my position. Because how did I know whether they were nice men or not?"

Hammond swallowed.

"I was so frightened," went on Annie, "that very cautiously I slid down to the floor, and the first thing I felt was that great hammer. So I picked it up and held it. To defend myself, you know, if need be."

"Sure," said Hammond, nodding briskly so that his glasses slipped down his nose. "Sure. They simply dropped the hammer in the back of the car without seeing you and then took the car to escape."

"No," said Annie, wrinkling her nose. "I don't think so. I think it was the other man."

"The other man?" Hammond's jaw dropped again, but he caught it up firmly. "What other man?"

"The man that came first. Before I got in the Barrett car."

The dazed expression once more spread over Hammond's face.

"Annie," I said patiently, "be more explicit."

Annie pushed herself up on her pillows. She patted her hair that the nurse had combed into a smooth roll. "Now let me see," she meditated. "It was much earlier. Before I got sleepy. In fact, it was right after you went in, Jane. The firemen were still running about and all. It was raining, and this man came up to the Barrett car. Where he came from I don't know. But I heard him open the door, throw something in—it was heavy because it struck with a thump—and then he went away."

"Did he drive away? Did you hear a car? Or did he go back into the factory?"

"I don't know," said Annie. "He just disappeared into the shadows."

"But the men in the car," I insisted. "Goodness, Annie, what happened? Who were they?"

"Nothing happened," said Annie with dignity. "What could happen? And I don't know who they were."

"Oh, come now, Annie," begged George. "Just go on with your story. You picked up the hammer . . . ."

"And the man in the front seat—not the driver, but the other man—heard me and he yelled and used very bad language, and the driver went right down into the ditch and up again so that no one was hurt, although it knocked me clear into the corner, and my hat fell off and got under my feet someway and—"

"Annie," I implored, "we don't care about your hat. Go on."

"Well, I did," said Annie. "They stopped the car, and I explained very calmly how I happened to be there. I think," she added thoughtfully, "that they felt better about it then. The one man, the one that yelled, seemed to think at first that I was a—an apparition. Then they told me that I must sit quietly and they'd let me out in Chicago, and I did and they did and that's all."

"What did they look like?" asked George.

"Like men," said Annie. "Just ordinary men. A head, two arms, two legs."

Her indifference was overdone. She moved restlessly, and her eyes would not meet mine.

"Annie Edwards," I said sternly. "You are not telling the whole truth. Those men didn't release you at once. They threatened you with harm if you told who they were. Probably you promised not to tell. But you'd better disregard that."

"I'll say so," said Hammond solemnly. "After all, Annie, you're in a spot. You have possession of the weapon that killed Barrett. How will a jury know that you didn't use it?"

Annie was now whiter than the pillow slip, but her lips shut in a thin pink line.

"You won't like being on trial. You'll have to get a lawyer, a good defense lawyer," George went on.

"And think of your friends," I remarked. "Everyone will flock to the trial. The Tuesday Club will eat it up. You'll be in all the papers."

Annie moaned feebly and shivered. Captain Hammond changed his tactics.

"You don't need to be afraid," he said persuasively. "No one can hurt you right here in your own house. I'll keep a man on guard if you say so. And you don't have to tell us, anyway. I can guess. Let's fix it like this. I'll tell you, and you nod your head if I am right. O.K.?"

Tearfully Annie nodded.

"One man was short and skinny and quiet-talking. That's John Storm. And the other, the squatty fellow with long arms and curly black hair, was Jappy Carillo."

Again Annie bobbed her head.

"Well, that's fine," said Hammond with satisfaction. "That's just fine. Now you just stay here and get a good rest. It was a bad experience for you; I'll say that. But you don't need to worry because we'll have both of those birds soon, and they'll be behind bars. You can lodge a kidnaping charge against them."

"Oh, my goodness!" Annie squeaked. "I don't want to. Oh my, no! Why, I won't do it!"

"Well, it's the hammer I'm after," said Hammond. "Those tools usually have numbers or some mark of identification. I wouldn't be surprised, Annie, if that hammer solves the whole thing. Mighty important piece of evidence."

Annie tried to look glad, but all she said was: "Don't forget to have that policeman stay around here so that no one can get into this house."

George promised volubly, and I left the room, leading the way downstairs to get Annie's purse.

I was thinking with some satisfaction that George Hammond usually has to eat humble pie. Every time he gets smart I manage to turn up an important clue. Of course I suppose it was actually Annie who discovered the hammer, but if it had been left to her no one would ever have heard of it. Only my enterprise had made it available. I marched downstairs with my shoulders back in righteous pride.

But in the lower hall my feelings received a rude shock.

I looked at the hall table in amazement. I rubbed my eyes and looked again. The drawer had not merely been unlocked and opened. It had entirely disappeared. Only a yawning cavity appeared in its place.

CHAPTER TEN

"THERESA TOOK IT," I exclaimed in angry vexation.

"Now what would Theresa want with a hammer like that?" protested George. I could see that suspicious look sliding into his eye.

"She didn't want the hammer," I explained. "She wanted her insurance books."

"Huh?" said George. "Insurance books! Why?"

I simply could not go into that story. I turned from him and ran into the kitchen. No one was there. I hurried upstairs and went from room to room, but no Theresa.

"Botheration!" I said angrily and went back to the detective in the hall.

"I'm sorry, George." I tried to make apology. "I'll get it and bring it to you as soon as I find Theresa. She has hidden that drawer on purpose. I know she has. She and her old insurance agent."

"Now look here, if this is one of your crazy, cockeyed plants," began George, "I want nothing to do with it. The whole thing sounds fishy to me, anyway. I'm beginning to think you put Annie up to the whole business."

I opened the door.

"I don't expect thanks from you," I said frigidly, "but ordinary courtesy is not too much to ask. Keep your insinuations and accusations to yourself. You know you'll have to retract and regret. You always do."

He left in a huff, and I was left with my problems. I had intended to tell him about the key I had found in locker 168. I was going to explain my presence and my discoveries in Barrett's office last night. But now, darned if I would! I would figure out the puzzle myself.

Someone hid or dropped that key in Storm's locker. Was it Storm? Or the mysterious Carillo who may have had Storm's key and access to the locker? There was the strong possibility that Steve Boyd had seen me pick up the key. But why would he go to such lengths to regain his own letters? Had Barrett refused to return the precious plan and so invited his own death? Did Steve Boyd now have the envelope bearing the black cross? Did anyone have it, or had it been destroyed? And what in the world was the use of asking myself these questions to which I did not know the answers? I felt as stupid as Jack Benny on the Quiz Kids' program.

The doorbell rang, and I opened it to see Judith Barrett. She was in a hurry, with a fur jacket open over her plain black wool dress and a kerchief tied down over her brown hair. Her face was pale and thinner somehow, but her blue eyes were intent and purposeful.

"Jane," she said hastily, "I want to talk to you. Is anybody here?"

"Only Annie and Arthur and the nurse, and here comes the doctor," I said cheerfully, opening the door for that gentleman. "Come in, Doctor. Your patients are better today, I believe."

Dr. Hamilton nodded briskly and walked upstairs. I went into the living room, where Judith had taken a stand in front of the window.

"Everyone is upstairs, Judith. What can I do for you?"

"I'm just now beginning to take in this business, Jane," she said rather breathlessly. "The fact that somebody actually killed my father. The more I think of it the madder I get. I want that person caught. Caught and punished!"

"Naturally," I said soothingly. "We all feel the same way, Judy. We must discover the criminal, not only to punish him but to keep him from doing more harm."

"Him!" she said indignantly. "I don't believe it's a him. At first I did. I thought it was—but no matter. I know who did it, but I can't exactly prove it. That's what I want you to do."

"You know? Who?" I cried in pleased astonishment.

"Katherine Boyd," she replied at once. Her red lips curled scornfully, and she untied the kerchief and removed it. She shrugged out of her jacket.

"My goodness," I said weakly. I sounded for all the world like Annie. "It doesn't seem likely, Judith."

"It's more than likely. It's true," she said impatiently. "You tell Captain Hammond to arrest her and grill her or whatever they call it. She'd say it was spite if I accused her."

"But what makes you think she is the criminal?"

"The dog," she said.

"Dog?" I repeated.

Automatically I arose and let Win come into the house. I had been aware for some moments that he was scratching at the front door. There's nothing more annoying to me. The animal seemed glad to see me, although I don't know why he should, and then made a beeline for the kitchen. In my inner mind I decided that Theresa had gone to market and should be back any moment. Then I would retrieve Annie's purse.

"Go on," I said to Judy. "Why do you think that Katherine Boyd would commit such a crime?"

"The dog!" she said again and looked at me in an exasperated way, as if thinking that I wasn't nearly as smart as I was cracked up to be.

"I did let him in," I rejoined, as tart as she. "Now-"

"Oh heavens, not that dog!" she cried. "The china dog. The one on the edge of my father's desk. That was Katherine's, or rather it was mine, but she must have left it there."

I sank down to the sofa and tried to concentrate.

"I've had a very bad night, Judy," I said gently. "Would you mind explaining more in detail? I remember the china dog. You said it was yours, and I carried it home for you in my pocket. Now you say that dog belonged to Katherine Boyd."

"Yes," she said. "I mean no."

I threw up my hands in despair and prayed for enlightenment. The girl was as nervous and jittery as Annie.

"Listen," she said. "Let me start again. My grandmother had those darling little china dogs, and I was simply crazy about them. She always told me that I should have them sometime. Granny absolutely promised me. But when she died I was ten and Katherine was in her twenties, and she said she was the oldest granddaughter and she ought to have them.

"She took them and kept them, and I cried and the more I begged for them the more determined she was to keep them. I think it was mostly because Father got mad about it, too, and took a hand, and any opposition makes her furious. Always has. And she killed Father and left that dog there just for meanness."

I shook my head.

"There would have to be a stronger motive."

"She's hateful and jealous because Father made lots of money and Steve didn't. That is, he did, but she spent it. And now she wants more. I think she wanted money from Father and he said no—she went to see him Monday afternoon; I asked Grace Ashford—and she got angry and killed him and left that dog to be smart."

"She may have left the dog all right," I said slowly, "but perhaps she wanted to sell it to him or something like that. Hammond wouldn't arrest her on such slim evidence, Judy. But I'll look into it. I'll find out who put the dog there—and why."

"O.K.," said the girl. "I've got to run back. My aunt Elsa is here. Father's sister. She wants me to go home with her after—afterwards, but I think I'll just stay here until things are more settled. Aunt Elsa was afraid maybe the police would make me stay, but that's silly."

"You're under no suspicion," I said slowly. "You and Mr. Platt were at the country club all evening. Judy, are you sure that he was there all the time?"

She looked surprised and thought a minute.

"Yes," she said then. "Yes, I'm positive. We had dinner at seven-thirty. There was a style show from nine-thirty to ten-thirty, and Henry saw that." She smiled pallidly. "You should have seen Marge Gilmore. Henry laughed so about her. She modeled a red bathing suit, and it was listed on the program as Sand Sprite! Henry said she should have been labeled Blazing Balloon or maybe Bouncing Boiled Lobster! Really, Marge *should* reduce."

"Where were you when the call came about the fire?"

"I was dancing with Henry."

"Well, that's that," I said. "How are you and Bill Randall getting along?"

"We're not," she said, and her pale cheeks pinked a little. "There's something else, too, Jane."

"Yes?" I asked and waited.

"Henry Platt and I are practically engaged," she told me, "although it won't be announced for some time."

I suppose I betrayed my astonishment, for her voice promptly took on the tones of defense.

"Father wanted me to marry Henry. Not that he was insisting or anything like that. He told me that very day—Monday, I mean—not to decide, to wait. But he didn't like Bill. I thought it was because Bill was so cocky. But now I think"—she hesitated, and her eyes grew frightened—"I think maybe he knew something about Bill that I don't know."

I felt sorry for the girl, but I couldn't exactly reassure her.

"You'd be wise not to decide in a hurry," I said kindly. "Your father would want you to be happy."

"Yes," she agreed, but her eyes remained troubled. "The gossip is—perhaps you've heard it—that Katherine is running around with Henry. I asked Henry and he said—well, he didn't really say much of anything, just that I mustn't believe the idle talk and women like Katherine need admiration." Her mouth twisted rebelliously. "Henry treats me as if I were a child."

"He is quite a bit older than you," I suggested.

"But Bill Randall isn't much older, and he treats me as if I were a moron. He'll find out he can't boss me around." She jumped up and pulled on her jacket. "Where's my dog, Jane? Katherine won't get her hands on him again in a hurry. And if she's having an affair with Henry I pity her if Steve finds out!"

On the threshold, with the brown china spaniel in her hands, she shot back a meaning look.

"You wanted a motive, didn't you? Let me tell you, if Father had discovered anything between Katherine and Henry—well, telling Steve would be one of the last things he'd do."

She ran out, and Dr. Hamilton came down the steps behind me.

"See here, Jane," he said testily, "Arthur's up to something. I caught him putting the thermometer to his hot-water bottle. Trying to fake a temperature. I told him to get up. There's nothing the matter with him or with Annie either."

But Arthur insisted that he was still sick.

"I'm very weak," he said. "And as for the thermometer—it merely slipped from my mouth. Could I help that?"

I decided to confine myself to the murder case.

The quickest way to find out things is to ask questions. I put on my hat and coat and walked down to interview Katherine Boyd. She lived in an apartment building in the next block.

It was a warm spring day. Tulips were pushing up thick buds. Birds hopped and chirped gaily. I neither hopped nor chirped. My head was heavy; my ankle was still lame, and even my mind was tired.

Katherine Boyd didn't look tired. She looked angry and excited, practically hag-ridden. Her eyes were narrowed above bluish circles, and her thin white hands were never still.

An enormous bowl of deep crimson roses stood on the coffee table.

"How lovely," I said sincerely.

"Yes, aren't they?" she said, her painted lips taking a wry downward curve. "It's perfectly innocent and correct to send flowers to any lady of your acquaintance."

"What?" I said, puzzled by her intonation.

"Never mind." She shrugged. "I'm talking to hear myself. What can I do for you, Miss Edwards? I suppose you're on the hunt for the murderer of my respected uncle?"

"Yes, of course I am," I replied. "Can you help me with a bit of information?"

"I?" She opened her eyes and laughed a little in what I considered extremely artificial amazement. "I don't know a thing about it."

"You went to see him that afternoon," I came back coolly. "You returned that night. The watchman saw you leave at ten o'clock."

It was a bold shot, and it had its effect.

She began to tremble, and all her natural color faded away until two ghastly semicircles of orange rouge stood out in prominent relief upon her cheeks. She tried twice to speak, but no words came. Then she said scornfully, "He did not!"

"Oh yes, he did," I said, very cheerful, now sure of my ground. "He told me so."

"I didn't see Uncle Austin," she said with determination. "Not at night. I dropped in during the afternoon to sell him tickets to our charity tea. Ticket selling always infuriates him. That's why I always ask him. But I'll deny to my last breath that I was there at night. My word is as good as that watchman's."

"You've as good as admitted it to me," I pointed out calmly. "You might as well tell me the rest of it. If you didn't kill Barrett you need not fear. I won't repeat it to the police unless it's absolutely necessary."

"Of course I didn't kill him," she snapped. "Would I be running around at night in overalls with a can of naphtha?"

"The killer may not have started the fire."

"I had an appointment with Mr. Platt that night at nine-thirty."

"H'm," I drawled with intention, and she had the grace to be embarrassed.

"It isn't anybody's business but my own," she said defiantly.

"It might be your husband's," I wanted to say but didn't.

"When I got to Henry's office he wasn't there. The light was on, and I thought he must be somewhere in the building and I sat down to wait. And then I heard Uncle Austin talking. He was in his office down the hall, and the door was open. I didn't want to see him, so I left."

"You didn't go into his office?"

"Absolutely not. If your watchman saw me at all he saw me leave Mr. Platt's office."

"But if you had an appointment why wasn't he there? Why did he go to the country club dance?"

A quick spasm of anger contracted the slender red-tipped fingers in her lap. Then she relaxed again and smiled.

"Pressure, my dear. He had to squire the boss's daughter. I made the appointment in the afternoon—I had something of a private nature to discuss—and later he sent me a wire to break the date. But the message wasn't delivered to me until morning! I suppose they telephoned and no one was here, so they simply didn't bother. Typical of Rockport. Such a town!"

I am fond of my native city, but I let that pass.

"Didn't you see anyone at the factory on Monday night?"

"Your brother Arthur at the gate."

"Oh, dear me," I mourned silently and decided, if her information proved irrelevant, to ignore the whole thing. To think that Arthur hadn't said one word! Devoutly I hoped he hadn't admitted anyone else that night and I determined to question him again as soon as I reached home.

"Did you hear what Barrett was saying?"

"No. I just heard his voice. He might have been talking to Henry, but I don't think so because I didn't hear any answer. I believe Uncle Austin must have been talking on the phone."

"About the little dog," I began then.

"Dog? What dog?" she said suspiciously. "I haven't a dog."

"The little china dog that belonged to your grandmother."

"Oh, those. I don't have them any more. I sold them a couple of weeks ago."

"Them? How many? Are they valuable?"

"I had two. They're valuable if you're interested in antiques."

"To whom did you sell them?"

She hesitated.

"I've got to know," I advised her firmly. "It's important."

"I sold them to Henry Platt," she said smoothly. "And why does that concern you?'

"Henry Platt is interested in antiques?"

"No. He collects animals, porcelain and pottery, no metals. Not necessarily antique. He has a case with a nice arrangement in his apartment."

"Then the dogs are not intrinsically valuable—I mean, would anyone kill Austin Barrett to get them?"

"Oh heavens, no!"

"But how about Judith?" I pressed her. "Selling them out of the family—"

"She has enough," she broke in icily. "Too much, the spoiled little brat. Really, Miss Edwards, you presume—"

She pricked up her ears, and I heard the click of a lock. Julian Norbury came into the hall and paused at the arched entrance to the living room. He took one quick glance at the pair of us before the fireplace, muttered the briefest of greetings, and went on down the hall.

"Oh, I want to talk to him," I said to Katherine. "Mr. Norbury!"

But Mr. Norbury made no sort of reply to my call.

"You see," I explained to his sister and I watched her while I made the statement, "your brother was also at the Barrett plant on the night of the murder—and he left after you."

She moved her foot in its open-toed sandal and sheer nylon stocking and stared at it. I knew that I had surprised her.

"I saw him myself," I continued. I wanted her to know that I was sure of my facts. "He came out of the main gate after the fire had started. I'd like to ask him why he was there and why he has said nothing about the matter."

She rose slowly. Her dropped eyelids concealed all expression. She smoothed her skirt over her narrow hips with a characteristic gesture.

"I'll ask Julian," she said and went away.

She was gone for some five minutes, and I looked around the attractively furnished room. Into the commonplace apartment she had managed to introduce a clear original color scheme, a judicious mixture of blue and yellow and a bit of red that was definitely becoming to her. I looked at the Audubon flower print over the Governor Winthrop desk.

"Julian can't come now," Katherine Boyd said, startling me with her quiet entrance. "He is taking a bath. But he says you must be mistaken. It was someone else you saw. He was at Red Green's Bowling Alley all evening the night of the fire. He has witnesses."

I was suddenly very angry. "You tell Mr. Norbury," I said, "that it will do him no good to avoid me. I know him and I saw him. I've already mentioned it to the police. Red Green, indeed! If Mr. Norbury is honest and has nothing to conceal why doesn't he want to talk to me?"

As soon as the words were out of my mouth I could see that there was more than one answer to that, so in some confusion I took my leave.

Nevertheless, the thought of Julian Norbury plagued me. There was fear or guilt or both in his avoidance of me. But he couldn't elude me for long— not in a town the size of Rockport, not after I had made up my mind to meet him.

I plodded down the steps and turned back up Greenwood Avenue and met young Don Lane, a teller in the Rockport National Bank, coming down. He had an odd expression on his face as he recognized me, and it deepened as he glanced at the house from which I had come. He reversed his course to fall into step beside me.

"Jane," he said, "I know you're busy on this Barrett murder. I'd like to mention something, but it would be worth my job if the boss knew I'd told you."

"Don Lane," I said firmly, "you know perfectly well that I am not one for idle talk. If you know anything pertinent the police should know it. If you know anything that might be pertinent and again might not be I'm the one to know it."

He laughed. "You've got something there. I feel like a gossipy old woman to repeat this, but it seems funny, that's all. I know my neighborhood gossip just as well as anyone else. I know about what Steve Boyd makes. And I'm pretty sick of hearing Julian yap that Austin Barrett owes them plenty and his money came from picking Steve's brain and all that. Well, where would Katherine Boyd get two thousand dollars in cash? Because that's what she deposited with me last week."

"Interesting. I won't mention it though."

"Don't think I will. I want to keep this job as long as the draft will let me. I don't even want to know the answer—but if she knew something about the murder plan and was paid to keep quiet, why, there you are; do you see?"

I saw and I mulled the matter over as I went home, but mulling never does seem to do me much good.

The telephone was ringing as I entered, and Theresa was bearing down upon it.

"I'll take it," I told her coldly. "And wait a minute. I want to talk to you."

George Hammond was on the phone.

"Jane," he said in a certain creamy tone that makes me hiss, "I thought you'd like to know that I've got the hammer."

"You have?" I sputtered. "Why, where did you get it?"

"From Theresa. Now there's a woman you can depend on."

Theresa, standing beside me, caught his voice and bridled consciously, but when my icy stare registered she recovered herself.

"I took the thing out to the plant," Hammond was going on, "and as it turns out, it's a right nice clue, Jane. Very nice indeed. They got ways of tracing those tools, and that particular hammer—guess whose it is?"

"My sakes alive, this is no time for a guessing game," I said impatiently. "Speak up. Whose hammer is it?"

"It belongs," said George triumphantly, "to Steve Boyd."

CHAPTER ELEVEN

CONFUSED? I SHOULD SAY I was. My suspicions were turning so quickly in this case, I was dizzy trying to follow them. The only way was to investigate each clue as it was presented to me and let the best one win.

I turned to Theresa as I replaced the telephone.

"The lock on the table drawer," she said blandly, "was broken. I took it to be fixed, and it's quite all right now."

I looked at the hall table. The drawer was in its place. I opened it, and there was Annie's purse. I opened that. Naturally, no hammer. Detective Captain Hammond was ahead on that round.

"I think you'd better know," said Theresa hastily, "that Arthur is asking for the minister."

"The minister?" I echoed, startled and diverted. "Why does he want the minister?"

Arthur is not exactly a pillar of the church, although as a small boy he used to recite in Sunday school remarkably well. His fair cherubic countenance brought tears to many an eye as his sweet soprano soared in "Jesus Wants Me for a Sunbeam."

Ah me! I sighed for those days long past.

"He says," went on Theresa, "that he needs spiritual consolation. And he sent away that nurse like I told you he would."

I went upstairs. Annie was up and dressed and in the act of dragging her dresser across the room. She wanted it near the door in case the necessity for a barricade suddenly arose.

"Don't be afraid, Annie," I said reassuringly. "Unless the Chicago police move a lot faster than George Hammond, Storm and Carillo are safe."

Arthur looked very healthy. In fact, as I entered the room, it seemed to me that he concealed what looked like a thick Dagwood sandwich beneath the counterpane. But at sight of me his face lengthened and he looked most lugubrious.

"What's this fuss about a minister?" I asked at once.

Arthur sighed and passed a wavering hand across his brow.

"Jane, I feel that I may not be long for this world. I have a foreboding, a presentiment—"

I yanked the bedspread and knew I was right. Three slices of bread, ham, lettuce, onions, and I don't know what all.

"A presentiment of indigestion," I said grimly. "You can't digest that meal without exercise. Dr. Hamilton says you're all right. Up with you and back on the job at the Barrett Company."

Arthur collapsed upon his pillows and waved feebly at the sandwich.

"I don't want it," he moaned. "Take it away. I must have been out of my mind. I'm delirious; that's it. You know, Jane, I have a very high temperature. And I cough—why, I coughed all night long!"

"That," I said tartly, "was a snore. I heard it. Why don't you dress and come to the inquest? You're supposed to testify."

But he turned pale green and closed his eyes, so I left.

As it happened, the inquest was postponed. There had been new and important developments. The Rockport *Times* had extras on the streets. Theresa heard the news on the radio. The Barrett car had been found and was being returned to Rockport. John Storm and Jasper Carillo had been arrested in Chicago, had been brought back to our own city jail.

I had reassured Annie too soon.

Along with everyone else who could worm into an inch of space I crowded into the courtroom for the hearing. It was my first look at Carillo, and for all I cared it could be my last. He was a broad, swarthy, curly-haired man with unusually long, strong arms and an impassive countenance. Nor was John

Storm prepossessing. Gloomy and somehow malignant. No wonder Annie was barricading herself in her room!

The lawyers did a great deal of talking and arguing. The judge was constantly rapping for order. The upshot of the matter seemed to be that both Carillo and Storm were to be held in jail pending further inquiry by the grand jury. They admitted stealing the car. The great discussion concerned their status as suspects in the murder case.

They had an alibi. They asserted they were together throughout the evening, first in Storm's room and then in a tavern on Second Street. After that they went to Carillo's trailer. He didn't have a car, just a trailer in which he lived. They made up the plan to "borrow" a car and go to Chicago. That the car happened to be Austin Barrett's was coincidental.

"How would we know His Majesty's car?" sneered Carillo, and the judge rapped sharply with his gavel.

"But you must have known it," the state's attorney prodded Storm. "Your mother works at Barrett's home . . . ."

"She doesn't ride in Barrett's limousine," replied Storm in a voice that was quiet and yet so disturbing. "I didn't recognize the car."

"Where did you get the key?"

John Storm smiled and produced a thin wire contrivance from his pocket.

"This works very well," he observed. "The door, of course, was open."

There you have it. You couldn't believe either one of them on a stack of Bibles. But how could you prove anything? Hammond didn't try. Not then. He put them both in the city jail. Neither objected nor seemed to care. Probably under the circumstances a larceny charge seemed a mere detail.

As they left the room I looked at them hard and tried to decide if either of them could be a sab cat. To judge from appearances, yes.

Not long afterward—I had a few errands in the ten-cent store—I walked right into a wordy little battle in Hammond's office.

"You know we can't handle things that way!" George was protesting vigorously. "I don't care if it is an emergency. You've got to have respect for the law . . . ."

"All right! You don't need to shout!" said Henry Platt, backing away. "I've got respect for the law. No one is more law-abiding than I am. It was merely a suggestion."

"What was?" I ventured, entering the room. George stared at me sourly. Platt wasn't so secretive.

"Hello, Miss Edwards. I was just asking the captain here if John Storm couldn't be let out on bail and come to work. He's an expert on his job," he explained. "I need him and fifty more like him. Besides, he was hard to manage because he simply could not get along with Austin. I think maybe I can kid him along until we get this order out. Hammond, you know that machine tools are crucial to defense. Even the draft boards are exempting skilled workmen."

"How about Carillo?" demanded George darkly. "I suppose he's another expert."

"Keep him until he rots, for all I care," Platt said cheerfully. "I don't remember ever seeing that fellow before. I know he's the one we fired for drawing three paychecks. If he's a thief maybe he's the murderer. He could have had Storm's key and used his overalls and put that naphtha can into Storm's locker."

"Yeah. And then Storm would go off with him real chummy-like for a trip to Chi," growled George.

"He would if he didn't know what Carillo had done," maintained Platt.

"He's on to it now," George pointed out. "He knows all about the suit and the goggles and he says they are his. But he didn't wear them that night, and neither did Carillo—and that's his story."

"Yes. Well," said Platt doubtfully, "I'm sure I can't figure it out and I haven't time to try."

He nodded to me and was on his way, but I followed him down the corridor.

"Oh, Mr. Platt," I said, "just a moment. I wanted to ask about your dogs."

"Dogs?" he repeated blankly. "I haven't any. I live at the Rockport Hotel, you know."

"The china dogs," I explained.

"Oh," he said, "those." And looked at me with more interest. "Yes. I have a small collection of porcelain animals. And it was a queer thing about those dogs. But the affairs of the past couple of days have put it completely out of my mind."

"What was queer about it?"

"They were stolen. I had them at the office on my desk. Amusing ornaments. Three or four days later one of them disappeared. We looked everywhere. I rather suspected one of the office girls or perhaps the cleaning woman. Not of stealing, you understand. I thought it might have been knocked down and broken. But now the other one has disappeared, so apparently the thief wanted the pair."

I wondered if Austin Barrett had been retrieving his daughter's property. If so, where was the second china spaniel?

"Do you think the person who took the dogs committed the murder?" I asked Platt.

He looked amazed.

"I can't imagine why," he said then, somewhat amused. "That seems to indicate a crazy person. Because one dog was taken at least a week before the fire and the other one that night or maybe the Saturday night before. I don't remember."

The corridor outside Hammond's office was gray and quiet, and Platt was plainly anxious to be rid of me. I understood that he thought me a time waster. But I had not finished with the fascinating canines.

"You bought the dogs from Mrs. Boyd," I said slowly. "Why did you pay her such a sum? Are they worth two thousand dollars?"

A dark angry flush came up under his skin.

"The dogs are authentic and nice old pieces," he said stiffly. "But—I hardly know how to answer you, Miss Edwards."

He did look acutely miserable, but I wanted a reply.

"It seems peculiar," I murmured. "In view of the murder . . ."

"But this has nothing to do with that," he bumbled unhappily. "Mrs. Boyd is a woman of luxurious tastes. She really needs money. You see, I know what Steve makes. He's a good man, but his uncle couldn't depend on him. Erratic. And Mrs. Boyd is—persistent. It wouldn't be very gallant of me to say more, Miss Edwards. You must know that Judith Barrett and I are—are very close friends."

Perhaps those stumbling phrases are not informative but, combined with my knowledge of Katherine's character, they made sense. Platt had indulged in a flirtation with Katherine Boyd and was now trying to get out of it. Whether or not she misinterpreted his interest was beside the point. Nor did it matter how serious the affair had been. The point was that he wanted to devote himself to Judith and was trying to buy Katherine off. The dogs were only a symbol, sort of a receipt.

"I see," I said dryly. Very dryly. I do not care for the so-called ladies' man. "Had Judith seen those dogs on your desk?"

"No. She seldom comes to the factory."

"It does seem odd, Mr. Platt, that you would buy from Katherine Boyd the family heirlooms that Judith has been wanting and claiming for years."

A very strange look came into his face. He was honestly astonished.

"What do you mean?"

"The dogs belonged to old Mrs. Archibald, grandmother of both Katherine and Judith. Judy says the old lady promised them to her, but Katherine took them because she was the elder. It's been a sore point for years."

"I didn't know," he said. "I certainly did not know. I never heard Judith mention them, and Mrs. Boyd didn't tell me that."

A black look passed over his countenance, and I knew that my suspicion had entered his mind. Ten to one Katherine Boyd had planned the whole thing for devilment. Now she had the money, and Platt's purchase of the dogs from her was quite likely to make a rift between him and Judith.

"Well, let's hope they turn up," I said lamely and let him go.

I returned then to George in his office.

"When are you going to question Steve Boyd about the hammer?" I demanded.

"When I get good and ready," George snapped like the old crab he can be upon occasion.

I swung majestically around and left the place.

Wouldn't you think he could have told me that he had already gone over the whole matter with Boyd?

"The hammer is mine all right," Steve Boyd had said, his heavy face closed and thoughtful. "Go ahead and send it to Chicago. See what they make of it. I didn't kill Austin. Though God knows I got plenty mad at him plenty of times. But you haven't got anything more on me than on others, and you know it. Granted that I could have come in the back door with my key. I could have come in the front door, anyway, couldn't I? Granted that I did wear overalls and goggles and could have knocked Richards out. Granted that I had a motive. It isn't enough. And I've got a notion of my own I'm working on. I'll see what it amounts to and I'll be in to talk to you tomorrow or next day."

Why couldn't George have been a gentleman and told me that? Then I would have reciprocated with the story of the key to the cabinet and the letters and papers I held concealed in my spring hat. But probably it wouldn't have altered matters one way or another. There were a good many angles to the story. It just had to work itself out. As it was, I kept what I knew to myself and, what with spies, inventions, and china dogs, my mind was certainly curdled.

I went home and was gratified to find Annie at the dinner table. She had heard of the imprisonment of Storm and Carillo and had consequently removed her barricade and decided to pick up the lost stitches of her life.

"That Carillo is an ugly mug," I observed as she took a generous slice of ham and bedecked it with raisin sauce. "And that Storm isn't one I'd ask to tea. Don't know as I blame you, Annie, for being afraid of them. But we can breathe easily tonight with that pair behind the bars."

And yet that very evening I was to undergo another hair-raising experience, to make the unnerving discovery that I myself was under hostile observation.

"Arthur says what he really needs is a hot toddy," Theresa reported as she brought in the dessert. "He says it's the one thing that will really knock out his cold."

"He's still working on the theory of spiritual consolation, I presume," I said. "No hot toddies in this house. Hot lemonade, if he wants it."

"He won't," predicted Theresa.

Feeling that it is always best to gather up loose ends, I rang up Grace Ashford after dinner.

"You remember that pair of dogs on Mr. Platt's desk?" I began.

She emitted a gusty sound of disgust.

"Could I forget them?" she asked. "He raised the roof when the first one disappeared. Practically accused me of breaking the thing. But he didn't make such a fuss about the second one."

"After all, compared to a murder, I suppose a theft seemed picayune," I observed. "Is Mr. Platt in full charge of the Barrett Company now?"

"I should say so. But then, he has been for a long time. He told me today not to worry about my job. I'd be kept on."

"I don't suppose I should say this on the phone," I hinted delicately, "but—well, there would be no motive for the murder in that quarter, would there?"

Away from the office Mrs. Ashford was a good deal more frank and to the point. But she preferred initials to names and was still dramatic.

"Oh, my dear, I don't *think* so. Mr. P. is a *hard* man to work for—demanding, you know, but most efficient. He has his own way in the management. The directors are handpicked. Mr. B. thought Mr. P. was a little bit of all right. Besides, you know Mr. P. owns a *big* block of stock. It was he who put up the money for Mr. B. to buy out Steve Boyd a few years back."

"Oh, really? Well, thank you, Grace."

Next I called Judith.

"I made that inquiry, as you suggested," I told her, "but I have no actual evidence as yet. But I'm still checking the story, Judy, so do me a favor. Put that dog away and don't tell a single soul that you have it. I think that you and I may be the only two people in the world who know that you took that animal from your father's desk on Monday night. And that may mean something before this case is settled."

She promised faithfully. I returned to the living room, and the evening waned as I listened to the radio. News of the war on every station. Ifs and buts.

Theresa came through on her way upstairs. "The country is full of them commentators," she complained. "What's become of all the good recipe hours?"

I sat alone for a long time. Then I became aware that the dog Win had arisen from his rug near the fire. A growl rolled deep in his throat. He regarded the windows with suspicion. Involuntarily my eyes followed his, and I felt my hackles rise. Our back parlor has three windows in a deep bay that look out upon our side yard. I was abruptly certain that someone lurking outside in the darkness was gazing in upon me as I sat in that lighted room. I guess everyone has had that feeling, and it's not one to cultivate. I made no move to indicate my suspicion, but I picked up the evening paper, glanced, unseeing, at the headlines, tossed it down upon the table, and then moved in casual fashion into the hall.

"Come on, Win," I hissed at the dog, who lumbered after me. "Get him, Win! Sic 'em!"

Win for once was anxious to do my bidding. He was at the door before I could get there myself. I noiselessly turned the key and opened the door. He was out like a shot. Around the house he dashed, uttering a long bay that would wake the dead.

A muffled gasp came to me. I heard a muttered imprecation and then the sound of thumping footsteps.

"Get him, Win!" I shouted. "Good dog!"

Such a reversal of my usual form of address might well have confused the dog, but I don't suppose he listened to me. Certainly he's not in the habit of so doing. At any rate, he tore around the house. Almost at once I heard a loud crash from the direction of my cold frame and an echoing scream from Theresa, whose room is on the back of the house. Then running footsteps sounded down our paved alley. The dog stopped barking and all was silence.

I hurried to the kitchen, intending to go out that way and view the scene. But Win, triumphant, was already at the back door. As I opened it he bounded into the kitchen. He had something in his mouth, a tribute that he laid at my feet. He wriggled with panting eagerness, and I gave him an apologetic look.

"Win," I said solemnly, "it may be that I have misjudged you. It may be."

I took some meat from the refrigerator and gave it to him and turned to see Theresa behind me.

"Annie is moving her dresser again," she said grimly, "and that steak is for tomorrow."

"Never mind, never mind," I said. "We can buy more steak. Win deserves a reward. He has done a noble work. He has obtained an extremely valuable clue."

I held up a goodly sized strip of blue wool cloth.

"Look at that, Theresa!"

"I see it," she returned unmoved. "Doesn't look like much. Not even big enough for a quilt patch."

"Someone was prowling about this house tonight," I said. "Someone who fears my investigation was spying upon me. And well may he fear me now! As soon as I match this piece of cloth to a torn suit I shall know the miscreant."

One would think that that was enough excitement for one night.

We had more.

At two in the morning Theresa walked in her sleep. At least she claimed to be asleep when Arthur awoke, turned on his bedside lamp, and saw Theresa standing at his dresser with a revolver in her hand.

Arthur says that the revolver was pointed at him and, naturally, he made loud and frenzied protests. The yells brought me immediately, barefooted and sleep-dazed, to the doorway. And sleep fled as I saw Theresa drop the gun with a thud into the top dresser drawer.

"It's enough to give a body nightmares," she defended herself passionately. "There's that awful revolver lying there day after day when he should have returned it to the Barrett Company. There's him, a big able-bodied man, lying there in bed day after day when the doctor says to get up. There's me carrying up trays day after day—"

At this point she became conscious of her nightgown and curlpapers and fled, still muttering. I hope she was not blaming poor Arthur for the physical weakness that he cannot help. She may have been asleep. It is quite possible.

I cannot deny. I will not judge. All I know is that Arthur was up and dressed before eight o'clock next morning.

CHAPTER TWELVE

THE MORSEL OF DARK BLUE cloth filled me with triumph. I felt somehow that it was a clue of major importance. A conviction was born in me that I would discover and identify the garment from which it had been rudely torn. And I was quite right. But by that time I was no longer exultant. Much water had gone under the bridge by then.

Win's exploit made me dog-conscious. From the lusty hero of the back-yard fray my thoughts kept returning to the inanimate dogs. There was something about the way those porcelain pets kept slipping in and out as though they were endowed with life that made me wonder. Katherine had sold the dogs at a fantastic price. Someone had stolen first one and then the other. And Judith had picked up one from her father's desk, where it might have been a mute and helpless witness of his murder.

Where then was the other dog?

I went to Judith's house to take up this point. It was barely past the break-fast hour when Susy opened the door to me. I stepped into the hall with its allover dark red rug, its upcurving walnut stair rail, its prim armless Victorian chair. The living room was lighter, a charming setting for Judith, with a white mantel, shimmering green walls, soft, full ruffled curtains looped back from the Venetian blinds.

Susy with her quick step left me and went upstairs, and in a moment Judith came running down.

Her pale brown hair was rolled back above her smooth forehead. Her beige sweater and flannel skirt admirably fitted her slim young form. The lipstick and the heavy clanking gold necklace she wore seemed more suitable for her than somber black and made it apparent that she was trying to reconcile herself to the inevitability of death.

"See here, Judy," I said briskly. "Where is that dog of yours? I'd like another look at it. I'm interested."

"What did Katherine say?" she queried.

"She sold the two dogs two weeks ago."

Judy frowned, sat down on the divan, and tucked one foot beneath her.

"Sold them!" she ejaculated scornfully. "That's a tale, isn't it? Fishy, if you ask me."

I made up my mind. Also, I made sure that no listening ear was about. The hall was empty.

"Aunt Elsa is upstairs," Judith volunteered, watching me. "And so is Susy. And Mrs. Storm is busy in the kitchen."

"Listen to me," I said then. I told her that Henry Platt had bought the dogs and had seemed honestly ignorant of her claim to them. I described their disappearance.

"Now why," I demanded earnestly, "would anyone steal them? And why would one of them be left on your father's desk? Apparently it was on Henry Platt's desk during that day, as he didn't miss it until Tuesday."

"It's perfectly intriguing," she murmured, her blue eyes wide. "I don't see any sense to it. I simply can't imagine, Jane. Wait a minute."

She sprang to her feet and ran upstairs, her steps so light and airy that I thought with regret of my own avoirdupois. Not that I am fat, you understand, but I'd have to count calories until I was blue in the face even to approach Judy's weight. She was back in a jiffy, the brown dog held carefully in both hands.

"It's what they call Rockingham," she explained. "Do you know anything about old porcelain?"

"Not a thing," I admitted cheerfully. "Although we have a pair of Staffordshire figures and a luster pitcher that Annie does a lot of talking about."

"One of my great-greats was a potter," Judy told me. "On my mother's side. Granny told me about it. Often. He was John Archibald, an Englishman who started a pottery in Ohio in 1830. He was one of the first potters west of the Alleghenies. He made mostly coarse, salt-glazed stoneware utensils and white earthenware. There's very little of his work left about. But these dogs are later. He made them for his little girl. This is what they call Rockingham, or sometimes mottled or tortoise-shell ware. It's because of the brown glaze that is applied to the base; do you see?"

I looked at the dog, and the dog seemed to return the look. He was some sort of a spaniel—I could tell that—and seemingly a very aristocratic one. He sat on his haunches on a molded base. His hair was curly in great detail of modeling, and his eyes were round. His head was turned at right angles to his body. The base upon which he sat was ornamented all the way around with curlicues in relief. His color, suitably enough, was a deep brown.

"The two of them stood on Granny's mantel and on her granny's before her. My granny always kept them filled with peppermints. You know those round, hard white kind that make your mouth feel first hot and then cool?"

"Yes, I know," I said absently. "But where in the world—? Did you say she kept them in the dog?"

"Yes," said Judy matter-of-factly. "His head comes off. See?"

With one twist of her facile young wrist she removed the spaniel's head and disclosed the yawning cavity in his body. The head with its long curly ears was made with a sort of extra neck, exactly like the papier-mache Easter bunnies of my childhood.

Judith pushed the rabbit head—I mean the spaniel head—back into its place. Now the head faced to the front.

"Let me see that thing," I commanded abruptly and took the dog from her extended hand.

Carefully I removed the head and placed it on the low coffee table in front of the sofa. Then I put in an exploring finger and turned the open carcass of the dog toward the light. Judith exclaimed as I drew out a slip of paper.

"Why, Jane, what's that?"

I put the dog on the table and took my find to the window. But even with the morning light full upon it I did not understand what I held.

"It's a notation of some sort," I told her. There was no concealing it from her because she was looking over my shoulder and breathing on my neck. "But I don't know what it means. Do you?"

"It looks like a code," she said raptly. "You know, Jane, it really does."

My hand actually shook, and I felt in unhappy retrospect that crashing blow that had felled me in the Barrett office. The crooked cross, the mysterious blueprint, the stolen dog.

"Judy," I said slowly, "be still." I retreated and sat down upon the sofa. Outside a cardinal whistled, and I caught a flash of red. I heard steps off in the kitchen and a familiar thud that was the refrigerator door. Inside the cheerful room there was silence. There was only poor, puzzled Jane Edwards clutching a slip of paper and pretty Judy Barrett waiting with suppressed impatience for her to speak.

"I think we're onto something pretty big, Judy," I said at last as impressively as I could. "It looks to me as if we'd have a chance to perform a patriotic duty as well as punish the person who killed your father. There's more behind this than personal hatred or petty revenge. And we'll have to be careful, very careful indeed, not to muff it."

I spread the paper out again in the palm of my hand. There were four lines of letters and figures:

ES4P7AS5U5S56E
ACR4E7E1E4F5C6T6
2C
SC6127DSPT4L5E6NPT5DSE

The thing looked complicated. I began to feel misgivings. "Bill knows ciphers," said Judith excitedly. "He told me once that—"

"Heavenly day, no! No !" I burst out with dismayed intensity. With my free hand I caught hers. "You must not say one single word to Bill. Nor to anyone else. Not to your aunt Elsa or even to the police. Promise me, Judith. It's important. If you don't I'll—I'll—"

"O.K. Don't get so excited," she said a little reluctantly. "I promise."

"This must go to Washington," I said. "You know, Mr. Platt was right— but don't say a word to him either! But he wanted to get the federal men in here long ago, but your father wouldn't be bothered. And since then Hammond has been so set on convicting John Storm that he's blind as a bat to anything else. I'll take the paper. You put the dog away and forget it."

I could only hope as I went out to begin a busy day that she would heed my words and keep her promises.

The inquest was run off formally that day with the usual verdict of death at the hands of a person or persons unknown. Announcement was made of the funeral services for Austin Barrett at two o'clock on Saturday.

"That's so Platt won't have to give the men any extra time off to attend the funeral," John Storm cynically observed to his mother. "Wonder what he'd do if I jumped my bail. He's got me out to keep them humping on the number one line. At that, I don't hate his guts like I did Barrett. Platt's hard and he'll work hell out of the men, but he's willing to pay."

Mrs. Storm carefully put the glass she was drying upon the shelf.

"Be sure to be at the funeral," was all she said.

I didn't know that Hammond had released Storm, and of course Annie didn't either. There she was, taking the mulch off the perennial bed, when Storm strolled past on his way from the Barrett house.

"Good morning," he said to her and doffed his hat politely. Annie gave one look and a frightened bleat and sat down on the tender young columbines. She claimed that Storm gave a nasty kind of chuckle as he passed on.

"He's a dangerous man," she said with conviction as we sat at the lunch table. From her earlier refusal to talk Annie was progressing now to a loquacious stage. She described her encounter with the auto thieves with what I regarded as highly colored mendacity. "I wouldn't put anything past him. He's a spying sort. Moves slowly, speaks softly."

A most disquieting thought struck me. When had Storm been released on bail?

"Annie," I interrupted, "what kind of a suit did he wear today?"

"I could only see the trousers," Annie pondered. "He wore a light tan topcoat. But I think the pants were navy blue."

Suddenly I felt that my accumulation of secrets weighed too heavily upon my conscience. Skilled as I am at taking care of one thing with my right hand and two or three with my left, I felt that I was coming up against superb difficulties. After all, there are only twenty-four hours in any day, and I have to have some time to eat and sleep. Dangerous though it was, I would have to transfer some of my burden to George, and heaven help him if he blabbed to the wrong person.

Just how far should my confidence extend? It was out of my power to hand over the key to the office cabinet since this was already gone from my possession. I knew he would scoff at the piece of blue cloth. I could not find it in me just at the moment to hand over the slip of paper I had taken from the china dog because ciphers have always had an amazing fascination for me, and I wanted to take a whack at this one. Besides, if it baffled me George Hammond certainly could do nothing with it. I would have a try and then if I failed send for the experts in Washington. This process of reasoning left nothing but the letters written by Steve Boyd and the blueprint for the unnamed machine.

Having come to this decision, I went upstairs and straight to the cellophane hatbox on my shelf. Then I passed a hand over my eyes and took another look. Then I yanked the thing down from the shelf and acknowledged the startling truth.

The transparent box was empty. Not only were the papers gone, but my spring hat had disappeared.

Rushing to the door, I bawled angrily downstairs.

"Theresa!" I screamed. "Who has been in this house?"

And then my eye slid through Annie's open door. I caught the flash of color, and this time it was no red bird. My sister was preening before the mirror, trying on my hat.

"Annie Edwards," I gasped, leaning weakly against the door-frame, "tell me quickly—"

"You know, Jane," she said thoughtfully, "perhaps you'd better give me this hat. It does something for me."

"I'll do something to you," I cried violently. "What did you do with those papers I had hidden in it? You've betrayed your country, Annie Edwards, and if you were in Germany you'd be put in a concentration camp."

Annie hastily removed the red hat and turned a shaken face to me.

"I—I have not," she said. "I did not. I don't know what you're talking about."

"Where are my papers?" I repeated sternly.

"Oh, those!" she said then, relieved. "Really, Jane, you talk so extravagantly—you frightened me. Why, let me see. I left them there on the shelf. Or no, I didn't. I put them on your table."

I dashed back into my room. The table was bare of papers. The wastebasket beside it was empty.

I ran pell-mell downstairs.

"What's the matter now?" I heard Arthur call peevishly from his room.

Theresa was peeling potatoes.

"Where are my papers?" I demanded. "Did you take a bundle of old letters and papers from my room?"

Theresa regarded my haste and my excitement with disapproving eyes.

"I threw them out," she announced brazenly. "I thought that was why you left them on the table. And will you please stop imitating a hurricane? I've got a cake in the oven, and it's likely to fall."

"You're likely to fall too," I cried wildly. "Oh, why didn't I give those to George Hammond right away? Oh, why do I live in such a house with such a family? No privacy. No—"

"If you're making that row about those old letters," said Theresa icily, "you can stop it. Go out to the garbage can and get them."

I waited not a moment, and a good thing it was. As unlucky—or perhaps lucky—chance would have it the garbage had just been collected. But the truck had not yet turned the corner and, with its odoriferous burden, was yet within my sight.

"Wait!" I shouted and tore after the vehicle. "Wait!"

The driver could not hear me above the roar of the truck's motor, but as he made his last stop in our block I caught up to him.

"Important papers!" I gasped. "Thrown out in the garbage."

He made no reply in words but with a quietly resigned air mounted the back wheel and gazed over the edge. Then he turned to me.

"If it's a bunch of letters with a rubber band around 'em," he said doubtfully, "they seem, ma'am, to be pretty—er—soggy."

"I don't care if they're pulp," I cried recklessly. "I must have them."

But, dried out in the kitchen oven, they turned a pale toast color and seemed none the worse otherwise. Even the blueprint, which was now a richer shade. Although George Hammond sniffed uneasily as I spread them before him upon his office desk.

"What are they?" he asked. "Don't seem to be sprinkled with any of that there attar of roses."

But he lost his genial air as my tale was unraveled.

"Why you don't get killed I don't know," he marveled. "You must have nine lives."

"If I do," I retorted smartly, "it's the only catty thing about me. Now what do you propose to do, George?"

"Why, talk to Boyd again," he replied promptly.

So there we waited and discussed and argued until Boyd, his pear-shaped face heavy and watchful, came in.

That interview seemed odd and unsatisfactory to me. As I looked back upon it later I wondered why I had this feeling. Steve Boyd was frankness itself and yet . . . There was a curious blankness about his heavy-lidded eyes, or perhaps it was the way he had of opening and closing his hairy, muscular hands, or maybe it was simply that the shadow of coming unfortunate and tragic events was already gathering thick about us.

His invention, he told us, was a new sort of minesweeper.

"It's absolutely foolproof," he said. "It's simple to make, easy to operate, and one hundred percent efficient. The Navy is so sure of it that they are already constructing it in utmost secrecy. The various parts are being made in various plants. There is only one complete set of plans—outside of the one in my head—and that is in Washington."

"Then the blueprint I recovered from Barrett's cabinet?"

"One essential part. The part we are going to make here. But only Austin and myself knew of that blueprint. No department head, no foreman, no secretary, not even the general manager knew of its existence—or so Austin assured me."

"He was mistaken or deceived," I said slowly, and Steve Boyd turned that pendulous jaw of his and blinked those little eyes until I wriggled. "Someone knew because someone tried to get it. The person who killed Barrett and might have killed me."

"That blueprint had better be destroyed," Boyd told Hammond. "I've already written to my superiors."

But Hammond refused.

"The blueprint and the letters are evidence," he said doggedly. "I'm not saying I distrust you, Mr. Boyd, but you can see that I've got to watch every step. Nothing will happen to those papers in the safekeeping of the police."

Boyd got to his feet then. He was a strong, powerful man.

"Very well," he acquiesced. "We'll all go on keeping our eyes open. Let me congratulate you, Captain, because you are not acting in expensive and maybe ruinous haste. The enemy work slowly, but they're sure. It's easy to do enough damage to cause expensive delay in a factory. A workman with a monkey wrench, a little emery dust—maybe just a telephoned tip. I think that bomb was put in the office to scare Barrett. Little things aren't important enough to start a big investigation, but they terrify. They accumulate."

"Murder isn't a little thing," grunted George.

"No," acknowledged Boyd. "The murder of the president of the Barrett Machine Company is big enough to raise an awful howl and finish its perpetrator. That's why I wonder if it actually links up with this spy stuff—or if there is something else."

He looked at me with those hooded eyes, and I felt myself wondering if he knew about the message in the dog and if he knew that I knew and if his wife knew, or his brother-in-law, and if the dogs were first sold to Platt and then stolen with a definite purpose.

While all this was running through my mind Steve Boyd was saying good-by and was well on his way out of the office.

"So you let Storm out of jail," I said promptly to George, thinking it was as well to introduce a new subject.

"I got to thinking," he said seriously. "Platt wanted Storm out, and that left Carillo in, but why should Carillo be the goat? He has a pal, fellow named Jackson, works for the railroad, who came in to go his bail. There's no particular evidence against Carillo for the murder. It's all against Storm. The larceny case doesn't come up until the grand jury meets next week. So I'm watching them both."

"And they're watching me," I felt like saying as I remembered those boring eyes through my window last night. But I gave no voice to that suspicion, feeling sure that I had the evidence that would in time identify that culprit.

Steve Boyd was standing on the steps of the city hall. Something in his position, the set of his thick shoulders, the forward thrust of his head, stopped me in my tracks. His gaze seemed to be directed across the street. I stared past him and in a moment I saw what he saw.

A sedan, such dark maroon as to be almost black, was parked along the curb, and Henry Platt had the door open, waiting for his feminine companion to descend. As she did so Steve Boyd started slowly down the steps. I followed him. Katherine Boyd was walking with Henry Platt toward the entrance of the Rockport Hotel.

"She must be having lunch with him," I said to myself. My stomach told me the time, but a glance at the clock on the tower of the city hall behind me confirmed it. It was about twenty minutes past noon.

Steve Boyd stalked across the street against the red light, amid black looks and imprecations of angry drivers. I dashed after him when the light turned green and caught up with him as he entered the hotel. Not that he was aware of my presence. He advanced with firm intention across the lobby and into the dining room, where his wife was seated at a small round table and Henry Platt was pulling out his chair.

Steve Boyd walked right up to them, pulled out another chair, and sat down. For a moment no one spoke. Then I heard Katherine Boyd's carefully pitched voice.

"Hello, dear," she trilled. "Finished the conference just in time, didn't you?"

Well, I was stumped. After all, how did I know the three of them had not met by appointment? I didn't trust Platt; I didn't trust Katherine, and when you came right down to it I didn't trust Boyd. For all I knew that stuff about patriotism he had just handed out might be the old malarkey, as they say. I determined to reserve my judgment, maintain my independence. In the meantime there was no reason in the world why I shouldn't sit down at a nearby table and have my own lunch. And there was one very good reason why I should. I was extremely hungry.

I walked in and foiled the efforts of the waiter to lead me to a side table. I sat down close to my acquaintances. Henry Platt saw me, bowed affably. Katherine Boyd saw me, narrowed her eyes, and bowed stiffly. Steve Boyd never gave me a glance.

I ordered trout *meunière* and green salad and meringues with strawberries and felt pleased to think that my investigations had for once led me into very pleasant places.

Then I saw another actor in our drama.

Close against the wall, his eyes so bright as to be almost feverish, I saw Julian Norbury. His luncheon was on the table before him, but his gaze and his attention were for the group of three whom I watched. His seat was more inconspicuous than mine, yet was in better range to overhear a word if Katherine raised her voice or if Steve's temper made him incautious. And then the thought came to me that now I really did have Julian Norbury cornered.

I left my place and walked over to him. He didn't notice me until I sat down, and then a look of dreadful fury crossed his face and gleamed from his sunken eyes. It was gone almost at once, but if ever I saw hate transform a human face I saw it then.

I had no time to frame an opening sentence, for as I pulled out a chair opposite him and sat down he jumped up.

"You see, Steve"—suddenly Katherine's voice at its sharpest struck right into me—"there's really nothing to fight about now, or is there? Because I must be the woman scorned. Henry tells me that he is going to marry Judith."

My head jerked around, and I saw that Steve Boyd was standing up. His lowered head and reddened eyes brought to me a picture of a bull about to charge.

Platt sprang up too. He flung one imperative glance at the waiter advancing and said something to Boyd in a low, commanding tone.

It didn't do a bit of good. Steve Boyd's fist shot out and connected. Henry Platt went down with a dull thud upon the crimson carpet.

CHAPTER THIRTEEN

KATHERINE BOYD LAUGHED, a high, strained, almost hysterical laugh.

"You damn troublemaker!" Julian Norbury snarled at Steve Boyd.

His brother-in-law's great fist automatically clenched and half drew back. Norbury cringed, but Boyd, visibly controlling himself, stepped away. Norbury swallowed hard and stooped to investigate the extent of Platt's injuries.

"We can't have this! Gentlemen! We can't have this!" bleated the headwaiter. The napkin he held in his agitated hand was shaking. He waved it frantically, and the rest of his cohorts at once formed to shoo back the other scattered lunchers who were surging forward in pleasurable excitement.

Henry Platt, with Norbury's aid, stumbled to his feet. At first he didn't look particularly angry. He seemed confused. Until I noticed his eyes, slitted and gleaming, and his tightened mouth, quite colorless in his livid face.

"Sit down," urged Norbury. "Drink some water."

But Platt shook him off. He smoothed back his hair. He settled his tie. One hand tenderly caressed his jaw.

"That was a mistake, Boyd," he said then thickly.

Boyd gave one inarticulate grunt, turned on his heel, and swung out of the room. His wife gave a small quickly strangled cry. From under her lowered lids her eyes blazed at Henry Platt.

The rest of us stood like statues.

Henry Platt picked up the glass of water he had refused and drank deeply. The ice cubes clinked against each other. Katherine moved, reached for her gloves, her purse, and with the accustomed act regained her self-control.

"I'm sorry, Henry," she said smoothly. "Let me present his apologies. And mine."

Julian Norbury, handing a bill to the waiter, was plainly intent upon departure.

"Mr. Norbury," I exclaimed in a panic, "don't you dare run away from me this time. I want to know—"

He turned a dark look of fury upon me. Actual hate flamed from his sunken eyes.

"My dear, good Miss Edwards," he hissed. Yes, actually. "If you annoy me further I shall—exterminate you!"

And he fled. Platt gave one hard-eyed glance at Katherine and followed.

"A nice note!" I snapped in righteous dudgeon. "Did you hear that, Mrs. Boyd? Your brother threatened me. An open threat. You can understand now that—"

"Oh, stop your cackling!" said Katherine Boyd rudely. "Mind your own business. Neither of those fools has good sense. We didn't even have lunch," she complained to the waiter. "Well, put it on Mr. Platt's bill, anyway."

She drew on her suede gloves, touched her dotted black veil, adjusted her face to its usual proud complacency, and sailed from the room.

I have never been so affronted in my life.

But what use to waste the delicately browned trout? The meringues were excellent, neither too hard nor too chewy, although not quite up to Theresa's standard. Pretty soon I was drinking a second cup of black coffee and felt better. After all, the laws of cause and effect would attend to Katherine Boyd. She would get her comeuppance someday.

The thing to do, I told myself solemnly, was to stay on the track and not be drawn off by these flare-ups. Personalities must not deceive me. Why should I bother my head with Platt's amorous caperings? If Katherine Boyd's cupidity involved a try for a new and richer husband what could I do about it? And Steve Boyd's husbandly jealousy could leave me cold.

The murder was the thing. Was the quarrel between Boyd and Platt related to that murder? I thought of that quick and furious blow. Assuredly Steve Boyd had a vile temper. But I also knew beyond reasonable doubt that Katherine was a vain, cruel, selfish woman who would stop at nothing to gain her ends. Fear of discovery and consequent punishment might deter her from murder, but moral scruples never. As for Norbury—the oftener he refused to talk to me the more certain I was that he possessed pertinent and guilty knowledge of the crime if, indeed, he was not himself culpable.

Most of all I wondered about Henry Platt. The expression on his face as he arose from his ignominious prostration made me recoil in retrospect. Malignant. Venomous. I mouthed these adjectives and shivered. Barrett's death gave Platt control of the company for all practical purposes. But that control was already in sight with his proposed marriage to Judith. To kill Barrett was unnecessary. Besides, Platt had an alibi for the night of the murder. The dinner, the style show, the dance at the country club less than a mile away from the plant.

I cleared the whole mass of suppositions from my mind. The message in the dog. That was the essential clue. Upon those lines of cryptic letters and numbers I must focus my most intense mental efforts. Puzzle out that code and capture the spy at the Barrett plant. Find the man who stole the dogs and then, no doubt, we'd have the murderer as well.

Back home I put the square of paper before me on my table and studied it carefully.

ES4P7AS5U5S56E
ACR4E7E1E4F5C6T6
2C4
SC6127DSPT4L5E6NPT5DSE

No doubt it was simplicity itself—after you knew the code.

I began writing the letters of the alphabet in various formations. I numbered them in different series. I listed them in all sorts of combinations. But no go. I could get no comprehensible words.

Four lines. Fifty-five symbols. To an intellect like mine it should have been easy. But it wasn't. I covered sheets of paper with sets of figures. I tried various code words, such as dog, spaniel, Rockingham, Barrett, and others. No light came. I did not have the clue.

At last, weary and disappointed, I gave up. I composed a letter to the Federal Bureau of Intelligence, Washington, D.C.

Because it's wrong to waste time on this thing, I kept telling myself. This is not a simple crossword puzzle. Every minute is giving a traitorous wretch time to plan a disaster of enormous scope. I may be aiding him to wipe out the Barrett plant with its capacity to aid our country in time of need.

Still, after I wrote the letter I couldn't bring myself to mail it. I put it under the paper in my table drawer. The message itself I concealed within my vanity case to take the place of the key I had used and lost. I had already made several copies of the printed lines, and those I hid at various points inside the room. One, I recall, I secured with a paper clip inside the lamp shade. Even if Theresa's passion for housecleaning impelled her to dispose of any discovered scraps one copy should be safe.

I went downstairs and out upon the porch. It was a beautiful day, warm and full of the promise of summer. Win capered in canine joy about the lawn. Arthur, arrayed in pale gray with a new green hat, burst full-panoplied upon my sight.

"Do you need the car?" he inquired affably. "I thought I'd use it."

The glow of health was on his cheek. His step was springy.

"I certainly do need the car," I said acidly. "But may I compliment you upon a quick recovery? Yesterday at Death's door and today just out of *Esquire*. Theresa can out-doctor Dr. Hamilton. I'll drive you to work if you like, but aren't you rather dressed up?"

Arthur coughed slightly, a hollow echo of the hearty reverberations he had been achieving during the past few days. It was more an apology than a cough.

"Oh, I'm not going back to Barrett's," he explained brightly. "I told them to go ahead and fill my place. But don't look like that. I'm going to work all right. I wouldn't think of remaining in idleness. I have my social security to consider."

"And what work do you intend to do now?"

"I haven't quite decided," said Arthur confidentially. "And yet—why should I hesitate? Why should I not use my talents to solve the great problem? You know and I know that there's something rotten in Denmark. Dirty work at the crossroads, skulduggery in the—"

"In plain words," I broke in, "what are you talking about?"

Arthur leaned closer.

"The sab cat!" he whispered. "I'm out to get him. With my inside knowledge of things at the Barrett plant it won't take long to trail the rascal. I give myself three days at the outside . . . ."

"Arthur!" I cried, aghast. "Don't think of such a thing. You've tried detecting before, and it brought us nothing but trouble."

"I could say the same about you, Jane," he said in gentle and pained reproof. "My country depends on me, and I must do my duty as I see it."

"You've come close to disaster twice in this affair," I warned him. "First the bomb and then the fire. The third time may be worse."

But I protested to empty air. Arthur was gone. He didn't take the car. He knew I was firm about that. I stood on the porch and watched him strolling down Greenwood Avenue, bowing to Mrs. Gilmore, waving a hand to Mrs. Horton, and trying at intervals to persuade Win, who gamboled at his heels, to return. Fervently I hoped the dear fellow would find pleasurable but innocent occupation and forget his well-meant but troubling intentions.

As Arthur's portly form faded from view I saw a familiar maroon car drive up and stop at the curb before the Barrett residence. It was Henry Platt. I had watched the car in very much the same manner a couple of hours earlier as Katherine Boyd had descended from it at the hotel.

Henry Platt was vital and erect, seemingly none the worse for his knockdown at the hands of big Steve Boyd. Just the same, it must have done something to his disposition. He paused at the door, and I could see Susy admit him. I lingered on the veranda, wondering what he was saying to Judith and she to him and vexed because there was no possible way of finding out.

Really, there is a great deal to be said for those dictaphones I am always reading about in detective stories. I began to think of one behind a picture frame in the Barrett domicile or, better, under the davenport in the Boyd living room, and then I suddenly came back to actuality as the Barrett door opened again and Judith and Henry Platt emerged.

I don't know what impelled me to follow them. Certainly there is nothing more boring than driving down one street and up another, trailing a perfectly ordinary car containing two people chatting in a perfectly ordinary manner. Yet that is exactly what I did.

They made some stops. At the Rockport National Bank, Platt went in and stayed five minutes. At Smiley, Florist, Judith entered and stayed fifteen minutes.

Then they drove to Mill River Park and, naturally, parked. I parked, too, at a considerable distance and berated myself for a fool. There was no possible chance for eavesdropping. The open road offered no concealment. I had nothing to do but sit and think and I was notably unsuccessful at that.

In short time Judith and Platt finished their conversation. I heard the motor start and I made haste to start my own car. If the couple I was spying on should chance to observe me I wanted to be in motion, as if on business bent. But they went on ahead of me, and I drove in back of them as before.

Then another car passed me. It was a green sedan being driven rapidly but not, I believe, at excessive speed for the park drive. I did not observe the license number, nor did I see the driver. All I know is that a loud, explosive sound suddenly made me jump six inches. It was repeated, and I realized that the green car had passed Henry Platt's sedan and was disappearing around the curve ahead.

Almost at the same instant the dark maroon car seemed to swerve. It swayed slightly to the right and then shot abruptly across the road to the left. There came to my shrinking ears the sickening sound of crumpling metal, and the sedan came to a stop, its nose against an oak beside the road.

CHAPTER FOURTEEN

MY KNEES WERE GELATINE, AND my heart was an acrobat. Sometimes I think I ought to run for President; I am so frequently confronted by emergencies. I yanked up the brake, turned off my motor, and was out of my car before the sound of the crash had fairly died away. But swift as I was, Henry Platt was quicker. He jumped from his seat and ran around to open the door on Judith's side.

"Is she hurt?" I gasped as I arrived, panting.

He gave me one of his quick, dark glances and didn't bother to answer. At least, I don't think he was speaking to me. He was saying ugly words in a low, ugly voice. In between he gulped in air as though his very breathing was painful.

Judith seemed to be unconscious, a small, inert heap. Her head with its soft, curled brown hair lolled upon her knees. But even as Platt lifted her out and gently put her on the grass that was thick here and quite green she stirred and moaned and opened her eyes.

"She was jerked sideways as I hit the tree, and her head struck the door handle," Platt explained briefly. "If we only had some water . . ."

I felt her pulse, and it seemed to be beating along in a fine, busy fashion, and in a moment she opened her eyes a second time and said in her sensible way: "I'm all right. What hit us, Henry?"

"It was that green sedan," I said indignantly to Platt.

He frowned at me and twisted the corners of his mouth. I knew he meant to keep quiet, but Judith is a strong, healthy girl, and I know a revolver shot when I hear one.

"Pish and tush, Mr. Platt," I said independently. "This is no time to pamper delicate feelings. Where did those bullets go? Was someone trying to kill Judith—or you?"

"Bullets?" said Judith in her natural voice and struggled to a sitting position. "That's right, Jane. I heard shots, and a car passed us. . . ."

"It was a green sedan," I began again and stopped, startled at the expression in the girl's blue eyes. Wide, they grew wider and filled with fearful doubt.

"Come on," I suggested, taking her arm. "Let's see if you can get up. I'll help you into my car."

But she put a hand to her head.

"Wait a minute," she urged weakly. "I had a nasty crack."

"Very well," I agreed. "Just rest for a little, and then I'll drive you both home in my car."

I walked around the wreck as I spoke and I saw right away that the bullet had struck a tire, causing Platt to lose control as the car swerved. It was a mighty lucky thing that he was driving slowly, for the crash into the tree was enough to demolish the radiator but not enough to seriously injure the occupants.

Henry Platt stared morosely at the ground and waited for Judith to recover.

"Are you hurt, Mr. Platt?" I then thought to inquire.

"I'm all right," he said briefly, but he put a hand below his throat. "The steering wheel struck me across the chest, but it's nothing . . . . "

"Look out!" I cried, interrupting him. "Get behind the car. Crouch! My heavenly day, that green sedan is back. Judy! Roll over here and—"

"It's stopping," said Platt, not moving from where he stood. "And I haven't a gun. Why, it's Bill Randall!"

"Bill?" echoed Judith, and her voice had a sudden irrepressible lilt to it. "Oh, Jane, you were wrong."

"I was not," I denied vehemently. "I particularly noticed the green sedan when it passed before. Whoever was in it shot at this car. Twice. You can see for yourself the hole in the tire, and the other bullet must be around here, too, and—"

My voice dwindled and my eyes, too, popped out until they looked like raisins steamed for the Christmas pudding.

For there was another man with Bill Randall. Big and bland and beaming in pale gray came my brother Arthur.

"Judy!" cried Randall. "Are you hurt?"

His inquisitive eyes swept over the damaged car and the glowering Platt. I don't think he paid much attention to me on one knee beside Judith.

"Bill," cried Judith and pulled herself up to stand, swaying dizzily, "tell them it wasn't you. You didn't shoot at us, did you? It wasn't your car that passed us, was it, Bill?"

Young Randall made no reply to all this. Her pleading voice died away, and incredulity wiped out all other expression on her pretty face. But her amazement was as nothing to mine.

With surprise changing rapidly to horror I saw my brother, nonchalant and swaggering, snatch from his pocket a blue steel revolver.

"Trouble around here?" he cried. "Who's shooting? Where?"

"Edwards, you fool," cried Randall. "What are you up to?"

"Give me that gun," ordered Henry Platt.

His voice cracked like that of an old top sergeant, and Arthur, looking dazed, at once surrendered his weapon.

"Why did you do this?" Platt barked at him. "My tire blew out; my car is wrecked. Don't you know we might have been killed? You're a menace to the public safety, Edwards, and—"

"I am not," protested Arthur, his voice hurt and his face flushing. "I only wanted to protect you. Judy said you were being attacked and—"

"Arthur," I interrupted and tried to make my voice sound as authoritative as Platt's. I didn't succeed, but Arthur is used to minding what I say. "Arthur, listen to me. Did you and Bill pass this way about five minutes ago?"

"No," said Arthur at once. "And I didn't shoot anybody. You can look in the gun, Mr. Platt. It's fully loaded."

"You could have reloaded," growled Platt. "Somebody fired at us from a green sedan. Miss Edwards saw it. Now here's the green sedan and here you are, roaming around with a gun. Have you a permit to carry that?"

"It—it belongs to the company," admitted Arthur, confused now and minus his nonchalance. "I—I was going to turn it in tomorrow."

"You'll turn it in right now," said Platt grimly. He pocketed the weapon. "Tests can be made of the bullets fired at my car. As for you, Randall, what are you doing here? Working hours at the plant aren't over."

"I don't punch a clock," said Randall coolly. "I had some business to attend to-matter of necessity."

His words were not at all apologetic, and I looked for Platt to wither him, but he said nothing. Judith flared up.

"Is that all the explaining you're going to do? Your arrival here is very apt, isn't it? Just as opportune as it was on Monday night. Only this time the— the victim—escaped!"

Randall's young face stiffened. He thrust his hands deep into his pockets.

"I didn't shoot at you," he said calmly. "Neither did Edwards. And that's all the explaining I'll ever do."

All the anger went out of Judith and left only pallid distress. She dropped my arm and turned to Henry Platt.

"Take me home, Henry," she begged. "I—I feel ill."

So home we went. Judith and Platt and I in my car. Arthur and Bill Randall in Bill's green sedan.

We didn't talk. I suppose we were each busy with our own unpleasant thoughts. I know I was. I didn't know whether to believe Arthur or not. I was inclined to. I wanted to, but if only I had noticed the number on that dratted car! But, after all, the town was full of green sedans.

At the Barrett house Susy opened the door. Aunt Elsa, a comfortably plump woman, met us with questions and lamentations, the loudest being that she expected callers at any moment.

"I'm all right," Judith said. "Jane will stay with me. Don't bother, Auntie."

Henry Platt telephoned at once to Dr. Hamilton and then to George Hammond.

I settled Judith in the pleasant bedroom with the maple furniture and went down to the kitchen to fill an ice bag. Mrs. Storm was at the sink picking over strawberries.

"I hope," I said to her impulsively, "that your son is at work this afternoon. Someone shot at the car when Mr. Platt and Judith were driving in Mill River Park. We might easily have had two more deaths."

She didn't turn, but she kept on washing those berries until I wondered if there would be any flavor left.

"Mr. Platt?" she said then in her strongly accented voice. "Is that the man at the telephone?"

"Why, yes," I said, surprised. "Don't you know Henry Platt, the general manager of the Barrett Company?"

She shook her head.

"I keep to the kitchen," she said. "Susy waits on table."

She put the berries in a bowl and picked up a towel to dry her hands. I thought she seemed to be speaking with no realization of the meaning of her words.

"But John"—I brought her back to the subject as I screwed on the top of the ice bag—"he's at work, isn't he?"

"No," she said. "He is on the second shift. So is Carillo."

I went back upstairs and waited until Dr. Hamilton arrived and prescribed for Judy. Bed, sleep, ice for the rapidly swelling lump on her head.

"Captain Hammond came in when I did," the doctor reported to us. "Henry Platt went off with him. You'd better stay at home, my girl, until this mess is cleared up. I'm going to tell your aunt to keep you here."

"And what do you make of it all, Doctor?" I asked.

"Nothing," he said succinctly. "It takes all my time to repair people without checking on who's trying to carve them up. Some fool with a grudge against Platt took a potshot at him. I wouldn't try to link it up with Mr. Barrett's death."

But most people would connect the two deaths. It seemed quite reasonable to suppose that the killer who had neatly disposed of Austin Barrett had now turned his attention to the next in line, Henry Platt. And that made it look like fifth-column activity right enough. With Barrett and Platt both out of the way production at the Barrett Machine Company would undoubtedly be seriously delayed. It might be easier to get the plan of the new minesweeper, and if Steve Boyd were the next to go ... But I shook myself out of that line of thought.

"They've gone out to inspect the car, of course," I said to Judith. "I hope they dig out a bullet to photograph, because that will certainly exonerate Arthur. Arthur wouldn't shoot at anyone. A ridiculous accusation!"

Judy agreed in a small, listless voice.

"And I think you are too hard on Bill Randall, Judy," I continued. "If he was with Arthur this time he, too, is innocent."

"Take one of these pillows away, will you?" she asked, not too pleasantly. "Somebody shot at us. You can't get away from that! And don't mention that man's name to me. He's conceited and s-sly, and I hate him!"

But tears welled into her eyes.

There was nothing to say. Goodness knows I couldn't give Randall a clean bill. As far as I knew, he was just as likely to be the subversive agent as anybody else. Certainly, as Judy had pointed out, his arrivals were always suspiciously apt and opportune. Only Judy did look very young and pale and woebegone, and I felt very sorry for her.

"Where did you put the dog?" I asked briskly, more to take her mind off her troubles than anything else.

"He's under my dressing table," she sniffled and dabbed at her eyes with a wispy handkerchief. The ice bag on her head slid off, and I leaned over to rearrange it. "What did you do with the slip of paper?"

"I wrote a letter about it to Washington," I said.

And so I had. The letter was safely under the paper in my table drawer.

I lifted up the pink-flowered skirt of the dressing table, and there sat the little dog, perky and brown, on a shelf.

I took him in my hands and turned him carefully about, and then my gaze sharpened and clung.

"Judy," I said, "is there a pencil and a sheet of paper up here?"

"Over on the desk," she said. "Why?"

I took the dog with me to the desk. Rudely I turned him upside down with due regard for his detachable head. Then I copied the mark that showed indistinctly in the clay. Because of his brown glaze it was difficult to make out the inscription, but finally I had it down to my satisfaction.

"There," I chirped to Judith and I did not try to keep the pleasure out of my voice. "I wouldn't wonder a bit if this isn't—?"

"Miss Judith," said a voice at the door. A polite tap accompanied the words.

Mrs. Storm stood there. Her gaunt countenance was dreadfully pale, and the blank look in her eyes was intensified.

"What is it?" asked Judith from her pillow.

"May I go out? Susy is out, and your aunt with her callers is busy. I have an important errand . . . ."

"You look ill, Mrs. Storm," I said sympathetically. "Is there anything I can do?"

"No," she said, and neither her eyes nor her thin lips relaxed. "No. I must go. For a short while."

"Oh, of course," said Judith impatiently. "Run along."

The woman stood just inside the door, and her eyes when they left Judith glanced rather wildly about the room. When they came to the little brown dog upon the desk they stopped. Not that the expression of her face changed. I did not mark a flicker of curiosity or interest, and yet there was something that made me think the presence of the brown china spaniel caused surprise.

The next instant Mrs. Storm had disappeared.

I picked up the porcelain dog and concealed him safely beneath the full, crisp skirts of the dressing table.

What had so shaken the woman? Surely not the dog. She had been queer, I now remembered, as I filled the ice bag in the kitchen. Had she had a telephone call? Would it not be wise for me to follow her?

I was conscious of an interchange of words below stairs, and the next instant the front door closed. Then footsteps sounded in the upper hall, and I looked up to see Bill Randall in the doorway, his concerned face just visible above an armful of pink roses. Aunt Elsa had sent him up.

"Gosh, Judy," he said desperately, "I'm sorry. You know I didn't do it, but it rubs me the wrong way to have you question me. I can't be yapping my head off in front of a frozen face like Platt. Gosh, I'm glad it wasn't worse. I'll get the one who did this if I never do anything else."

He sounded intense and sincere. Judith bit her lip. She wasn't drowsy now. Her small hands were clenched under the sheet. I could see them twitch.

"The roses are lovely," she said in a small, polite voice. "Jane, will you find a vase downstairs and put them in water?"

What could I do? Although I crammed those stems into a water pitcher in double-quick time, when I puffed up the back stairway he was already on his way down the front. And he slammed the door behind him. A loud, angry bang.

"For pity's sakes, what happened?" I demanded. "That was a mighty brief call."

"Throw those things out," Judith snapped when she spied the roses. "Brief it was all right, but too long at that. He didn't need to come up here just to tell me all over again that what he does is none of my business."

"What's that?" I asked, still staring and holding aloft the roses. But she flopped over in the bed and pulled up the pink puff. The ice bag slid off again, and she picked it up and hurled it to the floor.

"I don't want the damn thing," she cried pettishly. "And shut the door as you go out. I'm going to sleep."

CHAPTER FIFTEEN

CAPTAIN GEORGE HAMMOND searched for the bullets and found them. The first one was lying on the grass beside the road, some fifty feet behind the car. The second had punctured the rear left tire and had been deflected by the metal rim. The detective shook it out of the limp inner tube.

"Seems as if the assailant was a mighty poor shot," I meditated. I had gone back to the scene of the crash in Mill River Park because I deemed it my duty to see that the police were on the job.

"And that ties it up with Arthur," put in Officer Blake, who was present. "And I bet that's why he bumped off Barrett with the hammer. If he'd used a gun he might have missed and—"

"*What* are you saying, Mr. Blake?" I queried with an upward soaring of my iciest tone that always makes him flush and stutter.

"I meant the murderer, Miss Edwards," he said. "Not *necessarily* Arthur, although I do claim that—"

"I wonder if this fellow actually tried to kill Platt," broke in George diplomatically. "Maybe it was a warning. Suppose he wanted something from Barrett and couldn't get it and he knew he couldn't get it, so he killed Barrett. Now he stands a chance to get it from Platt and is trying to scare him into it."

"Get what?" I asked practically.

"Well, of course we don't know that yet. Might be certain—er—a—papers. " By which circumlocution I knew that all had not been confided to Blake. "Might be certain labor demands. Might be an attempt to hold up production for a time. Even the slightest delay in the production of machine tools means something nowadays. And it seems to me if a fifth columnist is behind this it must be Carillo. Jappy Carillo. With a name like that he must be Italian, don't you think?"

"No, I don't," I said dryly. "When I think I think to some purpose. What's in a name? He might have been born Mike Murphy or Izzy Erbstein for all I know about him. What you ought to do, George, and what you haven't done is to investigate the past life of every person even remotely connected with this case."

"I have," protested George.

"Yes," I said witheringly. "As thoroughly as you investigated Julian

Norbury. Look them up. Where did John Storm come from? And his mother. And Carillo and Randall and Platt. Even Grace Ashford. She hasn't lived here all her life. As far as the Boyds are concerned and Julian Norbury—maybe all three of them are converts to totalitarianism. I've heard that there are lots of proselytizers on those Florida beaches. What you ought to do, George, is—"

"What I got to do now," said George with sudden practical energy, "is find out just where everybody was at three or thereabouts this afternoon."

As it turned out only Arthur and Bill Randall had an alibi. And George suspected even that. He is loath to accept Arthur's unsupported word for anything. But when he is so openly skeptical how can he expect Arthur to tell him the truth? Arthur opens up to confidence like a flower to the dew.

My brother's story was that Bill Randall had picked him up about two forty-five. He was then standing at the corner of Third and Main. Bill was driving and said that he had an errand to do.

"What was the errand?"

Arthur didn't know that. As they were going through Mill River Park they had come upon the wreck of Platt's car. They had stopped and heard about the accident, and naturally Bill had forgotten about his errand. Probably wasn't anything important.

The police didn't believe that. They pointed out that the errand could not have been trivial since Randall had left his work for the afternoon. But that didn't impress Arthur. Work never does.

Had they been following the Platt car?

No. Arthur was very firm upon this point. They had not. The Platt car was not in sight, nor had it been mentioned.

But of course, as Hammond observed at this juncture, Randall could have known that Platt had taken Judith out for a drive and, had he wanted to locate her, Mill River Park was the first place he would try.

At three o'clock Jappy Carillo had been asleep in his trailer in the camp near the Barrett factory. So he swore to the policeman who aroused him at four o'clock.

John Storm had been asleep in his room above Becker's Drugstore. There was no confirmation of this. All the druggist would say was that he had seen Storm come down the stairway at five o'clock.

No one checked on Mrs. Storm. Not then.

Steve Boyd, when interviewed, was in his working clothes in the machine shop. He said he had come out on the two-o'clock bus. But he had not punched in, and no one could swear to the exact time of his arrival. And when he learned that Platt and Judith had been fired upon he shut up like a clam and would say nothing.

It was almost six o'clock when Officer Blake rang the bell at the Boyd apartment.

"I was at home before two o'clock," Katherine told him evenly. "I had a severe headache and I took a nap."

"My gosh," groaned Blake wearily. "Another one. You'd think this was Sleepytown. I've already talked to the lady downstairs, Mrs. Boyd. She says your car wasn't in the garage all afternoon."

"It was parked in front of the apartment," said Katherine.

"But she said you always park in back and use the back stairway."

"I didn't this time. There's no law about changing your mind once in a while, is there? Especially when you're forced to live with curious cats!"

"Then you've got no witnesses to prove you were at home," said Blake, writing it all down laboriously. "Mrs. Gilmore in the next block says that she spoke to you as you were driving up to your house here, and that was at five o'clock."

"That was the second time," retorted Katherine, her eyes blazing, though her face was cold and set. "I had my nap and then I went to the Self-Service Grocery to do some marketing. And tell Sarah Gilmore to mind her own business. God knows I didn't want to speak to the fat old busybody!"

That for Mrs. Gilmore, who is president of the Rockport P.T.A. and the push behind every drive. Fortunately she did not hear of the remark.

While the policeman was there Julian Norbury came in. Seemingly upset by the shooting, he put as many questions to Blake as Blake did to him.

"Listen," Blake said finally. "You can read all about it in the papers. I don't know who shot at them. If I did I wouldn't be asking you where you were, would I? Now, come on, what's your story? You can pick it up after that fight at the hotel."

"Annoying little contretemps," said Julian lightly. "But nothing to it. A personal difference. Henry wasn't bothered. I went out with him and apologized for Steve, but he didn't pay any attention. His mind was on something else."

"Yeah. I'm not tracing his mind. Where were you after that?"

"I was in Red Green's Bowladrome."

"Stick around close to home," Blake advised him. "I'll check on that."

And twenty minutes later he had telephoned to Norbury.

"Your story didn't click. You got no witnesses. The pin boys don't come on until four o'clock, when school is out, and the girl at the fountain says she didn't see you."

"Can I help that?" said Norbury sulkily. No doubt even then his hands were twitching and his deep-set eyes were burning with the intoxication of his purpose. "That little snip never sees anybody over twenty-one. That's my story and I stick to it."

He banged up the receiver.

Even Mrs. Ashford couldn't prove her whereabouts. Platt had told her to take a couple of hours off, and she had been shopping.

So when Blake, hungry and tired, had reported back to Hammond's office he was not much the wiser. But by that time the bullets had been photographed. Arthur was eliminated from consideration and his story given the credit it deserved. For the bullets were small—.32 caliber. And the gun Hammond had taken from my brother was a .38.

"Now we got to find that revolver," Hammond said glumly.

"And if it doesn't do me any more good than the hammer I might as well save my efforts."

But the revolver was to remain hidden for a long time. When it did turn up it furnished the finale.

Of course I knew nothing of all this until later. At the time I was deep in a problem of my own. Throughout the late afternoon, as the shadows lengthened on the young grass, as Officer Blake accomplished his interviews, as Annie crept timorously forth to indulge in an osteopathic treatment, hoping that soothed muscles would also bring soothed fears, I was behind the locked doors of my bedroom. Bent over my table, I was absorbed in a new effort to read the message hidden in the china dog.

There was upon the dog in Judith's possession a mark, the stamp or trademark of the early potter. Above and below this stamp a childish hand had scratched other letters. Pressed long ago into the soft clay, they still remained to identify the original little-girl owner. The stamp and the name looked about like this:

FANNY
ARCHIBALD
POTTERY
SUE

I counted those letters. I wrote them down in a neat row and I eliminated all those used more than once. This left seventeen letters. But numbers were also employed in some way or other in the cipher. During my previous sessions with this code I had decided that, in all probability, the numbers had been used to represent the vowels. No number higher than seven appeared in this particular message. Presumably then, the numbers from one to seven might easily refer to the letters a, e, i, o, u, w, and y. Adding seven to seventeen gave me twenty-four. Still not enough to correspond to the twenty-six letters of our alphabet.

I sighed and muttered. I groaned aloud and walked up and down my room and made a rat's nest of my smooth coiffure.

"Hold on, Jane," I said then to myself in a firm tone. "How many words require the letters x and z? Comparatively few. Assuredly, for most communications, a synonym without those letters could be found. Omit x and z. Twenty-four letters then.

"And now I have twenty-four corresponding symbols. If only the message is written in English I've got something."

The message in the dog read as follows:

ES4P7AS5U5S56E
ACR4E7E1E4F5C6T6
2CR
SC6127DSPT4L5E6NPT5DSE

I wrote out the letters of the alphabet, omitting *x* and *z*. Under them I placed the letters of the potter's mark and of the name Fanny Sue, taking each letter in the order in which it came. I substituted numbers for all vowels. Like this:

A B C D E F G H I J K L M N O P Q R S T U V W Y
1 F A N 2 Y R C 3 H I B L D 4 P O T E S 5 U 6 7

My heart was jubilant within me, but still I could not decode the message. Yet there was enough progress to show that I was on the right track.

And then suddenly I saw. I had to reverse the numbers of the vowels, using 1 instead of 7 for the letter *y,* and so forth. And my alphabet read like this

A B C D E F G H I J K L M N O P Q R S T U V W Y
7 F A N 6 Y R C 5 H I B L D 4 P O T E S 3 U 2 1

When I had the message decoded and spaced I was shaking like a leaf. For the meaning was perfectly plain.

"Stop activities. Chgo (Chicago) says FBI here. Who? They want promised prints."

That was the message that had been placed in the china dog upon Austin Barrett's desk. Who had put it there? And why had Barrett been struck down? And where was the other dog?

I had not the faintest glimmer of an answer to any of these important questions, but I felt grimly certain that ultimately I would get it. I had taken the first long step.

Although I felt triumph surge within me as I read that message, stronger still surged a growing alarm as I contemplated the possible ramifications of this plot. I don't mind keeping things from George, but the FBI is a horse of another hue. I combed my hair, put my notes in my purse, and planned to startle the self-satisfied detective of our local force immediately after dinner.

I was terribly excited and when I found myself dabbing rouge on my nose and powder on my cheeks I tried to practice self-control. I found comfort in thinking what I'd say to Hitler if I had a chance. This exercise in blistering phrases always soothes me, so that by the time I went downstairs I was comparatively calm.

Annie had returned from the osteopath but was not in the best of spirits. Theresa was positively sullen. Dinner, she announced gloomily, was ready, and if we didn't come right away she'd throw it out, as it would soon be no good to anyone, man or beast.

"And the strawberry shortcake too," she added darkly, although we were hastening our steps.

Annie had been apprised of the shooting and was a prey to fears and fancies. Arthur, pleasantly affable, was already in the dining room and had placed his portable radio on one end of the table. But Annie, no ad for the osteopath, leaned over and turned it off with one savage twist of the knob.

"News, news, news," she said bitterly. "What's the use of listening? You'll just hear worse day after tomorrow. Bombs are falling; political systems are falling; Yugoslavia is falling——"

"So is the soufflé," said Theresa crossly. "Eat it and keep still."

Arthur and I conversed politely through the meal. The subject was scientific farming. Arthur had decided to give up searching for the sab cat and contemplated a return to the land. Since he scarcely knows a parsnip from a potato in its native uncooked state this project did nothing to increase my fears. In fact, I encouraged Arthur.

It took me a long time to explain to Captain Hammond about the dogs and the message and the cipher and all, but I was patient and, I believe, thorough. He listened, goggle-eyed.

"You'll turn my hair white," he said finally.

"What hair?" I asked pointedly.

"Let's get it straight," said George, paying no attention to that crack. "This message now—you're sure you've got it translated right? Seems far-fetched to me. These things don't happen."

"Of course they happen," I snapped. "Just because they've never happened to you is no proof of their nonexistence. As for the code—figure it out for yourself. Isn't it perfectly clear?"

"As clear," said George glumly, "as politics in central Europe."

"Now consider," I went on sensibly. "Those dogs were in the possession of Katherine Boyd. She sold them to Henry Platt, who collects china animals. He used them as ornaments on his desk."

"Fancy offices those birds have out there," said George reflectively. "I wonder how my desk would look with a couple of these here now penguins . . . ."

"Both dogs," I proceeded sternly, "were stolen. One is found on Barrett's desk. As far as I can see, no one knows that but you and Judith and I—and the person who put it there. Now, for heaven's sake, George, don't let that out to reporters."

"I'm not spilling any of this stuff," said George sourly. "It might backfire on me, and I don't want the horselaugh—dogs and codes and—"

"Where is the other dog?" I demanded.

George looked blank.

"George, think," I besought him, praying for patience. "There must be two people concerned. Somebody put the message in the dog for someone else to read."

"That crack about the FBI," said George worriedly. "I've heard they have men in every one of these important plants, wherever they have big defense orders. I was reading a news story just the other day about a federal man working as a draftsman at the Douglas plant in California."

"George," I said, carefully keeping my temper, "this isn't California. There is a dangerous spy at work right here in Rockport. A clever person who will stop at nothing to deceive us. We must take nothing on faith. Perhaps Austin Barrett was not the loyal American we thought. Perhaps that minesweeper talk of Boyd's was all eyewash. We've got to run every trail to its end. This afternoon, for instance . . . Who shot at Henry Platt? Have you traced that green sedan?"

"No," admitted George. "But how can we without the license number? There's pretty near as many green sedans around as shamrocks in Ireland. I'd say it was Boyd's, but his wife claims she had it all afternoon."

"When I saw Katherine Boyd an hour or so earlier," I remarked dryly, "she would have drilled both Platt and Judith on sight—if she had had a gun."

"That Mrs. Ashford drives a green coupe," went on Hammond. "But Carillo doesn't have a car, and neither does Storm."

"I wonder if Norbury could have been driving the Boyd car while Katherine was taking her nap," I puzzled. "I'm sure he's mysteriously involved. There's a look about him. He runs from me every time I come near him."

"I could make a remark there," said George, heavily facetious.

"But you'd better not," I returned coldly. "Julian might well be on the payroll of some foreign agent. He might have suggested the dogs as a secret means of communication. *And he was in the Barrett plant Monday night.* How did he explain that, George?"

George gave a little jump but spread on the sticky, placating smile that he thinks will appease me but which only serves to prove his duplicity.

"George Hammond!" I cried accusingly. "You didn't question him at all. Why, you lackadaisical "

"I did too!" protested George self-righteously, but his tone was too unctuous. "I certainly did! He denied it. Said he wasn't there that night, and it was only your word against his. Not that I believe him instead of you, but Jane, where are you going?"

I was halfway down the corridor.

"To gather rosebuds," I called back with biting scorn. "Time, I believe, is still a-fleeting."

CHAPTER SIXTEEN

MY DESIRE TO TALK TO Julian Norbury did not lead me to the Boyd apartment. Further words with Katherine held no attraction and would, moreover, be useless. And a brief period of thought told me that Julian would hardly be at home this early in the evening.

I drove to Red Green's Bowladrome and parked at the curb. This sporting establishment was a two-story building halfway down one of our older and more unsavory business blocks. Recent remodeling had given it a new front of black glass. A large neon sign blazed red and green. There was a smoky, crowded soda fountain in the front section and in the rear a row of bowling alleys with seats for bowlers and spectators. Upstairs was a so-called billiard room where horse racing was known to be the center of interest. Naturally I had never been up there, but I was willing to go in my zeal to promote justice. This heroic effort I was, however, spared.

My hunch was quite right. As I walked up to the heavy, swinging glass doors I looked through and spied the object of my search coming toward me. Just as I saw him he glimpsed me. I saw recognition in his glance and involuntarily I stopped dead in my tracks. His sunken eyes were gleaming black. His pale, carved face was crossed with an expression of murderous hate. I halted, but he didn't. Gathering up an astonishing and unsuspected amount of strength within his thin body, he slammed back that heavy door with prodigious force, striking me amidships and hurling me aside.

Julian Norbury beside me was as Tom Thumb to Joe Louis, but the results of our meeting were in reverse. I staggered backward and sat down with a jar that injured both my dignity and the end of my spinal column. At the moment only a gasp escaped me. Nor did Norbury pause. Offering neither aid nor apology he darted down the street.

Then amazingly I felt a small hard object on my tongue and I spat out a front tooth. At this new wrong a righteous wrath rose up within me. My breath came back with anger, and I bawled out at the top of my voice.

"Help! Murder! Police! Stop that man!"

There wasn't a pedestrian on the street, but of course everyone inside the Bowladrome heard me. I wonder that George Hammond in his office or Theresa in her kitchen at home didn't hear me. Men and women and boys began to surge to the doors. But they were too slow. Struggling painfully to my feet, I tottered after Norbury.

I was in time to see a car pull out of a parking space halfway down the block.

It was a green sedan.

People from the Bowladrome were crowding about, curious rather than helpful. I saw the flaming hair and the rubicund face of the proprietor, but I paid no attention to his shouted questions. Jumping into my car, I hurried it into motion. For my sharp eyes had seen that the traffic light at the corner was red and, if human effort could be of avail, I intended to overtake that green sedan and pursue it to its lair.

It must have been Julian Norbury who shot from its shelter that afternoon. He might be out to attempt such dastardly deed again, but this time Jane

Amanda was at his heels. My tongue felt the vacant space between my front teeth, and I boiled anew. It is a mighty good thing that the tooth was only an artificial one on a pivot. Had it been my own original, I declare I would have torn Julian Norbury limb from limb.

Where was Norbury bound? For he was already on his way out of the Bowladrome when I approached. That desperate face of fury may have been for me but, on sober second thought, I doubted it. I was just an added sting, you might say.

Norbury drove out Elm Street in just the opposite direction from the Barrett factory. I rolled along at a safe distance in the rear. Soon we were in the country. We passed Mount Hope Cemetery, the headstones showing ghastly gray in the darkness. I lowered the window. Rain was in the air, and the wind was sharp and gusty. Occasionally a pale moon emerged from the banked clouds, only to dive again into their shelter.

When we reached Mill River Park, Norbury turned off the highway, and I felt sure that he was going to revisit the scene of the afternoon shooting. But no. The green sedan passed the spot without a pause. I gave a look at the oak tree. That's about all I had time for. I noticed that Henry Platt's car had been removed.

Putting on a little speed, I managed to come closer to the advance car. My eyes aren't what they used to be, and I couldn't see Norbury in the driver's seat. I hoped desperately that I was not following the wrong car. Perhaps a young romantic couple. Was I wasting all this precious time while Julian Norbury went free and undisturbed about his business? No, I refused to credit such thought. Awkwardly I drove with my left hand while with my right I fished out the notebook from my purse and scrawled down the license number. At least I could now locate the owner of *this* green sedan.

Emerging from the park, my quarry now took the road through the forest preserve. I dropped back far enough so that he would not suspect pursuit. Besides, this stretch of road was lonely and dark. We met few oncoming cars, and the farther I was from Norbury the better I felt.

Later I was to bitterly regret this caution. Had I overtaken the green sedan I would have prevented another tragedy. Or would it merely have been postponed?

I thought I knew now what was in Norbury's mind. Wherever he was going, he was taking a roundabout way to it. For this road circled about and went back to Rockport, past the Barrett plant. It was a favorite drive in the summertime. But it was much more of a ride than I had bargained for tonight, and I began to cast an apprehensive eye upon the gasoline gauge.

I gripped the wheel and grappled with the whole vexing problem as I continued to follow the beckoning red taillight. It seemed indubitable that Julian Norbury knew the answers to many questions that were troubling me. I set my teeth, those that remained to me, in determination. This time, I vowed grimly, Julian Norbury would talk. This time he would not escape me.

But he did.

We were almost back to Rockport when the thing happened. I heard a sound, a sudden cracking sound that might have been a shot. The motor was humming rather loudly and I couldn't be sure, but then I saw the car ahead of me slacken speed and turn off the road, running safely along on the shoulder.

Mechanically my foot sought the brake of my own car. Events were not occurring in the proper sequence. If, this afternoon, Julian Norbury had shot at Judith and Henry . . .

The car ahead of me came to a full stop. It was in front of a farmhouse. The lights were switched off, and at once the vehicle merged into a black pool of shadow cast by an enormous pine. The moon chose that moment to go under a cloud. I peered from my window, but I could see nothing, absolutely nothing. There was no sound, no movement. And something about the still, dark car terrified me.

I had stopped about two hundred feet behind the sedan, well off the road. For once in my life I was hesitant and at a loss. If the sound I heard had been a shot and Julian Norbury were injured . . . On the other hand, how could he be? And if I approached that car only to have him pounce . . .

I shuddered, but at the same time I was sliding from my seat and marching right along. Jane Amanda Edwards can be depended upon to be governed by her conscience and not by her alarms.

"Yoo hoo, Mr. Norbury!" I called pleasantly.

There was no reply, unless you count the sudden, angry bay of a hound from the shadowed farmyard. I loitered and stared at the outlines of the farmhouse, the barns, the silo.

And then suddenly wings were on my feet and I was running right up to the green sedan. With sudden clarity I understood what had happened. Julian Norbury had known from the beginning that I was trailing him. Now he had succeeded in throwing me off his trail. He had slipped away under cover of darkness after giving me a merry chase. Perhaps he was off to a rendezvous. The city limits were only a mile away.

I was almost brave as I looked through the car window. But my courage waned at once, and I shivered with dreadful cold. For huddled upon the front seat, upon the driver's side, was a crumpled figure. I could hear hoarse breathing, a bubbling sort of breathing that made me ill and dizzy.

I slid a hand in and flipped the light switch, and abruptly the horrifying truth was plain before me. I *had* heard a shot. Julian Norbury, seriously injured, was there in the green sedan.

"Mr. Norbury," I said again, and this time my voice was but a frightened whisper. I tried to raise that lolling head and saw that he had been wounded in the chest. There was a powder-blackened hole and a dark, sticky area spreading rapidly over his gray vest.

But as I moved him some pressure seemed to be relieved, and he lifted heavy lids from senseless eyes.

"Mr. Norbury," I said loudly, as though the poor man were deaf. "I'm going to drive you to a doctor."

His pale lips opened and he spoke.

"I can topple you down," he said. "I can crush you."

His voice faded and he stared at me.

"Mr. Norbury!" I cried urgently. "Who shot you? Tell me. Who?"

But there was no understanding in his glazing eyes.

"You're wrong, Katie," he said reprovingly. "Wrong. The dogs . . ."

His eyes closed. There was a horrible gurgle in his throat. He shuddered violently, with a sharp contraction of all his muscles, and was still.

I could not feel a pulse. By no possibility could I have felt for a heartbeat. No breath seemed to pass those bleached lips. I laid him gently down.

"Help," I thought numbly. "I must get help. I must get help . . . ."

I ran to the path leading into the farmyard and fumbled with the fastening of the gate, but that watchful dog bore down upon me with such a repetition of his bark that I backed away. Besides, the house was so dark and silent, it could not be tenanted.

Then I heard the hum of a motor, and a car approached from the south as I had done. I ran back to the road and shouted, but to no avail. The motorist shot past. I could not blame him. With all the news stories about holdups, no one wants to stop on a lonely road. Nothing for it but to drive back to town myself. Or perhaps I could find a gas station or a house with a telephone.

I was about to open the door of my car when I began to wonder about Julian's assailant. Had he escaped or was he now observing me under cover of darkness? It was not a cheering thought.

At that moment another car came from the direction of the city. I stood directly in the beam of my own headlights and raised imploring arms in a gesture of supplication. If only the driver would stop, I would not ask him to descend but only to telephone.

The car, a small coupe, slowed and then swung off the road to stop on the opposite side. I ran across the stretch of concrete.

"Thank you," I began breathlessly. "There's been an accident here. Could you please go back to the nearest phone and—"

"Why, Jane Edwards," a voice said cheerfully, and yet I could detect panic and fear beneath. "What has happened?"

It was Grace Ashford. It was my turn to wonder.

"What in the world are you doing here?" I demanded, curiosity making me forget haste.

"I live—not so very far away," she said, gesturing in the general direction of the town, "with my sister . . . ."

"But it is late, and this deserted road—and you're alone." I must have been quite unnerved to babble in such fashion.

"I like to ride alone at night when I have something to think out," she said simply. "And tonight I had to think. But what's happened to you? Run out of gas?"

With that I made a sharp return to my senses.

"Julian Norbury has been shot," I said. "I think he's dead. Go back and call the police and the doctor and the ambulance. I'll stay here with him. Hurry!"

She was an efficient woman, accustomed to obeying orders with no questions asked. She shifted into low, and I added: "And listen! Get this. Tell Captain Hammond not to come out here until he first locates every person under suspicion in this murder case!"

But she didn't do that. Or at least she said she made the attempt but that Hammond wouldn't listen but hung up on her. It sounds just like him. Maybe it would have made a difference in the end, but maybe it wouldn't. Anyway, Hammond was the first one to leap from the radio squad car as it drove up.

I had been sitting on the running board of my own car, waiting and watching. I had made one more inspection of Julian Norbury and then had turned off the dome light in his car.

He was dead.

George had the police squad and the ambulance men work with gloves.

"There won't be any fingerprints," I said drearily. I was very low-spirited, very sad.

As it turned out, my own prints were the only ones found on the car, and they were on the door handle.

"It would make a swell suicide," said George longingly, "and would wind up the case. If we could only find the gun . . ."

"You won't find a gun in that car," I maintained morosely.

Nor did they, although a careful search was made.

"What are you lisping about?" George said to me then.

"I'm not lisping!" I denied indignantly, but I knew he spoke the truth.

"By golly," said George, throwing the beam of his flashlight upon me and observing me with new interest, "you finally managed to get yourself into a fist fight. Who hit you? And what does the other fellow look like?"

I closed my lips over the evident gap in my front teeth. With a supreme effort—it took all of my will power—I remained silent.

"How did you happen to be out here?" the captain asked more sensibly.

So I explained as well as I could.

"I thought that Norbury was alone in the car. He didn't stop anywhere. Whoever shot him was in that car when Norbury left the Bowladrome. Now why would he drive away out here and let his companion shoot him?"

"He didn't expect it, of course," said George sagely. "Fellow sits beside him. Could pick his time and his place, shoot with his right hand, turn off the ignition with his left, and still be quick enough to guide the car off the road and stop."

"Then he sneaked out and ran away in the darkness, George. You must look for tracks as soon as day dawns. You'll be mighty busy in the morning, George."

"And what will you be doing?" inquired my friend suspiciously.

I turned the key and started the motor.

"Nothing for you," I rejoined tartly. "I have an appointment with my dentist."

CHAPTER SEVENTEEN

THERE WAS NO FURTHER ACTION during the night, unless you count a brief thunderstorm just before dawn. It was accompanied by a heavy downpour of rain that effectually obscured all tracks.

"Not that there would have been any," observed George gloomily. "This killer is too wily. Probably slinked along that little ditch with the car between him and you . . . ."

"It was black as a pocket just there," I snapped irritably. "I couldn't see a thing that wasn't directly in front of my headlights."

My disposition had not been improved by an early visit to my dentist. Dr. Roscoe could see no great haste in furnishing me with a new tooth. But I delivered a few well-chosen words, and he silently plastered in a makeshift and told me to return next day.

"That's the trouble with you women," he said then cheerfully. "Open your mouth and lose a tooth. Keep it shut and you're safe. Did you know that Edison didn't invent the first talking machine? God did. But Edison made the first one that could be shut off."

He laughed heartily, and I left in disgust. Ancient wheezes bore me. He is Annie's friend, not mine. She holds a local record, I believe, in gum boils, dying nerves, and fractious wisdom teeth. My tongue felt nervously of my new tooth and I prayed earnestly that it would last out the day.

"There might have been tracks," I said then to Hammond. "If Norbury's companion had been a woman and had worn high heels . . ."

"Yes," said George, "or if his companion had been a three-toed sloth or maybe a one-legged guy like that Long John Silver or—"

"I'm wondering," I said thoughtfully, "about Mrs. Ashford. She was right on the spot. And where was she on the night of the Barrett murder?"

"Claimed to be home in bed," said George. "And far as we can make out, that's where every mother's son and daughter was last night. Except Storm and Carillo. They were on the job at the factory and no hooey about it. They got plenty of witnesses. That sure knocks my case. It's as nerve-wracking as a—"

"As a dentist's drill," I meditated. "George, I can't blame myself enough for not getting closer to that car. To think that I tried to stay far enough in the rear not to be seen."

"Yeah. Well, we all make mistakes. Even you. The car is Steve Boyd's. I suppose you know that. Norbury borrowed it after dinner. Steve and his wife claim to have stayed home. Went to bed early. Both of them. Norbury was hanging out at the bowling alley where he got a telephone call. Red Green told me that, but he didn't know any more. Norbury stuck around for a while, touchy as a snapping turtle. Then he went out and you raised a holler. Red Green said that upset him so he didn't sleep all night."

"Fine," I said absently and arose. "I admit my blunder, George, but it has only increased my sense of responsibility. I am out to find the killer, no holds barred. I shall leave no stone unturned, no avenue unexplored—"

"Hey, now," said George in alarm. "Don't take it too hard. Don't you go putting your foot into anything else."

"Nothing can stop me," I declaimed. "Not storm or hail or any of those things the mailmen brag about facing. Not ambush or eyes in the dark or lost teeth or—"

Officer Blake came in, so I went out.

"My God," I heard him say with feeling, "how that big patootie can talk! If we could turn her loose on Hitler he'd crawl back to Berchtesgaden, lock himself in, and be glad of the chance to stay there."

That was Saturday. At two o'clock the funeral of Austin Barrett was held and his remains interred beneath the ground at Mount Hope Cemetery. There was a large crowd, of course. Many business associates and civic representatives as well as family friends and throngs of the curious. But the whole thing was conducted quietly with decorum.

Later that afternoon an inquest was held to determine the cause of Julian Norbury's death, and that, too, passed off in decent methodical fashion. The verdict was murder, and adjournment followed. I testified, and so did Red Green and Steve and Katherine Boyd. The questioning was brief, and the Boyds were visibly relieved when it was over.

But the worst was yet to come for them. Naturally George was keeping mum before the public when it came to the really absorbing facts like the new minesweeper and the china dogs, but that didn't keep him from grilling both Steve and Katherine thoroughly and long.

I didn't hear any of it. It was very private. Just Hammond and a policeman to take notes. And the same questions over and over.

"Whom did Julian meet last night?" "Why?" "What do you know about his affairs?" "What did he know about yours?"

Nothing. That was the sum and substance of all the answers.

Steve was belligerent, as usual. But Hammond must have tried to ignore that. He must have tried to be very tactful and genial because he wanted as much information as he could get.

"Yes," Steve admitted. It was a muggy day, and he used his handkerchief to mop his forehead and the backs of his big hands. "Julian might have known about the minesweeper. Although it doesn't seem likely. He never paid any attention to what I was working on."

"He didn't, eh? Not interested?"

"Only in the returns therefrom," said Boyd wryly with a twist of his mobile mouth. "But it was impossible for him to have plans or parts or blueprints or tracings, because there weren't any for him to have. I told you this thing is so secret that it's not even being completed at any one factory."

And when Hammond asked him if he thought it likely the government had a secret investigator at the Barrett plant Boyd stared in open amazement.

"Might have," he said then. "I never gave it a thought. It's possible. But if he's there he's pretty cagey, isn't he? It wouldn't be Julian. He wasn't smart enough."

But whether Steve Boyd knew anything about his brother-in-law's death or whether he didn't, something had changed him. He seemed to be almost cheerful when he left. His step was springy. The brooding suspicion was wiped from his pear-shaped face.

Katherine didn't come out so well in her examination. She was very pat with her story. I suppose she had thought it all out in those sad hours when the news of her brother's death had first come to her. I can imagine her repeating it to herself, making herself letter perfect during those chilly, doleful hours at the mortuary, at the police headquarters, when she was doing all the needful things that have to be done under such circumstances. Perhaps she believed it herself by the time she was questioned. She was always one to evade consequences.

"There is only one explanation for Julian's death," she told them firmly. Her eyes were hollowed by exhaustion and, for the first time, her resemblance to her brother was marked. "He went out to the factory to see Uncle Austin on Monday night. That was true, although he denied it."

"How did he know his uncle would be there? Had he promised to meet him?"

"He said that Uncle Austin called him about ten o'clock and asked him to come out. He reached the office about twenty minutes of eleven. The fire was raging. He didn't see Uncle."

"Why did Barrett call him?"

"I don't know. I asked him that over and over. I wanted him to tell me just what happened that night. But all he said was, 'Keep out of it, Katie. This is deep stuff, and we want none of it. I'm sorry I went out there, and they can't prove that I did. I didn't kill Uncle Austin.' But," added Katherine, "I think he knew who did."

"What makes you think so?"

"Because after that he was afraid. He spent a lot of time at home in his room. He prowled about. I used to hear him walking up and down that bedroom until I would have to tell him to stop. And he was always writing things and tearing them up."

"These—things he wrote," Hammond urged her. "Didn't you see any scraps? Any words at all? Were they letters?"

But she didn't know. Or she said she didn't.

"He saw someone that night," she insisted. "That's why he was killed. I think at first he didn't mean to say anything because he hated Uncle Austin. But yesterday when he came in—it was about six o'clock—he was terribly upset. He had heard about the attempt to kill Judith and Platt. About the green sedan. And when I swore that I was at home taking a nap and Steve had been at work he asked for the car keys and went out again. That's the last time I saw him—alive."

"The green sedan," Hammond said then. "Wouldn't it have been possible for him to use it that afternoon while you were asleep and it was parked out in front?"

"I don't think so. There were only two sets of keys. And yesterday I had one and Steve had the other."

But if he had had an extra key made—it was, of course, possible.

They let her go then, but they suspected her. It wasn't so much what she said or what she had done but how she looked.

Her eyes were wary, and her tongue was glib. They were convinced that she knew more than she had told.

I scarcely need to say that the second murder put Rockport into fever heat. We were featured in every metropolitan daily and, for all I know, in the backwoods weeklies. After the two funerals the photographers thinned out pretty well, but crowds still gathered in the hotel lobby, in the city hall, and in front of the newspaper offices. They bought up each extra edition of the local papers, egged on by three-inch headlines that promised but did not provide information. The war was off the front page. Every policeman in town was busy for once in his life, and three announcers at our local radio station had to be treated for laryngitis.

Captain Hammond made frequent announcements.

"The situation," he said over and over with utmost earnestness but not a smidgen of truth, "is being cleared up rapidly."

To give him his due, he worked hard. And so did I.

To confuse the issue still more, the bullets fired at Platt's car did not match the bullet that killed Norbury.

"What of it?" decided George in deepest melancholy. "The guy has got two guns."

The days passed.

Judith's Aunt Elsa went home, but Judith remained in the white house on Greenwood Avenue. I saw her coming and going with her young friends. Henry Platt had his maroon car repaired, and sometimes I saw it parked at the curb. But I did not see Bill Randall. One day I stopped in to see Judith and I asked her about him.

"He's been away," she said somberly. "I don't know where. But he's back now, and what do you know? He's taken a room right here on the avenue with Mrs. Gilmore."

"He's living at Gilmore's?" I cried, astonished.

She nodded, and her old gay smile tugged at her lips.

"But actually. Mrs. Gilmore has enlisted for national defense, and this is her bit. One of her bits. You know how crowded the town is. But Mr. Gilmore is wild. He says how the hell can he get the bathroom in the morning when he needs it, and Marge is furious because she says she can get her own men without having her mother corral one. But you know Mrs. Gilmore. I don't see why on earth he wants to live there, but certainly I don't care!"

But I thought she did. Henry Platt's devotion might be very pleasing, but I never did take any stock in that old adage about an old man's darling and a young man's slave. Not that Henry Platt is old—but then, fortyish as I am, I well know how fortyish looks to twenty-two.

Judith didn't look well. Her pallor was intensified, and faint bluish smudges showed beneath her eyes.

"You're tired, Judy," I said gently. "Why don't you go away for a little trip?"

She shook her long curling bob.

"No. That's Henry's solution. I'm waiting. Something else will happen, Jane. Things aren't just going to stop here in a—a—blank. It seems like I can't go on living until the mystery is explained. You're waiting too, Jane."

I couldn't deny that. I still had the code message on my conscience. The letter to the FBI had not been mailed. A few more days, I kept telling myself, a few more days.

Judith had faithfully kept her promise to tell no one of the dogs. I had not risked telling her of Julian's last words to me. She was bitter enough toward Katherine. Besides, neither Hammond nor I had decided upon the correct interpretation of the words.

"You're wrong, Katie," he had said. "The dogs . . . ." And so Katherine was implicated. And before that he had said, "I can topple you down. I can crush you."

A definite threat of course. But to whom? If he were the secret-service man indicated in the cipher message his activities would doom him to death. Steve had scoffed at this theory. Katherine said that Julian had been afraid.

"Mrs. Storm is getting awfully queer," Judith went on in a lower voice, glancing at the doorway. We sat in the living room, where the sun made a bright patch on the rug. "She practically never leaves the house. Just revolves between her room and the kitchen. She would not go to Dad's funeral. She's always dropping cups and dishes, and once when Susy came in unexpectedly she screamed."

"She's been through a lot," I said. "It's the nervous strain."

"Yes. But you'd think she'd be relieved now. John is practically in the clear. I expect my attorney to get the stealing charge dropped. John is working every night and making money. So is Carillo. You know Henry gave a big raise out there to forestall any more strike agitation."

I tried to keep all details in my mind. Even my persistent optimism was beginning to wear a bit thin. From the beginning clues popped up, only to be explained and discarded. Or else they disappeared entirely.

Arthur's lunch kit had disclosed no fingerprints, nor did the neatly constructed bomb bear any distinguishing marks. The naphtha can, the overalls, the hammer, had journeyed to Chicago and duly returned from the laboratory, each bearing its own careful scientific description that threw no light whatever into our darkness. The overalls belonged to John Storm, and the hammer to Steve Boyd. The oilcan was company property. The very confusion of identification made them useless. Had we been able to prove the ownership of one article only, the police would have made an arrest. The key to Barrett's cabinet and the manila envelope I had seen in its bottom drawer had, of course, been destroyed long since. The green sedan from which Henry Platt and Judith had been attacked remained elusive.

About that time Grace Ashford began calling me at irregular intervals.

"Anything new?" she would ask brightly. "My dear, I hope it won't be one of those *unsolved* mysteries. It's awfully *queer!*"

And once she asked me if I had heard anything more about the china dogs.

"No," I said. "Why?"

But she said she had no reason for asking.

Richards, the watchman, had been released from the hospital and was continuing his convalescence at home. Although I visited him once again and took him one of Theresa's custards and although the police had questioned him several times, he could furnish no hopeful clue. A workman in overalls had come from the back door of the office and had struck him down. And he had identified the woman visitor at the plant that night as Katherine Boyd.

Steve Boyd's information about the blueprints had been confirmed by a letter from Washington.

"We deeply appreciate the efforts of the Rockport Police Department," the letter said in neat black typing, "and we assure you that there is no need to be concerned. The plans for the instrument mentioned are adequately protected."

"A polite slap in the face and an order to keep my nose out of it," said George, disgruntled. "But if there's an FBI man here he's sure hiding under the woodpile. I got to hand it to him for covering up his tracks. Now I got to smoke this killer out, and what with? Now all I got left is two bullets from a missing revolver, one bullet from another, a cipher message from somebody to somebody, both somebodies unknown, and Julian Norbury's last words. None of which, to put it mildly, are very goldarned helpful."

"And a triangular piece of blue cloth," I murmured to myself. "I'll find out where that belongs."

"What's that you say?" George demanded suspiciously.

"Skip it," I told him. "Just let me mutter."

There is a time when no news is bad news. We all had the jitters. Arthur was still trying to choose a vocation, and the house was littered with pamphlets. Annie planted all the gladioli upside down, but it didn't make any difference because Win dug them all up. Even Theresa was demoralized.

I remember she served a steaming boiled dinner on one of the hottest nights that spring. It was an awful April. What with London being bombed and strikes and fireside chats and Mr. Matsuoka flitting about, I was glad to see the month go.

Then May came in, and I found the other dog.

Not that the discovery brought me any joy. It was really odd the way the whole thing came about. Purely fortuitous. And like the beginning of the affair, largely due to my sister Annie. As I came in to lunch that day I noticed Bill Randall come out of the Gilmore's front door and walk down the avenue. He wore no hat, and something about the curl of his blond hair, or maybe the set of his broad shoulders in the bold, plaid sports coat, made my heart quite soft.

"I declare," I said to Annie. "Sometimes I think that Sarah Gilmore makes more trouble than a cankerworm in an elm tree. Helping the housing situation, stuff and nonsense! Defense project, my eye! She wants to get that young man away from Judy and give him to Marge."

To my intense surprise Annie burst into tears. Compared to my sister, the dying martyrs must have been gay and aggressive. Why she should take Bill Randall's matrimonial fate to heart was more than I could imagine.

"I'm a nervous wreck," she wailed. "I promised those dreadful men who kidnaped me that I would never tell and I did and I'm always afraid they'll come and t-take me for another r-ride, and I'm not doing my bit for my country, and Sarah Gilmore is and—"

"Oh, goodness, hush!" I said crossly. "Do buck up, Annie! John Storm has more to do than think about you. Jappy Carillo too. They're working every night, and the police are watching them. Have some gumption, do!"

Annie straightened and gulped down a sob.

"Police didn't help Julian Norbury. Don't you honestly think Storm and Carillo are murderers?"

"I don't know," I said honestly. "Hammond is giving them plenty of rope in the hope of turning up new evidence. Meanwhile you have absolutely nothing to worry about."

"Then," said Annie happily, "I'm going to get busy. I have a wonderful scheme to aid the starving Chinese. I'm going right over and tell Sarah Gilmore. She's not going to get ahead of me!"

Annie scurried across the street, and after a moment I followed. I didn't feel that I could do much for the Chinese, but I wanted to hear Sarah Gilmore explain how roping in a likely prospect for her marriageable daughter linked up with our defense program.

Annie, however, had already been admitted, and the screen closed behind her by the time I came along. With the privilege of an old neighbor I stepped into the hall. And then I paused. I could hear Annie explaining at a great rate behind the draperies at my left and I could hear Sarah Gilmore's hospitable voice that somehow matched her comfortably padded exterior urging Annie to take a seat on a sofa.

But as I took another step forward an unbidden thought hopped into my mind.

"Bill Randall must have the right rear bedroom," a still, small voice said to me. "Mr. Gilmore would raise cain if he was moved out of his, and I know that Marge still has the big front room because I saw her in it last night. Someone should tell that girl to pull down the shades. This is Thursday afternoon and the maid's day out, and there's not a chance in the world that anyone would know if you sneaked upstairs and took a look at Randall's room."

Oh, it was a mean, tempting little voice all right, and before I knew it I had heeded it and was on my way, treading lightly on the padded stair carpet, and hurrying a trifle in the bargain.

I was quite correct in my assumption. I stepped into the square room and shut the door behind me.

The wallpaper was sprigged with bright, chintzy flowers, and the curtains were white and crisp. There was a wide table and bookshelves and a very good lamp. There was an easy chair and an attractive but durable deep blue bedspread. I silently handed it to Sarah. This room would appeal to masculine taste.

The wastebasket was empty. With the closet I was thorough. But I could find no suit of heavy dark blue wool from which my three-cornered scrap had come.

Nor could I uncover papers or letters. I looked through the table drawer, and the lack of accumulation seemed odd. But perhaps Bill was a neat young man and didn't keep old letters. I turned up the edges of the rug and I felt behind the books on the shelf.

It took some time to inspect the drawers of the highboy because I was careful to put everything back as I found it. Then I turned to the dresser. On top were several snapshots of Judy Barrett, and I wonder how Marge Gilmore liked that? The drawers held the usual array of toilet articles, underwear, handkerchiefs, and so on. But in the last drawer I found things.

There was a leather-covered box. When I opened it I actually felt my eyes get round and strained. For the case held a pair of the nastiest-looking revolvers I have ever seen.

I decided at once to take them with me. I'd give them to Hammond for examination. My method of obtaining them might be embarrassing to explain, but, after all, it might well be that one of them fired the shot that killed Norbury. But I felt a little queasy. It was essential to have those revolvers tested at once, but along about that time I happened to think of the difficulties in making an unobserved exit. What Sarah Gilmore would say if she spied me coming from her guest room with a large leather case under my arm I shuddered to contemplate.

Hurriedly I turned to finish my task. I picked up a round object wrapped thickly in white tissue paper. It felt knobby and interesting, and hastily I unfolded the covering.

Then I gulped in honest dismay. For in Bill Randall's drawer I had found another spaniel of brown Rockingham ware.

Undoubtedly it was the mate to Judith's dog. There it sat and regarded me with impudently cocked head. I turned it upside down and saw the self-same potter's mark and another signature that little Fanny Sue Archibald had scratched there long ago.

The surface of the dog was glazed. There might well be a fingerprint on those brown porcelain curls. Taking a piece of the tissue to protect my own fingers, I pulled out the dog's head and felt inside the body.

Disappointment was my only reward. The cavity was quite empty.

Slowly I closed the drawer. Regretfully I wrapped the china animal in its concealing paper. My heart was heavy, for I could not help but believe that my afternoon's work had brought more sorrow to sweet young Judith Barrett. Bill Randall's possession of this dog argued that he must be one end of the line of communication that was operating against the peace and safety of our land.

Grasping the heavy pistol case under one arm and the small white-wrapped canine under the other, I turned to go. I began to reckon that perhaps the side door downstairs would be the safest.

My breath then caught in alarmed vexation. I felt like saying a censored word and I began to hastily concoct a likely story for Mrs. Gilmore.

Then I realized that those decisive steps on the stairs and in the hallway were not Sarah's. In another instant the door of the room in which I stood was pulled open.

Bill Randall confronted me.

CHAPTER EIGHTEEN

"AND WHAT ARE YOU DOING IN MY bedroom, Miss Edwards?" asked Bill Randall.

His voice was low, and it stung like the lash of a cracked whip. There is no denying that I wore a hangdog air, but I snatched at my dignity.

"I am merely doing my duty, Mr. Randall," I asserted coldly. "I am assisting the cause of justice."

"You are not an authorized officer of the law," he pointed out. His voice was still soft, but I marveled that he could so change in character. Yesterday

I had been picturing him as a lovelorn gallant. Today he seemed far more likely to be the conscienceless villain. He seemed years older, hard, and assured.

He shut the door behind him and stood with his hand on the knob.

"I'll have to call the police, Miss Edwards," he said then in businesslike fashion. "I can have you placed under arrest for breaking and entering. Or a more serious charge. If I am not mistaken that is my property that you have beneath your arm."

At that brazen assertion I lost my hesitation and braced up. The element of surprise had dashed me. I do not often lose my *savoir-faire*.

"Do call the police. Call Captain Hammond as quickly as you can," I urged. I straightened my shoulders and took a firmer grasp on my spoils. Under my left arm was the gun case, under my right the paper-wrapped spaniel. I wiggled my right elbow. "This dog will convict you. You are a nefarious spy, Mr. Randall, but it takes more than a clever code to guarantee your wicked schemes. What's more"—I wiggled my left elbow—"I haven't a doubt in the world that the bullet fired so treacherously into Julian Norbury's breast came from one of these revolvers. And before that there were the bullets directed uselessly, thank heaven, against Judith Barrett and Henry Platt."

Young Randall's face was quite blank. His eyes narrowed momentarily in thoughtful fashion. He leaned back against the closed door.

"Come along downstairs to the phone," I said peremptorily and moved a step forward. "You're in a spot now, my fine young man. You can't silence me. Mrs. Gilmore and my sister Annie are downstairs. This is no lonely country road, nor is it a silent, deserted office building. Harm me and you'll pay for it."

Randall laughed then, and I jumped in surprise. The full bubbling burst of merriment startled me.

"My dear Miss Edwards," he said, and his voice was suddenly warm and properly apologetic, "don't talk like that. I'm awfully sorry for what I said when I came in. Surprise, you know, and all that. Of course you're doing what you think best. Let's talk this over before we make a row. Far from wishing to harm you, I admire you. I'm only too glad to help you in your—your laudable efforts."

Now this right-about-face put me increasingly upon my guard. Much as I like appreciation (and who doesn't?) I like it properly spooned out, as it were, in prescribed doses and not dished up at random.

"My efforts get results," I told him crustily. "I've got results right now to present to Captain Hammond. You might just as well march. Downstairs with you."

"No," he said. "No." He set his firm, tanned jaw. "Listen, Miss Edwards. You're all wrong. Really you are. Take the revolvers, if you insist, although I swear that neither of them was used for murder. I have had those revolvers for years."

"I don't care if you got them in your stocking for your first Christmas," I said stonily. "I shall have them examined. If you are innocent why should you object?"

"I object plenty," he said abruptly, vehement. "I don't want to be mixed up in this dirty case any more than I have to. Do you suppose my father will enjoy my picture slapped on front pages all over the country? Do you think my mother wants to see her son labeled as a suspected murderer? She isn't very well—poor Mother. There's something about you that reminds me of my mother, Miss Edwards."

"Cut out the soft sawder, young man," I said, more grim than ever. "Let me out of this room."

But still he barred the way.

"How would this stunt be?" he proposed then. "I'll make you a proposition. I'll fire these revolvers outside and let you take the bullets to Hammond. You don't need to say where you got them. Please."

"Leaving you fully armed?" I objected. "Nothing doing. I keep the guns *and* this dog that you stole from Platt for your rascally purposes."

"I didn't," he said flatly. "And what do you want of the dog? What has it to do with the murder?"

"Where did you get the dog if you didn't take it from Platt?" I countered.

He hesitated, it is true, but only for a moment.

"From Judith Barrett," he answered promptly.

You could have knocked me down with that feather they're always mentioning. I backed up two steps and I didn't know where to turn. But was I going to allow this handsome young soft-soaper to bamboozle me? I was sure he told me a lie.

"Come on," I said briefly. "We'll go to Judith and prove your statement."

He opened the door, and I preceded him. He followed me quite meekly down the front stairway. In my darker moments may I always be able to recall the expressions on the startled faces of my sister and Sarah Gilmore as they turned from their conversation in the parlor doorway to regard us.

Randall was as mum as an oyster, nor did I say a word. Out the Gilmore door and down the cement sidewalk between the rows of young petunia plants. Turn to the right and up three doors to the Barrett house.

The pert Susy answered the bell and showed us into the living room, where Judith jumped up from the davenport to greet us. She seemed to be taller, but perhaps that was because she was so thin.

"What is it?" she asked quickly. "Oh, Jane, what has happened now?"

"Plenty!" I snapped. "You were right to suspect this man, Judy. You hit the nail on the head. He has the other dog, Judy, and he has the consummate nerve to say that you gave it to him."

Have I said before that both Bill and Judy had very blue eyes? At that moment there was something electric in the way their glances crossed, and something sizzled in the atmosphere as their looks met and clung.

The girl gave a choked cry, a strange cry compounded of certainty and awful realization as well as horror. She put her hand to the back of a chair and moved stiff lips, but no sound came forth.

"Tell her that's the way of it, Judy," Bill Randall urged. He stood there tall and compelling. His voice was strong and clear. "Tell her that I was only curious. That I wanted to examine the dog and you gave it to me. She intends to call Hammond and have me thrown into jail."

Judy dropped her head, and a long shudder made her quiver. The room was still, and we waited. Then the girl looked at me and spoke.

"What Bill tells you is true, Jane," she said calmly. "I gave the dog to him. It—means nothing."

I stared at her blankly, too amazed to say boo.

Randall took the parcel from my unresisting hand. But when he attempted to take the leather case I eluded him. I took a grip on the box and a firmer grip on myself.

"See here, you two," I said coldly. "There's something mighty queer about all this. Do you mean to stand there, Judith Barrett, and tell me that you gave him the first dog? The one we found the night your father died? Or did you also have the second? Are you a pretty, foolish cat's-paw? Are you being used by enemy interests? Are you—?"

"No," she cried. "Don't look at me like that, Jane. I gave him my own dog, the first one . . . ."

But there was a distraction in her voice that made me doubt her. Making up my mind in a hurry, I darted past her to the hall. Up the stair I went on the double-quick.

She ran after me.

"Jane Amanda Edwards!" she said imperiously. "Don't you dare go into my room! Let me pass. Do you hear?"

"I hear all right," I returned. "Nothing the matter with my ears. Nor with my conformation. The only way you can pass me, my dear, is to fly over."

While I am not fat in any sense of the word, my figure is well rounded, and my bulk well filled the narrow stairway from wall to balustrade.

I plunged into the bedroom with Judith at my heels, crying wildly. I yanked up the skirts of the dressing table and, just as I expected, the brown spaniel, his head turned inquiringly, sat there on the shelf before me.

Slowly I dropped the draperies and looked at the girl. But if I expected a penitent I was badly fooled. She flew at me like a demon, angry, frustrated tears pouring down her reddened cheeks.

"So I *am* a liar, and what are you going to do about it?" she screamed. "Go home! Go home! Get out of here!"

She pommeled my arm with small, hard fists and pushed me violently to the door. I tried to expostulate, but sheer surprise made me weak, and the first thing I knew I found myself outside the white paneled door and heard the key turn in the lock.

"I don't care what you do to me, Jane," she sobbed within the shelter of her room. "I don't care what anybody does. I won't say another word."

I didn't say another word either. Slowly and unhappily I stumbled downstairs and looked into the living room. I knew that only emptiness would greet me. Bill Randall, with the second spaniel, had already made tracks. Where he had gone and what he was doing I certainly could not at the moment guess. Therefore, I did not at the moment try.

Anyway, I still had the guns. I patted them almost affectionately. I went home and retired to a semi-secluded space out behind the garage where I examined the revolvers. They were loaded, so I fired them. Both of them. I tried to be careful. Indeed, I *was* careful. And the statement of Mr. Alexander, our neighbor across the alley, calling me a thief and a murderer, was entirely unjustified. Nor was I attempting, as he insinuated, to secure an inexpensive Sunday dinner. Could I help it if one of his prize White Wyandottes happened to get in the way? And after the silly hen had committed suicide I had to get the bullet, didn't I? Mr. Alexander can sue if he wishes, but surely if our boys can give up their homes and their jobs and go to camp for two and a half years Mr. Alexander can sacrifice one hen for his country.

And if he can't follow my reasoning that isn't my lookout!

It was supremely ridiculous of Mr. Alexander to send for the police. If, as he feared, the killer *had* been about the neighborhood what, in heaven's name, could Officer Blake have done about it?

Fortunately Annie remained at Gilmore's, where the two shots caused no commotion. Although she arrived home with her nerves intact she was extremely peevish because Sarah Gilmore had not waxed enthusiastic over the plan to help the starving Chinese.

"She wants me to join *her* Committee to Keep Our City Clean," grumbled Annie. "She says the trailer camp out near Barrett's is an abomination and an eyesore."

"If you wanted her help," I pointed out to Annie, "you should have made her think she started the whole thing. Why don't you join her old committee and show her up? She never finishes half the things she begins."

To think that thus idly I made the suggestion which was so soon to bear bitter and unpalatable fruit!

"All she thinks about is that roomer of hers," continued Annie. "She says she cannot conscientiously introduce him to her friends until she finds out where he goes at night. He does *not* visit Judith Barrett. She's made sure of that. And he does *not* spend his evenings with the Gilmore family. Mr. Gilmore claims to have seen him at night riding about with Mrs. Ashford, but Sarah doesn't believe that for one minute. It was probably one of those nights when Mr. Gilmore would have been better off at home."

"Probably," I said. "Where's Arthur?"

"He has a new friend by the name of Sam Smead. Arthur says he's a swell fellow. But, Jane, he lives in Trailer Town. And I don't like that. From what Sarah says, it's no place for Arthur."

In my anxiety to talk to Captain Hammond I did not give this latter item of news the attention it deserved. I was in haste to check the bullets from Randall's revolver. I had retrieved both of them, one from our garage after it had gone through the window and the other, as I have said, from the interior of Mr. Alexander's hen.

Patching up a story was a bit difficult. Softhearted means soft-headed, I've always said, but somehow I could not bring myself to betray Judith. Not for an instant did I believe she was criminally guilty. Soon I would find out what was behind her action. And I didn't think for one instant that Bill Randall would run away. That would be a dead giveaway. No, he would stay, and if he wanted to cross wits with Jane Amanda Edwards he was welcome to try.

"Really, George," I said with asperity, "you think up more questions than Dr. Gallup. All you have to do is check the bullets. If they correspond with the others I'll tell you where I found them—and the revolver."

"I'm doing the best I can," said George. He was very grumpy. "I got troubles enough without you coming in here all the time as mysterious as a meeting between Hitler and Mussolini. I've looked up every soul remotely connected with the case. I know their middle names and what they eat for breakfast. Far as I can see, there isn't much mystery about any of them except the Storms. John Storm is the man, I tell you." He checked off names on his stubby fingers. "Henry Platt, born in New York City, came here from New Orleans, 1933. Randall's from Providence. Had a mess of different jobs, but no trouble in any of them. Mrs. Ashford came from Chicago. I've got her whole history. Carillo turns out to be Austrian by birth, but he was naturalized twenty years ago. I can't find a darn thing out of the way with the Boyds."

"Well, what about John Storm?" I asked impatiently.

George leaned forward. I could tell he was excited.

"His mother is an enemy alien! Oh, she's registered O.K., but she never told the Barretts that she came from Hamburg in 1936. Nor that her husband was executed as a Communist leader by the Nazis . . ."

"But John is—"

"He's a citizen. Been in this country since 1925. But like father like son. I'm going to close in on him."

"But, George! The mother! Mrs. Storm was away from home until very late the night Barrett was killed. She could have worn John's overalls and goggles. She could have taken Katherine's sedan and shot at Platt and Judith. She could have knocked me out that night in Barrett's office and escaped. She could have met and killed Julian Norbury . . ."

"Yeah," said Hammond. "Yeah. But how can I prove it?"

"A step at a time," I said hopefully. "First eliminate all other considerations. Photograph those bullets now and give me an official escort to examine Henry Platt's room at the Rockport Hotel."

"Criminy sakes!" Hammond sat up, and his glasses slipped down. "What's the idea? We searched his room once. I can't go there again. He's a mighty important man."

"I'm beginning with him," I explained, because entering his room presents the fewest difficulties. "I have searched Bill Randall's possessions. I expect to search the belongings of Storm and Carillo and Boyd."

"I won't be a party to it," said George stubbornly. "No sense to the way you bother folks. I got a man on John Storm every minute. One of these days he'll slip, and then we'll have him."

"I can't wait for him to slip," I maintained. "You're too slow. You've had time to catch a dozen spies!"

George snorted angrily.

"I'm not," he pointed out sourly, "that there Martin Dies!"

I went along to the Rockport Hotel and, to my pleasure, found that gaining admittance to Platt's apartment was easier than I had foreseen. Had I realized this, I would not have bothered George in the first place. He takes such a narrow view. But, as it happened, the hotel manager was an admirer of my former exploits, a friend of Tim Allen's, whose dastardly murder I had avenged less than a year ago. Moreover, he took it for granted that I had police approval.

"You understand, Mr. Wilkens," I adjured him solemnly, "that this is a dead secret? I shall displace nothing in Platt's room and I want you to stand beside me so that you can be a witness if necessary. Of course this is only routine."

And so it was. I was trying now to discover the origin of the piece of blue cloth. I positively boiled whenever I allowed myself to think of the wretch who peeked into my window, who dared to spy upon my simple home life. I intended to check over the wardrobe of every person concerned if it took me all summer. After that I could trace the suits that had been given to rummage sales or consult the cleaning establishments and the tailors. Then . . .

But there I was, going up in the elevator of the Rockport Hotel with natty Mr. Wilkens, the manager. At the fifth floor we walked down a corridor, turned to the right, and stopped at room number 524. The monotonous brown carpet was thick and soft beneath our feet. The hall was silent and deserted, with that blank look hotel corridors always have.

"He gets home about five," Mr. Wilkens observed, unconsciously lowering his voice in the approved conspiratorial manner.

My ear pricked at a sudden noise. I hastily grabbed at the hand that held the key. Someone inside room 524 had made a sound. A book dropped, or perhaps a shoe . . .

"There's somebody in there!" I whispered hoarsely to Mr. Wilkens.

His face lengthened lugubriously but only for a moment. Then he brightened.

"It's only the maid," he said soothingly. "Couldn't be anyone else."

Again he stooped and fitted the key to the keyhole, and again I heard certain smothered noises inside the room.

"Maid or no maid," I said sharply to the hotel man, "you'd better be careful. This is a murder case, and I've been bopped twice already. If you're going to open that door wait until I get out of range. Dentists cost money."

He chuckled as if I had made a most amusing sally, turned the key, and pushed open the door.

Immediately a startled exclamation passed his lips and, exhibiting no particle of caution, he rushed inside. Hearing no one, seeing no one, I followed.

The room was empty. But books had been pulled from the shelves. The desk was cluttered with papers, and the closet door stood wide.

The long curtains at the open window which led to an outside fire escape were swaying gently in the breeze.

CHAPTER NINETEEN

I FLUNG BACK MY HEAD AND charged across that hotel room like any old war horse on his way to battle. But Mr. Wilkens, the manager, ran as well. He kept getting in my way, and then I got in his, and the result of that was we both arrived at the open window in the same split second. As though we had been drilled, we thrust our heads forward and turned them left and right as we peered down the fire escape. And all I got for my trouble was a sound crack from Mr. Wilkens' cranium.

"Good heavens, man," I cried, rubbing my temple. "I've got to see. Do you realize that the murderer just went out of here?"

He was rubbing his own head and backed away from me.

"I shall call the house detective," he said.

Even with the window to myself I could catch no glimpse of the escaping criminal, and I knew that by the time I could get downstairs he would be safely lost in the crowds on Main Street.

"Call the police," I shouted after Mr. Wilkens. "And call Mr. Platt."

While he was thus engaged I looked about the room. Through an open door I could look to a bedroom beyond. But the room in which we stood was a commodious and well-furnished living room. The walls were cream and the rug thick and rust-colored. The sofa was brown, and there were three or four deep easy chairs. A tall bookcase was well filled. The kneehole desk was of dark mahogany. The draperies were of patterned linen, trailing green ivy upon a pale ground. Between the two windows were shelves, long and narrow, five of them. There the china animals cavorted charmingly. I noticed gay striped zebras and giraffes. There were cats and dogs of various types. There were elephants and amusing pigs. Usually they went two by two, as in the Ark.

I could see that the Rockingham spaniels would have fitted into this assortment very well indeed. Too bad that Henry Platt had not been content to install them upon these shelves. Too bad that he had exhibited them upon his office desk. Such is vanity. Such is love of display.

"Mr. Platt says he can't come now," reported Wilkens upon his return. "He says he can't help it if there was a burglar. He's very busy at the factory and he won't be home until five. Wanted to know what had been taken, as if I could tell!"

"I'd give a pretty to know what he was looking for," I said thoughtfully.

"Who?"

"Why the man who was in here, of course," I snapped. "I'm going to look in the bedroom."

I inspected the contents of Platt's closet and dresser drawers. He had a nice taste in haberdashery, and Arthur would be most envious of his collection of cravats. But although I searched through the row of suits hung in meticulous array I could not find one to match the piece of blue cloth.

"Has Mr. Platt worn a dark blue suit lately?" I asked the manager.

"I don't know," he confessed, wrinkling his brow. "I'm not much on colors . . . ."

The house detective came with George Hammond and Officer Blake to take over. Captain Hammond was thorough. I'll say that for him. He poked about and called for photographers and fingerprint men. I regarded the whole business with jaundiced eyes. The bird had flown, and what he was after went with him.

"Probably got nothing to do with the murder case," George pronounced hopefully. "Just a coincidence. I don't think the guy had a key. He must have come up the way he got out. Platt must have left his window open. But I'll do a little phoning anyway."

But the little phoning brought little results. The only one of our suspects that he could reach was Katherine Boyd.

"And she's had plenty of time to get home from here," I pointed out.

When Henry Platt came in he seemed more curious than alarmed.

"I'm sure I locked the window," he said, his dark face thoughtful. "In fact, it's always locked. I never open that window except in midsummer. This burglar came in through the door."

"You don't seem worried about losing anything," said Hammond.

"Give me the bad news," said Platt. "What did he take?"

"How do I know?" growled George. "We're waiting for you to tell us."

Platt began to look around. He riffled through the papers on the desk and walked around in the bedroom, glancing through the contents of closet and drawers.

"Far as I can see, he didn't take anything," he decided. "I don't keep money around. What little jewelry I own is here in the top drawer. And my clothes seem to be as usual. It's very strange. I wonder what he was looking for."

He seemed innocent and genuinely puzzled.

"I suppose he didn't have time to take anything," I said. "Probably he'd just started to look around when Mr. Wilkens came to your door.'

"Oh yes," he said and nodded, but then his brows pulled down black and tight. "But why was Wilkens coming to my room?"

"Looking for the woman in charge of this floor, perhaps," I suggested to him. "He was passing along the corridor when he heard a noise in your room."

He seemed to accept this explanation, and then I said to him: "By the way, Mr. Platt, Bill Randall doesn't pay much attention to office hours, does he?"

I could see anger come and go in his eyes, and he had time to count to ten before he answered.

"Oh, he gets his work done," he admitted. "He puts in eight hours sometime or other during the twenty-four. Mr. Barrett," he added as though the words hurt him, "gave him that right."

When George went out I followed, and when I caught up to him he was looking very down in the mouth.

"I'm putting a man to watch that fire escape," he said. "Platt didn't seem to connect this with the attempt to shoot him or else he isn't letting on, but—what do you think about it?"

"Now, George," I told him gently, "just because I use my brain is no reason for you not to use yours. What do *you* think?"

"Whoever tried to get him in the park is still on the trail," said George heavily. "Who is it?"

I opened my mouth to speak of Randall and then I thought of Judy's white face and pleading eyes. No, not yet. Not until I was certain would I incriminate her.

"I never jump, George," I said sweetly and turned away.

"Jump?" he repeated vacantly.

"At conclusions," I said and went home.

The dinner hour was nigh, and I felt the need of sustenance. There was an atmosphere of hustle and bustle at the Edwards residence. Arthur was as full of business as an egg is of meat, and Annie was preoccupied, her lips moving the way they do when she is planning something. Theresa was vastly indignant at the manner in which we bolted dinner.

"That's calves' liver at seventy cents a pound," she informed us darkly. "It's not so easy getting it. I've had my order with the butcher for three days."

"It is delicious, Theresa," I said, and Annie echoed me mechanically. "If there is any left put it in the refrigerator and I'll have a sandwich when I get home."

But she only sniffed and was not much mollified.

My plans for the evening were well laid. I intended to inspect the living quarters of John Storm and Jappy Carillo while they were busy at the factory.

What Annie and Arthur had in mind I did not know. Had I inquired I might
have spared myself much mental torture later.

After dinner Annie skipped across to Gilmore's, where I could see Mrs.
Gilmore in the porch swing and Mr. Gilmore watering his pansies. Certainly
I had no qualms about my sister. If the Gilmore residence is not safe then,
indeed, is revolution upon us. Arthur swung off down Greenwood Avenue,
and I suspected nothing more harmful than a round of billiards and perhaps a
Coca-Cola at Red Green's place.

I made certain preparations. There is something about a murder case that
always involves a certain amount of nocturnal wandering. Tonight I wished
to be ready. I wore a dark coat and small dark hat. I took a flashlight and put
on my rubber-soled oxfords. I possessed Bill Randall's revolvers but no am-
munition, so after due thought I regretfully put aside those weapons. But I
took with me my fine collection of old door keys.

Downtown I parked in front of Becker's Drugstore, above which John
Storm lived. Of course there were many other occupants of the place. It was
an old brick building, the first floor given over to small shops and the second
floor rented out in single rooms and small housekeeping apartments.

I trudged up the dark inside stairway lighted by a feeble twenty-five watt
bulb. At the top I looked down the corridor lined with closed gray-painted
doors. At the third try I saw the name of John Storm printed in neat black
letters upon a card tacked to the side wall.

I knocked carelessly at the indicated door, expecting no reply and receiv-
ing none. Eying the lock with speculation, I saw with utmost satisfaction that
it was of the simple, old-fashioned variety. Pulling out my keys, I set to work.
The first key did not fit, and as I removed it I was almost bowled over, for the
door was swiftly opened and a figure confronted me. In a moment, however,
I recovered my composure and recognized the person in the room.

"Oh, Mrs. Storm," I said civilly, "is Mr. Storm at home? I would like to
have a word with him."

"He's at work," the woman said shortly. Her eyes glittered as I
nonchalantly returned my keys to my purse. But when I moved to enter she
stepped hesitantly aside.

The bedroom was poor and plain with an iron bed and a Marseilles spread,
cheap scrim curtains at the window and a thin, colorless rug. But it was very
clean. The curtains and the dresser cover and the spread were spotless, and I
could see that Mrs. Storm did not confine her housekeeping virtues to the
Barrett house but kept her son in cleanly comfort as well.

There was a good lamp casting a yellow glow of light upon a painted
table, a table that was heavily laden with books and pamphlets.

"Oh," I said in surprise, "what a lot of books. Is your son devoted to
reading?"

"To study," she said simply. "John's mind is for machinery."

I looked with more respect at the books. The titles confounded me. Why, that time bomb in Arthur's lunchbox would have been child's play for Storm, and the mysteries of the new minesweeper might well be no mystery at all.

"Tell me, Mrs. Storm"—I turned impulsively to the stiff, quiet woman— "why didn't you say you came from Germany? What sort of a life did you have in Hamburg?"

At once her gaze sought the floor, and she shook her head.

"I speak of it not," she said. "My husband there was killed. He was— how do you say?—anti-Nazi."

"Yes," I said. "He was a Communist? One of the party whom the Nazis attacked in the beginning?"

She hesitated a long moment and then said with dignity:

"With me that does not concern. Of politics I do not know."

"Maybe not," I said with significance. "But John does. And to find a haven in this country only to spread anti-American propaganda is shameful. To try to destroy the factory in which he is employed is—is vile!"

She seemed to brace herself. I thought she would for once burst into fiery speech but by an effort refrained.

"John only wants to work and to help other workmen to a living wage," she said. "America claims to give freedom of opportunity." And then some-how her feelings got the better of her rigid self-control. "There is," she said in her hard, queerly clipped pronunciation, "just so much a human being can endure. Just so much that a man can take. And if you ever come to the break-ing point, if once you allow yourself to give way, then after that you don't care much what you do. Americans that should remember."

The brief spasm of feeling passed, and her face was as gray and as closed as ever. Somehow I felt abashed. I could get nothing more from her. Not a word. And when at last I suggested that I look at John's wardrobe she agreed amiably enough, with the faintest of smiles tugging at her lips. When I in-spected the narrow closet I understood that smile. John Storm had one good suit of black and one of summer gray. The other garments were strictly for work in the shop. Not one of them was of navy blue wool.

It was still twilight as I descended the stairway. I remembered with regret my hasty dinner and visited the drugstore for a double chocolate malted milk. When I emerged the soft spring darkness had fallen. All the better for me. I did not care to be seen as I sauntered about Trailer Town and, if I should be forced to do a bit of housebreaking, it would be the easier.

I drove to the mushroom community, and after I parked my car I tried in unobtrusive fashion to locate the residence of Jappy Carillo. The first urchin I accosted was able to point it out.

Interested as I am in my fellow human beings, I looked about me with avid interest. Fronting on the highway was a row of cabins, the nucleus of a business block, with oil station, restaurant, automobile-supply store, and so on. Farther back were at least a hundred trailers and many tents. Ranged in rows they had crudely lettered signs with pretentious and humorous street names. Rosebud Lane. Tin Can Alley. Carillo lived at the far end of Piccadilly Road. To judge from the garbage cans, yapping dogs, and frequent mudholes, Annie and Sarah Gilmore and the Keep-Our-City-Clean Committee would have their work cut out for them. I felt sorry for the housewives forced to live under these changeable conditions and sorrier as I thought of them doomed to squirm under Sarah Gilmore's eagle eye.

I dodged between two rows of garments hanging ghostly on a clothesline and reached the Carillo trailer. It was of regulation type with a smoke pipe sticking from the roof and a door halfway along one side. There were small windows, but since it was dark inside I could not judge of the interior. I made a circuit of the habitation, tentatively tried a couple of windows, but they did not respond. And then I felt foolish, for when I tried the door I found it open. Evidently Carillo had no regard for locks nor for his possessions.

I stepped up into the tiny apartment and flashed my torch about. Everything seemed neat and shipshape save for a soiled cup and plate in the small sink. I let the light travel over the stove, the small icebox. There was a bunk at one end of the room with what seemed to be a heap of laundry done up in a red-checked tablecloth thrown upon it. Not much space to hide things, I decided, and then I noticed a narrow door that must lead to an equally narrow closet. I was moving toward this when I heard the scrape of footsteps outside.

Instantly I shut off my flash and stood there, my knees quaking. Perhaps Carillo was returning home. I heard the mumble of a low voice, and it seemed to be just outside the door. It seemed to me that my goose-pimples were as big as acorns, and my hands dripped clammy and cold. With each passing second I felt more certain that only trouble could result if I were discovered, and I thought desperately of concealment. To achieve the closet I had to pass the half-open door, and even if I did make the closet I doubted that a person of my width could get into it.

The bunk! It had, I recalled, a dark curtain that could be pulled across it, and certainly reason forbade that Carillo could be retiring at so early an hour. Of that contingency I sternly forbade myself to think. Swift and soft as any cat, I stepped backward and sat on the edge of that bed. The springs gave a loud protesting shriek, but the person outside paid no heed. From the sound of humming I deduced that Carillo was sitting on the steps. Smoking, perhaps, enjoying the spring night before he entered to bring quick retribution to a spy.

I heaved myself farther into the bunk and encountered the bundle of laundry. And then indeed I knew horror. For the bundle moved. I put out a trembling hand and snatched it back as from a fire. There was another person, a living, breathing creature, beside me in that dark and narrow prison.

Why I did not scream I know not. I think it was because, not too incongruously at that moment, a picture of that ugly bullet dug out of Julian Norbury flashed into my mind.

The other occupant of the bed panted and heaved to the very end of the confined space. I heard a gasp, and fearfully, not knowing whether I would see man or beast, my hand sought my torch and I pushed the button.

"Annie!" I hissed in a startled undertone.

"Jane!" whimpered my sister. Her eyes were big above the folds of the red-checked cloth. "I—I was investigating . . . . I—I thought you were the killer!"

"Sh!" I said. "He's outside!"

I had turned off my light, and even as I whispered those words I realized that they were not true. He was no longer outside.

He was inside!

I had barely time to draw the curtain in concealment. Annie once more pulled the tablecloth over her huddled form. The lights in the trailer flashed on.

We heard footsteps and muttered words, and then the creature opened the ice chest and gave a cheer of satisfaction. There came the sound of a bottle being opened and liquid being poured into a glass. I was extremely thirsty myself, and this did not add to my comfort. I crouched behind that dark curtain and did not move a muscle. I did not even try to peek. As for Annie, she was so petrified by fear that she did not even breathe.

The man drank in long gulps, smacking his lips between in obvious enjoyment. As I heard the gurgle of liquid into glass repeated I felt my apprehensions increase and pile up until I felt submerged. To remain longer with the swarthy Carillo an unknown quantity not six feet from me seemed unendurable. I moved cautiously to see if there was a possible rip in the curtain through which I could peer.

Simultaneously the unseen man burst into a low but rollicking song.

" `There is a tavern in our town,' " he caroled, and at the sound my veins were filled with ice, and poor Annie gave a convulsive jerk at the other end of the bunk.

" 'And there my true love sat him down,' " continued the singer.

Realization smote me, and with a mighty sweep I pulled back the curtain of the bed. At the same moment Annie threw off the concealing red checks of the tablecloth.

Seated at the tiny table before three bottles, two empty and one filled, sat my brother Arthur. One hand was curled about a foaming glass. The other wandered to his eyes and rubbed them in vigorous fashion. He blinked and decided to discredit his vision.

" 'I'll hang my harp on the weeping willow tree,' " he began again, but there was no heart in his song.

"Oh, Arthur," quavered Annie, "how glad we are to see you!"

I turned off the light. No need to advertise our presence.

"We must not be found here," I said shortly. "And no time for explanations now. Get yourself out of there, Annie. Arthur, replace that bottle of intoxicating beverage. Concerning it, I shall speak to you later. My car is parked near the gas station. Hurry to it. I shall follow you."

But Annie, with little cheeps of relieved words, was groping for her shoes. It seems she had taken them off upon entering, under the mistaken impression that quiet would facilitate her investigations.

"Look under the bed," I snapped. "And hurry. It must be late, and Carillo is likely to return at any moment. Arthur, pour that—that stuff in your glass down the sink."

But Arthur was in one of his most inconsequential moods.

"Waste not, want not," he declared oracularly and poured the beer down his throat instead.

I was making a hasty search of the minute closet. No suit of Carillo's matched my triangular sample. He seemed to run mostly to green plaids.

I felt Annie beside me. "Carillo?" she quavered, clutching my arm. "Don't tell me, Jane! This isn't his trailer?"

Then we heard great plunking footsteps upon the gravel outside.

"Oh, heaven help us!" sighed Annie. "Here comes the end."

"Nonsense," I whispered briskly, my brain alight with inspiration. "I have an idea. There are three of us and only one of him. Find that tablecloth, Annie. We'll capture him and make him confess. He can't see us in the dark."

There was no time for further parley. Annie, obeying blindly, thrust the tablecloth into my hands. I spread it, and as the dark bulk of a man advanced and stepped up through the narrow door I threw it over his head and pulled tightly.

Annie was a great help. She dived and caught an ankle, and the fellow went down with a terrific crash. Arthur, however, gave no assistance. In fact, some moments later I was to discover that he had crawled quietly into the bunk and fallen fast asleep.

The man on the floor thrashed about in really awful fashion. My shins were practically pulp from his kicks, and my ears were scorched from his sulphuric language.

Annie gave up then and crawled into a corner, and I began to fear that I should never be able to hold on when a dreadful foreboding smote me. I, too, left the profane thrashing monster to his own devices. I stepped back and leveled the beam of my torch upon him. And then I heard Annie's gasp and despairing groans. For myself, I was too spent to utter a sound, but I wished fervently that I were far, far away.

For the furious man, arising from his ignominious position upon the floor, was Officer Blake.

CHAPTER TWENTY

FOR A PERIOD THERE WAS silence, and, you may well believe, a silence fraught with shattering possibilities. With my usual thoughtful consideration I turned

my back to the policeman that he might have time to recover himself. I found
the switch, and the electric lights illuminated the small, cramped room.

Annie, trying to be of comfort, spoke to Officer Blake in a soothing voice.
"You know us, Officer Blake," she piped.

He gave her one disgusted glance. He let his blazing eyes rest upon me
and drift to Brother Arthur relaxed upon the bed.

"My God, yes," agreed Blake savagely, and it was dreadful to hear his
teeth grind together. "I do! And how! What d'ya mean, resisting the law?"

"We didn't," I disclaimed. "How were we to know you were sneaking
about in the dark? What did you come here for, anyway?"

"I've been watching this trailer for a week," he said bitterly, "and when I
bag somebody it turns out to be you."

"Watching!" I echoed with biting sarcasm. "If you'd been watching you
would have seen us come in. You weren't very much on the job."

"I was up at the lunchroom for a cup of coffee," he defended. "I'm supposed to watch Carillo and I was waiting until time for him to come from
work . . . ."

"Sh!" I hissed and turned out the light. "I hear something."

We listened. There was the sound of someone moving outside. The door
had closed as we greeted Blake. Curtains covered the windows, and we stood
in blackness. The movements outside weren't particularly stealthy, but I
couldn't make them out.

Blake was suspicious and moved his huge bulk silently to the window
above the sink. He pushed the curtain aside and peered out, but no one was
visible. And now everything was quiet.

I was near the door, and very cautiously I moved to be behind it in case
Carillo made a sudden entrance into his habitation. And it was then that I was
abruptly aware that the intruder stood just outside the door. I couldn't exactly
hear him, but I swear I could feel him. I am very psychic that way. Shakes and
shivers possessed me as I gave a frantic thought to shelter in case the killer
should suddenly begin to fire into the trailer. A fine squealing and scurrying
there'd be!

But he did not fire, nor did he knock or speak. I cannot think that he even
tried the doorknob, although he may have done so. The first intimation that I
had of any direct action was the click of the key in the lock. One second later
I heard a motor start up and a car depart.

"We're locked in," I observed with fatalistic calm.

Again I turned on the lights and observed Officer Blake. He was crouched
to one side of the door, his revolver out, his fish eyes goggling at me in the light.

"What's that you say?" he asked. Then with a bellow of realization he
sprang for the knob and shook the door. Naturally it would not open.

"What do you mean, you old cluck?" he cried to me. Actually, to me!
"Standing there and keeping mum while the killer makes us prisoners.
Carillo did it, and he's off now to murder again. You're under arrest, all

of you. You're—"

"You blithering idiot!" I returned with heartfelt sincerity. "How dare you speak to me in such fashion? Under arrest, indeed! Why don't you go over and get a job with the Gestapo? That's your style. Arrest, my eye! How are we to get out of here? That's the question now."

There were windows, but apertures of their size would never permit passage of a body of my size. Nor Blake's either, for that matter.

"Annie," I decided, "you must get through a window and go for help."

"Window?" said Annie, regarding the small square openings with utter distaste. "Indeed, and I will not. You'll not get me stuck in one of those things, Jane Edwards."

Later she admitted that her main reason for refusal to thus aid us was a run in her stocking and the fact that she had not worn her best slip. As though Officer Blake would have noticed. He was far beyond that.

"Well, there are other trailers near," I said then. "All we have to do is shout for help. Come on, we'll stand at the window on the south there and yell."

Blake really put himself into this chore, and I made my calls as far-reaching and as dramatic as possible.

"Help!" we called. "Help! Will someone come over and get us out?"

For some time no one paid any attention, and we grew breathless and discouraged. Finally Blake essayed one more furious blast. As one irked beyond endurance, a woman in a trailer down the field jerked open the door.

"Stop that racket!" she shrieked. "Fun is fun, and I don't mind you enjoying yourselves, but if you don't can that noise I'll go for the police."

Blake grew slowly purple, and then his color ebbed.

"There," I said with satisfaction. "Let's whoop it up. Then she'll go for the police and —"

"No," said Blake in a hollow tone. "No. Let's wait a bit. Someone will come along. We can think up some way . . . ."

"You could break down the door," suggested Annie. "Perhaps Arthur would wake up and help. We'll have to arouse the poor boy when we go home, anyway."

Arthur, at that point, swung over to his back and opened his mouth. He was enjoying his rest. Blake gave him one long despondent look and then, as though urged by the association of ideas, wandered over to the icebox.

"Keep away from there!" I said sharply.

"Jane," said Annie, "doesn't Arthur's friend Sam Smead live out here? Maybe we could call him."

"I do no more yelling," I said moodily. "I'm hoarse as an old crow right now. I'll see what I can do with the lock, and if that doesn't work we'll have to sit here until Carillo makes up his mind to come. He'll probably shoot us on sight."

I produced my collection of old keys and had the satisfaction of watching

Blake's amazed but speechless fury. But the lock was new and small. Twiddle my keys as I would, they could not open the door.

Everything passes in time, though in its passing it may scar. I shall not chronicle Officer Blake's frequent uncalled-for remarks. At last we heard a car stop.

"Not a word until we know who it is," said Blake.

"Don't be silly!" I said. "What difference does it make now? Whoever it is can go for help. If it's Carillo himself we'll simply apologize and—"

But Blake by this time was ugly and violently unreasonable. He had again turned out the lights. What's more, he took out his revolver.

"I said not a sound," he repeated with horrid emphasis. "It might be Carillo and it might not. It might be Captain Hammond. It might be almost anyone."

"Yes," I agreed sarcastically. "It might even be Eleanor Roosevelt. Probably this is one place she hasn't visited."

A car started and stopped. Other strange noises came to our straining ears. But no one tried the door. No one spoke an audible word.

Arthur breathed heavily and peacefully in the bunk. Annie sat frozen in the chair. Blake was poised between me and the door, and I simply stood still and waited.

As usual, the unforeseen happened.

We heard again the motor of a car, and then with a sudden mighty jerk our trailer started to move.

Annie screamed and Blake swore and Arthur snored, but the trailer went on. Staggering about, we endeavored to regain our balance. I caught at the window curtain near me and felt it rip uselessly from the rod. Blake was clutching Annie, whose chair had backed up against the ice chest. She retaliated by kicking him in the knee, and his wicked words resolved into a mere bellow of rage.

The unknown driver in the car ahead increased his speed, and the trailer careened around a corner. Lights flashed by. We hit a bump, and I bit my tongue and heard a terrific thump behind me. Arthur had fallen from the bed.

"Over the dam!" he cried out gaily, awakening at once. " 'The three ittie fishies swam over the dam!' "

"The river!" I thought. "That outlaw can let this trailer run down into Mill River, and we'll all drown like rats in a trap!"

Annie began to weep in loud, unrestrained tones, and I could see Blake trying to steady himself enough to look through the small window in front.

"Stop, in the name of the law!" he was calling out in a loud voice. "Stop at once or I'll shoot!"

But the noise of the motor and Annie's sobs and Arthur's contributions effectually prevented the driver ahead from hearing. The trailer continued to hump along over the meadow.

"Shut up, all of you!" Blake yelled furiously. "I'll shoot to kill!"

"Why, you insufferable bully!" I cried. "If you shoot me I'll—"

Then I became aware that the last part of his speech had been addressed to the oblivious and unheeding driver. He took aim through the window and fired. Upon the heels of the first explosion came an echoing one.

We were at that moment being rapidly towed along the side of the pasture where a deep ditch marked the path of a small creek. I learned later that the car ahead was struck in the rear right tire, hence swerved sharply aside. The driver wrenched the wheel around. Our trailer, pulled this way and that, parted abruptly from its traveling companion, backed into the ditch, and there, at an acute angle, remained.

Blake, who was halfway out the front window, stuck there. Annie, Arthur, and I, being already upon the floor, found ourselves sliding quickly to the rear, and the three of us were ultimately and unpleasantly wedged beneath the table.

However, it was not for long.

I shall pass over the language of Blake, the hiccups of Annie, and Arthur's pathetic efforts to assist us when he could not even help himself. It was not more than minutes until the man in front descended from his car, heard our plaints, and came to unlock the door. He stood by in amazement as, one by one, we crawled out.

Jasper Carillo stood by the door of his supposedly empty trailer.

He watched me emerge slowly and painfully.

"Were you in there?" he asked stupidly.

Blake followed me, and Carillo's eyes grew round.

"Were you in there too?" he cried.

Then Annie had to be drawn forth. Carillo said no more. But when Arthur was pried out Carillo looked as we used to when we watched a procession of Keystone cops emerge from one tiny Ford.

The pivot tooth upon which Dr. Roscoe had expended such loving care and I had spent good money had again become detached. I placed it in my purse and then helped Annie to walk up and down that she might relieve a cramp in her leg. There was no use saying a word because Blake was roaring and Carillo was attempting to explain that he was moving the trailer to a new location.

"I don't like the afternoon sun," he kept saying.

Finally when Blake had a good many words out of his system I spoke.

"It's all a mistake, Mr. Carillo," I said with what dignity I could muster. "I hope you will excuse our intrusion . . . ."

"And also your beer that she drank up," put in Blake with a leer, pointing back over his shoulder to the trailer.

"Wit needs a sharp mind," I said with icy hauteur. "Officer Blake," I went on to Carillo, "presumes to be humorous. I shall be glad to recompense you for any loss. My brother consumed the beverage, thinking that it was Coca-Cola."

Blake gave a loud, vulgar exclamation, and Annie said hastily, "Oh, but, Jane, I think Arthur didn't know quite what he was doing. He wasn't himself when he came in, you recall, and I'm sure he had been to that awful Sam Smead's and gotten mixed up and mistaken the trailer."

"Annie!" I said in a truly terrible voice, and she subsided. Arthur's weaknesses are his own and their results are my burden, but I shall bear it privately.

"Did you come back and lock the trailer a while ago?" I asked Carillo.

"No," he said, apparently frank. "I locked it when I left this afternoon. Tonight I borrowed this car to move my trailer."

The car was not a green sedan.

"The trailer wasn't locked when I came," said Annie with certainty.

I knew that was true. Annie might try to steal a march on Sarah Gilmore, but she is not one to pick locks.

I decided immediately that the person who had searched Platt's room had also searched Carillo's trailer. He had been close by, watching, hatefully cruel, and had imprisoned us.

With no assistance from Blake, Annie and I propelled Arthur to our car and went home.

The first news of the morning came from Captain Hammond. His angry voice over the wire was painful to my ears.

"See here now!" he said violently. "Those bullets you gave me don't match up with the bullet that killed Norbury or the bullets that were fired at Platt. And your neighbor Alexander has been in here, raising heavy Hades . . . ."

Gently I replaced the phone. I went to see Judy. At first sight of her, crisp in a flowered print, a foolish little blue bow atop her hair, I knew something had changed.

"I hope you're ready with explanations, young lady," I said grimly. "But before you begin—what did you do last night?"

"Lots," she said swiftly with a pleased gurgle of laughter. "I quarreled with Henry. I told him I wasn't going to marry him. You know, Jane, I think he was surprised."

"And well he might be," I retorted. "Did you also tell him it was all on account of the man who stole his pottery dogs and used them to convey seditious messages?"

She stamped a small and vicious heel.

"He didn't. Bill isn't the spy. I'll absolutely never believe that."

"You seemed to believe that he was the killer some weeks back."

"Just at first." She flushed. "I was all upset then. And I made Bill so mad that he—well, he's straightened things out now and he's ready to tell you too."

"Obliging of him," I snapped. "But where did he get that second dog?"

"He found it in Jappy Carillo's trailer."

CHAPTER TWENTY-ONE

ON THAT DAY OCCURRED certain other events which were to color and mold my determination. Not events, really, so much as small disconnected trifles that, taken together, helped to clear the way and plotted the course of my belief.

In the first place, Mrs. Ashford ran away. She didn't come to work that morning and she didn't answer her telephone. Her sister could not be found, and her friends at the office professed ignorance of her whereabouts. The upshot of all this was that Henry Platt progressed from a sharp vexation at the absence of a competent secretary to an increasing anxiety for her safety. Finally he called the police, and the usual steps were taken to locate the missing woman.

If George Hammond had taken but a moment to call me I might have saved him some tiresome detail, but there, he has to do something. I'm sure the taxpayers want him at least to put in his time. You can't teach an old dog new tricks, but if he had seen fit to consult me I could, as usual, have furnished him with pertinent information. The first news I had that the police were concerning themselves with Grace Ashford was the radio broadcast at noon.

This was some three hours after the postman had delivered mail on Greenwood Avenue. I had already perused the letter Grace Ashford had addressed to me on the previous evening. As I read it I could see the neat rows of her black pin curls and imagine her voice underlining certain words.

"I suppose," she said after the usual preamble, "that it is *perfectly* dreadful of me to skip out without a word to Mr. Platt, but he'll survive. There are plenty to take my place. And I would try *anything* to get away from the murder investigation and any more photographs. You see, Jane, I'm getting married again. I've been trying to make up my mind—you know I'm not the kind of a person to jump into things. I *think.* That's what I was doing the night I was out driving by myself, the night Julian Norbury was killed. And that is what I want to tell you about.

"I saw someone that night. A person—a man, I suppose, but it might have been a tall woman in slacks and a felt hat. The point is, he or she was *running* along the road on the way into town. Running steadily and easily but as though it was important to get somewhere in a hurry. Now that doesn't mean much, because I couldn't identify the person on a bet. But I was afraid to tell even *that.* Because I am sure that Julian Norbury was killed because he knew too much. He knew the *saboteur* at our plant. Norbury was always hanging around there. Certainly there was no legitimate reason, although he always pretended to come from the employment office. And after we had all the guards he would get in on the strength of calling on his uncle. Goodness knows Mr. Barrett never wanted to see him! But *on the afternoon of the mur-der he was in Mr. Platt's office and he was hiding in the closet!*

"I know. I saw him come out. Mr. Platt wasn't even in the factory—he hadn't come back from downtown yet—and how Norbury sneaked in I don't know. But as I entered the room he stepped out of the closet, and if ever a man looked *shaken,* he did. I believe that's when the second dog was taken and I think he saw who did it. I had an impression that someone had just gone out. There's no proof of this but my own *feeling,* but when you work in a place as long as I have worked there you get to know the sounds and all. And this impression was so strong that I went to the door and looked out. Down at the end of the hall Steve Boyd was turning the corner. Of course I didn't give the dog a thought *then,* but I did ask Norbury what he was doing there.

" 'Not a thing,' he said airily—you know how insufferably snippy he could be—and he walked out. At first I didn't think much about it, but since you asked me about the dogs I've been putting two and two together, as they say, and getting *nothing,* and then since Norbury was shot I've been simply *petrified.* But I'm out of it now, and please, Jane, don't let the police get on my trail. I'll write to you next week and give you my new name and address."

The second bit of information came from Annie. She brought it to lunch.

"Marge Gilmore," she said, "has a new bathing suit. She bought it this morning, and it is most modest and becoming. It's a dressmaker suit of black jersey. Marge says it looks like *Arsenic and Old Lace* to her, but she'll be d-darned—that is, *she* didn't say darned, but—"

"Never mind that," I said. "Go on."

"But she'll be darned if everybody in this town is going to keep on comparing her to a ponderosa or a baby boiled lobster. Ever since she modeled that red bathing suit at the country-club style show "

I had been bruising the mint in my iced tea, and just like that the idea struck me.

"Annie," I interrupted simply, "what a fool I am!"

Her jaw dropped, and she sought for words.

"Say nothing. That's a statement you'd better leave alone," advised Theresa as she put the dessert in front of us. It was a lovely froth of snowy meringue and lemon custard. "Angel pie, it's called," said Theresa, and her jaw dropped lower than Annie's as I arose and left it there on the table.

I went in a beeline to George Hammond.

"George," I said, "let's wind this up. I think I know who did it. I can't prove it, but I believe we can catch the rascal red-handed."

"Yeah," said George, "and lock him in a trailer, huh? I can't make head or tail of Blake's explanation of where he was last night, but—"

"Let it pass," I advised raptly. "We have followed many trails. Now there is a way out. George, consider the code!"

"The code?" said George and blinked.

"The dog," I said impatiently. "The message that said to lay off. Go easy.

The message that was on Barrett's desk."

"Yep," said George. "I sent it to Washington, but they've paid no attention to it. At least, I haven't heard yet . . ."

"We don't have to wait for them," I said impatiently. "Listen, George, who knows how to read that code?"

"Why, you do, I guess, and if you're right, why, I do and—"

"Nonsense!" I said sharply. "I mean the killer. He knows the cipher. He made it up, or his confederate did. The two people who used the cipher can read it. The dogs that were their private post offices have been confiscated. The present investigation has interfered with their activities:"

"We haven't got the second dog," said George.

"For the time being let's not talk about that," I hurried on. "I propose to send a message in that code to every suspect on our list. Except Mrs. Ashford. She's gone. If an innocent person receives the message, no harm done. He can't read it and will pay no attention. If the guilty one reads it and acts on it we'll have him."

"Yeah." George sounded dubious and smoothed his corrugated brow. "But he may be suspicious. He may think it's a plant."

"I'll make it so strong that he'll be afraid to disregard it. But there is no reason for him to believe that we have deciphered the code."

"Well, what are you going to put in the message?" George wanted to know.

That took some thought. George locked the door, and we figured it out together.

This is what we finally evolved:

6B6U6D PL B47N5DR PB7SY4TL 4BN L5BB A4L6 4T N56

If you want to refer to the cipher you may readily see that this message meant: "Eleven P.M. Loading platform old mill. Come or die."

"The time, the place, the threat," I sighed with weariness. "Not too much, but enough. A rendezvous at the deserted mill is really clever. Plenty of undergrowth near that loading platform to conceal your men."

"I hope we nab him this time." George was still skeptical. "I hope I'm not letting you pull me in over my head."

I ignored that.

"I'll type and mail these," I said briskly. "Then I'm going out and reconnoiter about the old mill. Tomorrow night we'll see what we sec."

"Tomorrow night you keep away from there," George warned seriously. "There's likely to be shooting. Remember now. You stay at home."

I kept to myself next morning. Annie was picking out a new crochet pattern. Arthur was distraught because Win had disappeared.

"He'll come back," said Theresa, mournfully prophetic. "No such luck as losing him. And he'll find nobody else fool enough to feed him porterhouse."

At three o'clock Hammond called up and said he'd had two inquiries. Henry Platt had called.

"I've got a queer-looking note here, Hammond," he had said brusquely. "Just a line of figures and letters. Certainly doesn't mean anything to me."

"What do you figure it is?" Hammond had asked.

"Darned if I know. Just the work of some crank, I think. But if you want to see it I'll shoot it down to your office."

Hammond had agreed to look it over, and five minutes later the telephone had again summoned him. It was Katherine Boyd. Her voice was high and hurried.

"There's something else going on, Captain," she said swiftly. "I think we ought to have more protection. I'm not going the way poor Julian went. Why don't you get some outside help in here? Depending on that addled, impertinent Jane Edwards—"

I don't suppose for one minute that Hammond came to my defense. But he led her on to tell the cause of her apprehension.

"There's somebody trying to frighten us," she said sullenly. "Both Steve and I have received threatening letters."

"What did they say?"

She was hesitant. "I'm not going to say any more until I talk to Steve tonight. But I'm telling you, watch out."

From the others there was no sign. I had sent the message to Bill Randall, John Storm, Jappy Carillo, as well as to Katherine and Steve Boyd and Henry Platt.

At nine o'clock I began to prepare. At nine-thirty I was ready to go. But my progress was somewhat delayed because Win's return coincided with my departure. He leaped upon me with such abandon that I dropped my flashlight and my car keys. Finding them necessitated going down upon my knees, and this action resulted in bursting the knees of both stockings. Naturally, with skirt lengths what they are, I was forced to return to my room, and as I came downstairs again I met Arthur in the hall. He insisted upon accompanying me.

"You need protection," he said loyally. "Where are you going? These night excursions are very dangerous, and a man should be with you."

"A lot of protection you were night before last," I said coldly. "Sleeping in that bunk while we were being dragged to kingdom come."

Still, his thought was sweet, and I let him come.

But when Arthur found out that we were bound for the deserted cotton mill on the lonely bank of Mill River he regretted his gallantry and he was most reluctant to continue. By that time I was driving out of town at a good pace. I had no mind to be late at the rendezvous.

"There's nothing to be nervous about," I assured him. "We will be protected by the police. We have nothing to do but get there and hide."

"Hide!" said Arthur bitterly. "And go seek, I presume? Really, Jane, you are getting childish."

We came to the edge of town, and I could smell the damp, fishy odor of the river. Then I approached the roadside stand backed by clumps of trees back of which a narrow dirt road wandered toward the abandoned mill. I didn't dare park right at that point because my car might be recognized by the one coming later, so I drove on over the bridge and left the car beside a thicket well off the road on the left side.

"Come on," I said to Arthur. "Let's hike back there and conceal ourselves. I want to see and not be seen this night."

But now Arthur was in fine fettle, and I had trouble subduing him. His spirit is naturally volatile and, all inspired by the adventure, he insisted upon singing "Down by the Old Millstream."

"If you don't keep quiet you'll find yourself with a bullet in you," I said in cold warning. That stopped him

"But it is down by the old millstream," he kept murmuring defiantly, as though that had anything to do with it.

We trudged along the rutted road. The weeds were more than waist high although it was so early in the season, and it was apparent that the place was seldom visited.

The building we approached was once a cotton mill, used to manufacture sacks and carpet warp and similar products. Its long rooms had been empty and idle for many years. Its boarded-up windows were sightless eyes hooded against the darkness. Beside the entrance a great cleft locust tree sent up forked and towering trunks. The loading platform was on the riverside and reached by outside steps. During the heyday of the place the products of the factory had been shipped by water.

"Really, Jane," grumbled Arthur, stumbling through the rank growth, "there must be snakes in here, to say nothing of chiggers. And if there is poison ivy or smartweed I'll be laid up for the summer. I think I'll go home now. I don't like it here."

"Will you stop that babbling?" I hissed, exasperated. I felt sure that Hammond and his men were already concealed and I didn't want them mistaking me for the murderer. Besides, I was having difficulty maintaining my own footing and I had thought of snakes long before Arthur mentioned them.

"There is a loose board in a window. We'll get inside and wait. And you might as well know that Austin Barrett's murderer is due here shortly. If he should arrive before the police and he hears you I'll not guarantee your life."

Arthur stopped talking at once and meekly followed my lead. We entered the musty cavern of the ground-level floor and climbed the inner stairway to the main room. The windows and the door opening to the loading platform had been boarded up, but on my reconnoitering trip on the preceding day I had arranged matters. The door was ajar, a mere crack, and a couple of nail kegs made seats.

Below the river flowed calmly, steadily, making little slaps at the planking.

The night was dark. Not a star gleamed. My eyes gradually became accustomed to the gloom, but the damp, decaying smell of the place was horrid.

A long peal of thunder broke the silence, rolled, and reechoed up the river.

"A storm," moaned Arthur, "and, in all probability, rats!"

"Shush!" I commanded and settled him on his nail keg well away from the door. I couldn't resist flashing my torch for the merest instant while I glanced at my watch.

It was ten forty-five. We had fifteen minutes to wait. We were not comfortable. There was too much of me and too much of Arthur for the nail kegs. Arthur mercifully dozed and, as he was sitting bolt upright, did not snore.

The thunder rolled again, and the wind stirred the fine-cut leaves of the locust. Through my peephole I thought I saw the swift and silent movement of a black patch on the water.

A boat? I had felt very safe, quite brash and reckless, knowing that Hammond and his men were lurking in the undergrowth not ten feet from the outside stairway to the loading platform. But suppose the conspirators came by boat? I had not thought of that possibility and I quickly discounted it now. Unless . . . Were they accustomed to using this place as a rendezvous? That seemed too wild a coincidence.

Still I sat tense behind my crack and stared down at that moving water like a kingfisher waiting for his lunch. But I could see no one. The river moved its inevitable way, and far below I could hear the murmur of its fall over the dam.

And then I became more fully aware of a sound that had been troubling me for some moments. It did not come from the river, nor was it behind me on the road. This sound was where it had no business to be. I could hear scrapings, faint but unmistakable, below me. Someone was moving about in the basement. Not really the basement but the ground floor, as I have mentioned. The room in which we were concealed was level with the loading platform above the river and was actually the second floor.

I didn't move. I scarcely took a breath. Arthur, too, was perfectly quiet, and I was thankful that sleep still claimed him. Had Hammond decided to hide in the room below?

Was Blake exceeding his orders? Were the conspirators deliberately disregarding the appointed rendezvous upon the loading platform?

I could imagine the stealthy steps coming up the inner stairway I had myself just trod. And then I heard the door at the end of the room slowly and creakingly open.

I pulled a lot of fresh river air into my aching lungs. Escape by means of the door beside me was impossible. Not I to abandon dear Arthur to danger. I felt for my torch. Could I identify the person lurking at the end of the room I could scream for the officers of the law, and when Jane Edwards screams she is heard.

But somehow things happened all at once.

Quick running footsteps outside. The boards pulled swiftly away from the window near me. A man jumped into the room. He was only a blur against the darkness, but I could hear his hoarse breathing.

Then George Hammond somewhere outside bellowed "Stop! Halt in the name of the law!"

At the same time the man near the window moved beyond me and turned on the torch he carried. I didn't even have time to twist my head before the light was out again. Viciously the intruder hurled the torch at the unknown still lurking at the end of the room.

"You dirty double-crossing traitor!" he screamed in a high, unnatural voice. "You've sold me out!"

And with the scream poor Arthur came to life. Startled out of his doze, he came to his feet with a mighty spring.

"Run for your life!" he bawled and suited the action to the words. Out through the door he bounded, pushing it aside as if it were made of straw, running as if it were broad daylight and he familiar with every step of the way. Three times I heard his feet descend with mighty thuds upon the outside planking, and then, to my expectant but still horrified ears, came a dreadful splash.

Arthur had fallen in the river, and I was in a dark room at the mercy of a murderer.

I had no time to shiver or shake. I had not time to run. Right upon the sound of Arthur's immersion came shouts outside. The police crashed out of their hiding place. Lights were flashing, and there was much running about to the river, to the road, to the mill.

And in the room above, where I shrank against the wall, an automatic pistol was fired. One shot, two, three, four, five.

Between shots a man snarled ugly words. He talked in a dreadful, panting voice.

"You won't see me burn for you. You won't turn me over."

The first shot was returned. But then a body slumped to the floor, and only the gun spoke.

And so the killer was himself killed.

CHAPTER TWENTY-TWO

I KNEW THEN THAT THE CASE was ended. As the shots ceased I rushed out of that dreadful room, flashing my torch down to the reaches of the river.

"Help! Help!" I cried then. "My brother is drowning!"

But even as my wild plea left my lips my heart rose up in beautiful relief. For there, just below the loading platform, I saw my brother. Encircled in the grasping green of water hyacinths, his despairing countenance was as palely purple as the blooms. He was submerged to the chin, and his face was piteous.

My outcries brought police, but it was none too easy getting Arthur out of the mud. And then he had to be helped down that awful overgrown road to the car. Officer Blake, detailed to assist, did so in a hateful, rebellious spirit. As though poor Arthur was to blame! Would one fall in the river on purpose?

It took much tugging and pulling and persuading, but at last we reached the road. Morosely silent, Blake stood guard over Arthur while I hurried over the bridge, secured the car, and drove back. Still silent, Blake loaded our sodden companion into the back seat.

"It's been nice seeing you," he said, and I whirled from the wheel, surprised and gratified. "And I hope to God," he added balefully, "that it never happens again!"

"He needn't have been so nasty," I said indignantly to Arthur. "After all, I had to miss out on the finale and I was the one who planned the whole exposé."

But Arthur only moaned, so I dared delay no longer. With Arthur's tendency to bronchitis I had a horrid vision of pneumonia. So I drove home and, what with getting Arthur into bed and explaining to Theresa and pacifying Annie and calling the doctor and fixing mustard plasters, I was well occupied most of the night. By morning it was apparent that Arthur was not going to be ill. He wanted his breakfast and he wanted to go back to sleep.

Therefore, it was not until the eight-o'clock radio broadcast that news of the windup of the murder case came to Annie and Theresa. We were in the dining room. Annie began to flutter and shriek, and Theresa for once was struck dumb. "I simply cannot believe it!" gasped Annie. "Aren't you surprised?"

"Of course I'm not surprised," I came back snappily. "I've known for some time, but I had no proof."

"For some time?" said Annie suspiciously. "How long?"

"Ever since Marge Gilmore bought that new bathing suit," I replied.

"Bathing suit?" quavered Annie. "Oh, Theresa, these terrible tidings have addled her brain . . . ."

George Hammond came in then, so jovial and smiling and expansive that Theresa was moved to bring in a fresh coffee cake by way of celebration.

"Jane, I want you to help me get the details down," said George happily and beckoned to a young man behind him. "In shorthand, see? You talk and Bob here can take it down, and I'll have a wedge of that coffee cake, Theresa. Got lots of raisins and nuts in it, hasn't it? And just a drop of coffee. Go ahead, Jane. I'll help out when you get stuck."

I regarded him as he poured cream into his coffee until the cup brimmed. But I talked. I was rather glad in my own mind to sum things up.

"The motive—that's what fooled me," I said thoughtfully. "In the beginning I thought it was carefully planned sabotage, a determined effort to end or

seriously delay machine-tool production at the Barrett plant. And so it was—
in the beginning. The murderer sought both to cripple the Barrett business
and to give the new minesweeper plans to a foreign government. But circumstances changed, and with them his desires. Greed was the sole motivation of
the killer. He betrayed his early allegiance; he betrayed his confederate; he
committed two murders to obtain money and power for himself alone.

"We have now identified the two foreign agents who used the brown
china spaniels to conceal their evil communications. But weeks ago Julian
Norbury identified them. Greed was also Norbury's ruling passion. For money
he had consented to search out and sell the minesweeper plans. But spy and
pry as he would, he could not find them. Early on that fatal Monday afternoon, before Henry Platt had returned from lunch, Julian Norbury stood concealed in Platt's closet. He did not see the theft of the second spaniel. He saw
a man put a message in it. Startled and horrified at this misuse of the dog, he
realized that his sister might be dangerously involved. He took the dog and
decided to deal directly with Austin Barrett. He must have telephoned Barrett
at home, and his uncle, linking this new information with some that he had
already obtained, told him to come to the office at night. But when Norbury
arrived about ten forty-five he was stunned and terrified by the sight of Barrett dead, by the licking flames in the room. All consciousness of the china
dog fled his mind. He dropped it on Barrett's desk and ran. I suppose after
that he was afraid to tell what he knew, or perhaps he was never afraid, only
greedy. And when he betrayed his knowledge, when he demanded money for
his continued silence, he was killed.

"The murderer did not believe that the message in the dog would be deciphered. Events had so rushed him that he hadn't been able to make frequent
use of his new secret receptacles. He felt safe to wait and stand back because
suspicion fell quite naturally (and some of it with his assistance) upon others.
So he didn't refuse to keep the appointment at the cotton mill. He did not fear
to do so. In case of discovery he reckoned upon his ability to foist suspicion
upon his companion in crime, as he had done once before. Only this time his
confederate had become convinced of treachery and perfidy, and he didn't
wait for the police to take over. He shot first!"

"Well, I'm glad it's all over," said Annie thankfully. "I don't need to
worry any more about meeting Jappy Carillo. He's dead."

"No, he isn't," said George, surprised, accepting more coffee from
Theresa. "He's in jail."

"But who shot whom?" cried Annie.

"Dear me," I said, "do I have to use words of one syllable? Haven't you
heard all this talk? Henry Platt is dead. He killed Austin Barrett and Julian
Norbury and was going to betray or kill Carillo, so Carillo shot him. Both of
them were foreign agents."

"Sab cats!" cried Annie.

"Exactly," I said.

"But what," asked Annie, looking dazed, "did Marge Gilmore's bathing suit have to do with it?"

"That's how I knew Henry Platt's alibi didn't amount to a hill of beans. It's not five minutes in a car from the country club to the Barrett factory. I've done a lot of asking around. Platt was seen at dinner. He was seen dancing, but during the style show he wasn't seen. Everyone, particularly Judy, was willing to swear he was there because he chimed right in with the crowd, giggling about fat Marge Gilmore in the red bathing suit. The man's a good actor."

"He should be," said George, "considering what Carillo has confessed.

"He's done espionage work in almost every country. He gave Carillo orders that came from a higher-up in Chicago. We'll get the whole organization now. Carillo tended to the small sabotage jobs when Platt gave the word. He slipped in the emery dust to wreck that precision drill. He fixed the bomb in Arthur's lunchbox. But he suspected that Platt was getting lukewarm. Platt saw a chance to marry Judy Barrett and get the whole works for himself. Platt liked to be a big shot in civic life here in Rockport. He fixed up the plot to kill Barrett, but he didn't tell Carillo. He sent Carillo to Chicago that night and suggested that he take Storm along and that he steal Barrett's car. Fast work was necessary, because Barrett had discovered Platt's real identity. He had intercepted a letter that contained just enough to make him suspicious."

"The letter that he marked with the hooked cross and the notation: 'Look into this at once,' " I interrupted. "That's why he discouraged Judith about Henry Platt that very day. Formerly he had been in favor of him, because ever since Platt took charge the plant has been making big profits.

"Barrett arrived at the office at nine-thirty. Katherine Boyd came some moments later. She had not received Platt's message canceling her appointment. She didn't see Platt. He came in the back gate and locked it behind him. He was in the locker room, putting on Storm's goggles and overalls and arming himself with Boyd's hammer. Katherine left before Platt came in, killed Barrett, and took the cabinet key from his watch chain. He didn't have time to search the files then. He poured naphtha about and started the fire. Then on his way out of the back door he met Richards and knocked him down. Replacing the overalls in great haste, he dropped the key, which fell inside the molding in the locker. Either he was not aware then of his loss or he dared not delay to search. At any rate, he hid until the coast was clear. He threw the hammer into Barrett's car as he passed, returned to the club in his own car. Probably he wore an enveloping raincoat. Next morning his plant was overrun with police, and no interest could be shown in key or cabinet. Anyway, I found the key and came that night. He foiled me there. He was there before me, and it was simple enough to knock me down and take the incriminating letters that Barrett had locked away. But I had the blueprints.

"After that events molded actions. Platt attempted to indicate his lack of interest in Carillo by getting Storm out for work but leaving Carillo in jail. Hammond spoiled that plan. Naturally Carillo was furious. On his way to talk to Mrs. Storm he saw Platt leave the Barrett house with Judith. So he went back down Greenwood Avenue and borrowed the Boyd sedan that was parked outside the apartment while Katherine napped. He shot twice at Platt's car just in warning. Carillo wanted no fooling."

"And at last we got bullets that match," said Hammond. "The ones in Platt's tires match the ones in Platt. All of 'em fired from Carillo's revolver. Carillo completely cleared John Storm."

"And his mother," I said, "is a tired, frightened woman who only wishes to work in peace. She recognized Platt the day Carillo shot at him. She knew him in Hamburg and she was scared stiff. He was a mighty bad man, and she was so scared she wouldn't tell John or Judith but kept to her kitchen."

"You know, Platt must have had everything planned for," said Hammond. "I've wondered . . . . That must be why he hired Arthur in the first place. He didn't want that front gate too well guarded."

"Keep to the subject," I said hastily. "Don't put that down, young man!" I interpolated to the stenographer. "Katherine Boyd must have been a general nuisance. Platt promoted the affair primarily to secure the invention, but when he found out that Katherine stood no chance of getting it for him he dropped her. Her visits to Austin Barrett were always for money. Now—"

"Now she's getting sense," put in Theresa. "Seems she appreciates her husband now. Since her brother was killed and she's been watched by the police the simple home life seems pretty good. She was up here yesterday, asking me for my recipe for boiled beef and horseradish sauce. It's Steve Boyd's favorite."

"About the only thing left to be explained," I began, but the words were still on my tongue when the bell sounded and Bill Randall and Judy Barrett walked down the hall and into our dining room.

"We're summing up," I said sternly, "and I've just come to your part. Let's hear your story, young man."

"Bill was the federal investigator," said Judy proudly. "Of course he couldn't tell until the spy was caught. Father knew it all the time. But that wasn't why he was so—so—"

"Unimpressed," said Bill, grinning. "Let's put it that way. I had to act like a dumbbell. He liked me all right, only there was just that difference in generations. And if he were here right now he'd give us his blessing."

"Mr. Randall," said Hammond to me, glancing at Bill most respectfully, "had worked out the whole thing, Jane, just as we had—"

"We!" I ejaculated.

"—only in a much quieter way," insisted George.

"But the windup was swell," Bill assured me. "You almost caught me that day in the hotel when I ran down the fire escape. That was about the tenth time I'd been through Platt's things. And the night, the Tuesday night you came to search the cabinet, you spoiled things for me. I had to miss out chasing the guy I'd been waiting for. But I got back at you on that trip to Trailer Town . . . ."

"You were the one who locked us in, you wretch!" I cried.

"Such a cozy little party, having such a merry time! I couldn't resist!" he said.

Hammond slapped his thigh and gave a mighty chortle.

"I'd have given five bucks to have been there," he began, but hastily changed to an incoherent mumble when he saw my face.

"I'm sorry, Miss Edwards," said Bill Randall with repentance. "You see, I had a key. I had searched that trailer before. I found that dog in plain sight on Carillo's table. I wanted it for the fingerprints that were on it. At first I thought he'd stolen the pair from Platt. I've got Carillo down pat. His record is quite complete at Washington under another name. In fact, I had the Platt data pretty complete and men coming to make the arrests when you sprang this cotton-mill rendezvous—and it's just as well. Platt is gone, the Barrett plant can go all out for defense, and Judith and I can get married."

I looked at him standing tall and smiling and self-confident and brave and knew that Judith would be happy and beloved, and I felt thankful to think we have so many millions of fine, upstanding young men just like him in our country.

Annie, sentimental as always, was dabbing at her eyes.

"Well, we've got everything and everybody settled," she said happily. "The sab cats are captured. Katherine and Steve are reconciled. Judy and Bill are happy. Dear Arthur—"

The postman rang, and Annie skipped to the door. She came back holding a large envelope in her hand.

"Arthur's first lesson," she explained. "His correspondence course. He has decided to become a rabbit fancier."

"A—a rabbit fancier?" repeated Hammond.

"Yes. Isn't it lovely?" explained Annie. "Just the thing for Arthur. The advertisement said one hundred percent profit. The work is easy and the results are sure. Now, everything is settled, isn't it, Jane? All we have to worry about now is how to pay the taxes."

"No," I said, puzzled. "Not quite everything."

I went up to my room and came back with my triangular piece of blue cloth.

"This," I said to George. "I've never been able to place this."

And I thought rather sadly of the risks I had run, the discomforts I had endured, in my dogged attempt to identify that scrap.

George took a long, thoughtful look. Then he went to the door.

"He wouldn't come in," he explained bafflingly. Opening the door, he bellowed, "Blake!" And when that officer entered: "Turn around!"

Blake, with his usual expression of distaste at the sight of me, obeyed his superior and presented a broad back. George, without apology or ceremony, hiked up the back of the policeman's coat.

And there, plain as day upon that vast posterior, neatly inserted and darned all about, was a long, triangular patch.

"All's well that ends well," said George Hammond.

THE END

More Recipes from Theresa's Kitchen

RHUBARB PIE

3 tablespoons flour	2 cups diced rhubarb
1 cup sugar	1 recipe piecrust dough*
1 egg, beaten	pinch salt

Preheat oven to 425° F. Sift flour, sugar, and salt together, add egg, and mix thoroughly. Stir in rhubarb pieces. Line a 9-inch piepan with pastry and spoon in rhubarb mixture. Trim and dampen edges of lower crust and cover with top crust, slashing generously to allow steam to escape or fashioning into a lattice. Press top crust firmly against lower crust with tines of a fork to seal. Bake at 425° for 10 minutes. Reduce oven temperature to 350° and bake another 35 minutes until golden brown. Let cool before serving, either plain or with whipped cream or vanilla ice cream.

*EASY PIECRUST DOUGH

2 cups sifted pastry flour	2/3 cup shortening
¾ teaspoon salt	4 to 6 tablespoons ice water

Sift together flour and salt and cut in chilled shortening with two knives or a pastry blender until mixture resembles coarse meal. Add water in small quantities as necessary until mixture can be molded together. Divide dough into 2 parts and roll each one out on a floured pastry board with a floured rolling pin to desired size. Follow instructions above for lining pie pan and covering pie. Makes two 9-inch shells or one 9-inch 2-crust pie. (For a richer pastry, use 1 full cup of shortening and the full 6 tablespoons of ice water. The crust will be flakier, but the dough is harder to handle and must be thoroughly chilled before rolling out.)

OLD-FASHIONED STRAWBERRY SHORTCAKE

2 cups flour	1/3 cup shortening
4 teaspoons baking powder	¾ cup whole milk
½ teaspoon salt	Butter
1 tablespoon sugar	Crushed, sugared strawberries

Preheat oven to 450° to 460° F. Sift dry ingredients together, mix, and work in shortening. With a knife, gradually mix in milk until a soft dough is formed. Do not overhandle. On a floured board, press and roll dough out until one-half inch thick. Bake on cookie sheets for 12 to 15 minutes. When done, split into two parts, butter, and fill generously with crushed, sweetened strawberries. Top with more berries. Cut into squares and serve warm with whipped cream. (For individual shortcakes, cut dough into rounds with a biscuit cutter.)

BANANA CAKE

½ cup butter, softened	1 cup white flour
2 cups sugar	1 cup whole wheat flour
1 cup mashed ripe bananas	1 cup finely chopped nuts
2 eggs	1/8 teaspoon salt
¼ cup sour cream	1 teaspoon vanilla
1 teaspoon baking soda	

Preheat oven to 375° F. Cream butter and sugar together, mash bananas with a fork, and add to butter mixture. Stir in eggs, one at a time. Dissolve baking soda in sour cream and beat in. Add the sifted white flour, the whole wheat flour, and the chopped nuts. Pour batter into two well-greased and floured layer cake pans and bake for about half an hour or until done. Place sliced bananas between the layers and sprinkle top with powdered sugar (or frost with butter cream icing if desired). Serve with whipped cream.

ANGEL PIE

4 egg yolks	3 tablespoons water
1 lemon, juice & grated rind	1/8 teaspoon salt
½ cup sugar	2 egg whites
2 tablespoons flour	2 egg whites

Cook the first five ingredients together over hot water, stirring constantly, until they are thick and smooth. Remove from heat and let cool. Add the salt to the whites of 2 eggs, beat until stiff peaks form, and fold gently into the custard. Fill a baked pie shell (see piecrust recipe on preceding page) with the custard. Cover with a meringue made with the remaining egg whites plus

1/8 teaspoon salt	4 tablespoons sugar
½ teaspoon vanilla	

Add salt to egg whites and beat on a platter or shallow bowl until stiff peaks form. Slowly add the sugar, ½ teaspoon at a time, and finally the vanilla. Spread on pie, making sure that meringue touches pie shell all around to prevent shrinkage, and bake at 325° for about 12 minutes.

RHUBARB SAUCE

Wash and peel rhubarb, cut into small pieces, and place in a non-reactive (enamel or china) bowl. Sprinkle with half again as much sugar as rhubarb and let stand 12 hours or longer. Place in a saucepan with no water (or just enough to keep it from burning) and simmer gently over low heat until tender. Can be served as a side dish with sausage or other meat, or, if flavored to taste with vanilla, as a topping for ice cream.

About The Rue Morgue Press

The Rue Morgue vintage mystery line is designed to bring back into print those books that were favorites of readers between the turn of the century and the 1960s. The editors welcome suggests for reprints. To receive our catalog or make suggestions, write The Rue Morgue Press, P.O. Box 4119, Boulder, Colorado (1-800-669-6214). The Rue Morgue Press tries to keep all of its titles in print, though some books may go temporarily out of print for up to six months. The following list details the titles available as of September 2001.

Catalog of Rue Morgue Press titles September 2001

Titles are listed by author. All books are quality trade paperbacks measuring 9 by 6 inches, usually with full-color covers and printed on paper designed not to yellow or deteriorate. These are permanent books.

Joanna Cannan. The books by this English writer are among our most popular titles. Modern reviewers favorably compared our two Cannan reprints with the best books of the Golden Age of detective fiction. "Worthy of being discussed in the same breath with an Agatha Christie or a Josephine Tey."—Sally Fellows, Mystery News. "First-rate Golden Age detection with a likeable detective, a complex and believable murderer, and a level of style and craft that bears comparison with Sayers, Allingham, and Marsh."—Jon L. Breen, *Ellery Queen's Mystery Magazine*. Set in the late 1930s in a village that was a fictionalized version of Oxfordshire, both titles feature young Scotland Yard inspector Guy Northeast. *They Rang Up the Police* (0-915230-27-5, 156 pages, $14.00) and *Death at The Dog* (0-915230-23-2, 156 pages, $14.00).

Glyn Carr. The author is really Showell Styles, one of the foremost English mountain climbers of his era as well as one of that sport's most celebrated historians. Carr turned to crime fiction when he realized that mountains provided a ideal setting for committing murders. The 15 books featuring Shakespearean actor Abercrombie "Filthy" Lewker are set on peaks scattered around the globe, although the author returned again and again to his favorite climbs in Wales, where his first mystery, published in 1951, *Death on Milestone Buttress* (0-915230-29-1, 187 pages, $14.00), is set. Lewker is a marvelous Falstaffian character whose exploits have been praised by such discerning critics as Jacques Barzun and Wendell Hertig Taylor in *A Catalogue of Crime*. Other critics have been just as kind: "You'll get a taste of the Welsh countryside, will encounter names replete with consonants, will be exposed to numerous snippets from Shakespeare and will find Carr's novel a worthy representative of the cozies of two generations ago."—*I Love a Mystery*.

Clyde B. Clason. Clason has been praised not only for his elaborate plots and skillful use of the locked room gambit but also for his scholarship. He may be one of the few mystery authors—and no doubt the first—to provide a full bibliography of his sources. *The Man from Tibet* (0-915230-17-8, 220 pages, $14.00) is one of his best and highly recommended by the dean of locked room mystery scholars, Robert Adey, as "highly original." It's also one of the first popular novels to make use of Tibetan culture. Locked inside the Tibetan room of his Chicago apartment, the rich antiquarian was overheard repeating a forbidden occult chant under the watchful eyes of Buddhist gods. When the doors were opened, it appeared that he had succumbed to a heart attack. But the elderly Roman historian and sometime amateur sleuth Theocritus Lucius Westborough is convinced that Adam Merriweather's death was anything but natural and that the weapon was an eight century Tibetan manuscript.

Manning Coles. The two English writers who collaborated as Coles are best known for those witty spy novels featuring Tommy Hambledon, but they also wrote four delightful—and funny—ghost novels. *The Far Traveller* (0-915230-35-6, 154 pages, $14.00) is a stand-alone novel in which a film company unknowingly hires the ghost of a long-dead German graf to play himself in a movie. "I laughed until I hurt. I liked it so much, I went back to page 1 and read it a second time."—Peggy Itzen, *Cozies, Capers & Crimes*. The other three books feature two cousins, one English, one American, and their spectral pet monkey who got a little drunk and tried to stop—futilely and fatally—a German advance outside a small French village during the 1870 Franco-Prussian War. Flash forward to the 1950s where this comic trio of friendly ghosts rematerialize to aid relatives in danger in *Brief Candles* (0-915230-24-0, 156 pages, $14.00), *Happy Returns* (0-915230-31-3, 156 pages, $14.00) and *Come and Go* (0-915230-34-8, 155 pages, $14.00).

Norbert Davis. There have been a lot of dogs in mystery fiction, from Baynard Kendrick's guide dog to Virginia Lanier's bloodhounds, but there's never been one quite like Carstairs. Doan, a short, chubby Los Angeles private eye, won Carstairs in a crap game, but there never is any question as to who the boss is in this relationship. Carstairs isn't just any Great Dane. He is so big that Doan figures he really ought to be considered another species. He scorns baby talk and belly rubs—unless administered by a pretty girl—and growls whenever Doan has a drink. His full name is Dougal's Laird Carstairs and as a sleuth he rarely barks up the wrong tree. He's down in Mexico with Doan, ostensibly to convince a missing fugitive that he would do well to stay put. The case is complicated by three murders, assorted villains, and a horrific earthquake that cuts the mountainous little village of Los Altos off from the rest of Mexico. Doan and Carstairs aren't the only unusual visitors to Los Altos. There's Patricia Van Osdel, a ravishing blonde whose father made millions from flypaper, and Captain Emile Perona, a Mexican policeman whose long-ago Spanish ancestor helped establish Los Altos. It's that ancestor who brings teacher Janet Martin to Mexico along with a stolen book that may contain the key to a secret hidden for hundreds of years in the village church. Written in the snappy hardboiled style of the day, *The Mouse in the Mountain* (0-915230-41-0, 151 pages, $14.00) was first published in 1943 and followed by two other Doan and Carstairs novels. "Each of these is fast-paced, occasionally lyrical in a hard-edged way, and often quite funny. Davis, in fact, was one of the few writers to successfully blend the so-called hardboiled story with farcical humor."—Bill Pronzini, *1001 Midnights*.

Elizabeth Dean. Dean wrote only three mysteries, but in Emma Marsh she created one of the first independent female sleuths in the genre. Written in the screwball style of the 1930s, *Murder is a Collector's Item* (0-915230-19-4, $14.00) is described in a review in *Deadly Pleasures* by award-winning mystery writer Sujata Massey as a story that "froths over with the same effervescent humor as the best Hepburn-Grant films." Like the second book in the trilogy, *Murder is a Serious Business* (0-915230-28-3, 254 pages, $14.95), it's set in a Boston antique store just as the Great Depression is drawing to a close. The action in the final book, *Murder a Mile High* (0-915230-39-9, 188 pages, $14.00), moves to the Central City Opera House in the Colorado mountains, where Emma has been summoned by am old chum, the opera's reigning diva. Emma not only has to find a murderer, she may also have to catch a Nazi spy. A reviewer for a Central City area newspaper warmly greeted this reprint: "An endearing glimpse of Central City and Denver during World War II. . . . the dialogue twists and turns. . . . reads like a Nick and Nora movie. . . . charming."—*The Mountain-Ear*.

Constance & Gwenyth Little. These two Australian-born sisters from New Jersey have developed almost a cult following among mystery readers. Critic Diane Plumley, writing in *Dastardly Deeds*, called their 21 mysteries "celluloid comedy written on paper." Each book, published between 1938 and 1953, was a stand-alone, but there was no mistaking a Little heroine. She hated housework, wasn't averse to a little gold-digging (so long as she called the shots), and couldn't help antagonizing cops and potential beaux. The Rue Morgue Press intends to reprint all of their books. Currently available: *The Black Coat* (0-915230-40-2, 155 pages, $14.00), *Black Corridors* (0-915230-33-X, 155 pages, $14.00), *The Black Gloves* (0-915230-20-8, 185 pages, $14.00), *Black-Headed Pins* (0-915230-25-9, 155 pages, $14.00), *The Black Honeymoon* (0-915230-21-6, 187 pages, $14.00), *The Black Paw* (0-915230-37-2, 156 pages, $14.00), *The Black Stocking* (0-915230-30-5, 154 pages, $14.00), *Great Black Kanba* (0-915230-22-4, 156 pages, $14.00), and *The Grey Mist Murders* (0-915230-26-7, 153 pages, $14.00).

Marlys Millhiser. Our only non-vintage mystery, *The Mirror* (0-915230-15-1, 303 pages, $14.95) is our all-time bestselling book, now in a fifth printing. How could you not be intrigued by a novel in which "you find the main character marrying her own grandfather and giving birth to her own mother," as one reviewer put it of this supernatural, time-travel (sort-of) piece of wonderful make-believe set both in the mountains above Boulder, Colorado, at the turn of the century and in the city itself in 1978.

James Norman. The marvelously titled *Murder, Chop Chop* (0-915230-16-X, 189 pages, $13.00) is a wonderful example of the eccentric detective novel. "The book has the butter-wouldn't-melt-in-his-mouth cool of Rick in *Casablanca*."—*The Rocky Mountain News.* "Amuses the reader no end."—*Mystery News.* "This long out-of-print masterpiece is intricately plotted, full of eccentric characters and very humorous indeed. Highly recommended."—*Mysteries by Mail.* Meet Gimiendo Hernandez Quinto, a gigantic Mexican who once rode with Pancho Villa and who now trains *guerrilleros* for the Nationalist Chinese government when he isn't solving murders. At his side is a beautiful Eurasian known as Mountain of Virtue, a woman as dangerous to men as she is irresistible. Together they look into the murder of Abe Harrow, an ambulance driver who appears to have died at three different times. First published in 1942.

Sheila Pim. *Ellery Queen's Mystery Magazine* said of these wonderful Irish village mysteries that Pim "depicts with style and humor everyday life." *Booklist* said they were in "the best tradition of Agatha Christie." *Common or Garden Crime* (0-915230-36-4, 157 pages, $14.00) is set in neutral Ireland during World War II when Lucy Bex must use her knowledge of gardening to keep the wrong person from going to the gallows. Beekeeper Edward Gildea uses his knowledge of bees and plants to do the same thing in *A Hive of Suspects* (0-915230-38-0, 155 pages, $14.00). Both are absolute delights, as are Pim's two other mysteries, scheduled for publication in late 2001 and early 2002.

Juanita Sheridan. Sheridan was one of the most colorful figures in the history of detective fiction, as you can see from Tom and Enid Schantz's introduction to *The Chinese Chop* (0-915230-32-1, 155 pages, $14.00). Her books are equally colorful, as well as showing how mysteries with female protagonists began changing after World War II. The postwar housing crunch finds Janice Cameron, newly arrived in New York City from Hawaii, without a place to live until she answers an ad for a roommate. It turns out the advertiser is an acquaintance from Hawaii, Lily Wu, whom critic Anthony Boucher (for whom Bouchercon, the World Mystery Convention, is named) described as an "exquisitely blended product of Eastern and Western cultures" and the only female sleuth that he "was devotedly in love with," citing "that odd mixture of respect for her professional skills and delight in her personal charms." First published in 1949, this ground-breaking book was the first of four to feature Lily and be told by her Watson, Janice, a first-time novelist. No sooner do Lily and Janice move into a rooming house in Washington Square than a corpse is found in the basement. In Lily Wu, Sheridan created one of the most believable—and memorable—female sleuths of her day. "Highly recommended."—*I Love a Mystery.* "This well-written. . .enjoyable variant of the boarding house whodunit and a vivid portrait of the post WWII New York City housing shortage, puts to lie the common misconception that strong, self-reliant, non-spinster-or-comic sleuths didn't appear on the scene until the 1970s. Chinese-American Lily Wu and her novelist Watson, Janice Cameron, are young and feminine but not dependent on men."—*Ellery Queen's Mystery Magazine.*